When the Stars Come Out

Also by Laura Trentham

When the Stars Come Out

LAURA TRENTHAM

St. Martin's Paperbacks

This is a work of fiction. All of the characters, organizations, and events portrayed in this novel are either products of the author's imagination or are used fictitiously.

WHEN THE STARS COME OUT

Copyright © 2018 by Laura Trentham.

All rights reserved.

For information address St. Martin's Press, 175 Fifth Avenue, New York, NY 10010.

ISBN: 978-1-250-13128-7

Our books may be purchased in bulk for promotional, educational, or business use. Please contact your local bookseller or the Macmillan Corporate and Premium Sales Department at 1-800-221-7945, ext. 5442, or by e-mail at MacmillanSpecialMarkets@macmillan.com.

Printed in the United States of America

St. Martin's Paperbacks edition / February 2018

St. Martin's Paperbacks are published by St. Martin's Press, 175 Fifth Avenue, New York, NY 10010.

10 9 8 7 6 5 4 3 2 1

Acknowledgments

Over the course of publishing going on a dozen books now (Wow! How did that happen?), I've thanked a multitude of people who've helped get me here: my parents, my husband, my agent, my editor, and all the people at St. Martin's Press. This time around I want to give props to two important contributors to my writing career that don't get enough credit—coffee and wine!

Chapter One

A bang shook the wall. No fist had come through the Sheetrock, and it hadn't been violent enough to be a body. Probably a chair then. The break room sat a dozen feet from where Willa Brown worked. Indistinct male voices came in spurts and sometimes on top of each other. Overall, a typical Abbott family meeting. Good thing no customers were milling around to witness the fireworks.

Willa ducked her head back under the hood of Vera Carson's Oldsmobile Cutlass 442. She wanted to do the car and Abbott Brothers Garage and Restoration proud, but even more, she wanted to do Jackson Abbott proud. While she'd learned the ins and outs of car mechanics from her father, she'd gained an appreciation of the classics over the last two years working with the brothers. Jackson in particular.

Another harder hit to the wall registered but she didn't look up from where she was finger-tightening a bolt. While she had the disadvantage when it came to brute strength, none of the boys could match her dexterity in tight places.

The office door shot open and bounced against the wall, deepening the impression of the doorknob. Mack Abbott went out the front door and Wyatt out the back.

Jackson stalked out and slammed the door shut, looking like someone had borrowed his '68 Mustang GT and gotten ketchup on the seats. If it were socially acceptable, Willa wouldn't have been surprised to bear witness to Jackson marrying his Mustang.

Although twins, Jackson and Wyatt approached life from opposite directions. Wyatt was the wild charmer while Jackson was quieter and more circumspect. If past behaviors held, Wyatt was headed to the barn out back of the shop to expend his anger on a body-sized punching bag that hung from the rafters. Jackson would bottle up his aggression and let it explode all over the dirt track. She almost felt sorry for whoever raced him next.

Jackson headed straight for her. More likely his destination was the Cutlass. That knowledge didn't stop her quick intake of breath as he drew close. He stopped next to her with his hands propped on the open hood, breathing like he'd gone for a sprint around the building. His anger vibrated the air around them. He definitely had a Mr. Rochester from *Jane Eyre* vibe going on. Dark, brooding, mysterious.

She was used to the Abbotts. In fact, their idiosyncrasies made her feel right at home. Growing up, she knew more about cars than most guys which did not help her cred with the girls, who'd been more concerned with pageants and cheerleading. It had been just her and her dad for so long that being around men felt normal. Melancholy reared up and bit her in the ass. Whenever she thought about her dad and the life she'd left behind—had to leave behind—regrets threatened to swamp her.

She put her father and her past out of her head and focused instead on her favorite subject—Jackson Abbott. If he was a textbook, she would name him *The Anatomy of the Perfect Male* or if she was in a philosophical mind-set,

Dwelling on Jackson. Her mind tended to dwell on him in her waking and sleeping hours.

Not that he saw her as anything but an employee. In fact, sometimes she wasn't sure he saw her at all. Like now. Even though they were three feet apart under the same hood, he ignored her. She thought about making a funny face to see how long it took him to notice. He probably wouldn't and her face would freeze that way.

She smothered a laugh and checked him out from the corner of her eyes, one of her favorite pastimes. He wore baggy gray work coveralls, same as she did, but in deference to the warm snap, he'd peeled off the top and tied the sleeves around his waist. His black T-shirt molded to his thick chest and emphasized his brown hair. His jaw was tight and his biceps flexed as he stared into the engine compartment.

"So how was the family meeting?" she asked in a sing-songy voice.

"Shitty." His voice was more hoarse-sounding than usual which made her wonder if he'd been doing most of the hollering even though that was unlike him. He was more the strong, silent type. Or the closed-off, brooding type.

Her chest tightened. Was the shop in financial trouble? Had the decision to expand into car restoration and the recent upgrades been too much of a strain? Oh God, were they going to fire her?

Where would she go? She didn't want to start over. Not again. Not when she'd finally found somewhere to settle for longer than a few months. Even though the Abbotts weren't her family, they were all she had. They drove each other crazy more often than not, but at least they'd stuck together and had each other's backs.

Unfortunately, she was the odd woman out in the equation. She straightened and faced him. "Am I being fired?"

"What?" Finally, he turned his attention to her. "Of course you're not fired. Where would you get that idea?"

She averted her face and pretended to work on something in the depths of the engine block. Her breath shuddered out. She didn't want Jackson to know how important this job was to her. Without it—without the Abbotts—she would be alone again.

"What was all the arguing about then?" she asked.

"It was about Ford. Ford and his need for something big, something quick. Instead of being patient and building our reputation through hard, honest work, he wants fast cash and is threatening to sell out if we can't buy him out."

"Why can't you and Wyatt and Mack pool your money and buy him out? That would solve a lot of problems." Now that her job was safe for at least another day, she could turn her worry outward for Jackson. He was more than mad. The gamut of emotions that flashed through his typical stoicism came too fast for her to interpret, but his voice reflected betrayal.

"We put most of our ready cash into the shop, and we're still repaying the loan for the addition. The question is, do we overextend ourselves for another loan, find Ford and appeal to whatever family loyalty he has left, or let things play out?"

Three years earlier when the brothers got serious about expanding into car renovations and not just repairs, they had added two more bays and specialized equipment like a metal-bending machine and a top-of-the-line welder. Those upgrades had been necessary but expensive.

To counteract the despondency in his voice, she forced a tease into hers. "Is there anything to really worry about? I mean, who the heck would be interested in buying this grease pit anyway?"

While she didn't garner a smile, tension leaked out of him like a drain being opened. The garage was actually the nicest she'd ever worked in. As the unofficial leader, Mack insisted they clean up after themselves. While she wouldn't eat off the floors, she'd certainly slept in dirtier places.

"You've got a point there. Ford likes to throw out empty threats to get a reaction out of Mack. Maybe it will blow over and things will get back to normal." The furrows along his forehead belied his words.

"What about Sutton?"

"What about her?"

"To be safe, why don't you see if she'll buy Ford's part?"

Sutton Mize was the daughter of a prominent family in Cottonbloom, Mississippi. She and Wyatt had come together over her ex-fiancé's car and had been inseparable ever since. On paper they shouldn't work, but seeing them together made everyone believers. However, there was no arguing the fact that Sutton changed the dynamics of the garage.

Suddenly it wasn't the Three Musketeers—Mack, Wyatt, Jackson—against the world. Willa had always cast herself as D'Artagnan, but with the addition of Sutton, Willa felt demoted and more of an outsider than ever.

"And if she and Wyatt end things? A vengeful ex who's well connected could wreck our reputation. Hell, Ford could wreck our reputation and drive the garage into the ground. Garages make or break on word of mouth, especially in a town like Cottonbloom."

Desperation stalked through her body. The feeling was only too familiar. Heat bloomed and a sickening wave of faintness passed through her, forcing her to unzip the top of her coveralls and flap the front to cool down.

"Hey, are you okay?" Concern for her replaced any angst he'd carried from the meeting.

"I'm fine. Fine." She half sat on the edge of the engine compartment. The wave of heat and nausea passed. Her skipped breakfast and lunch were coming back to haunt her. All her extra money and then some were going to repairs to her car. Her clutch was nearly shot, the exhaust was leaking, and her tires were bald. Considering where she worked, the irony of her problems wasn't lost on her. Black humor was the only kind she appreciated these days. But it was payday and since she wasn't getting fired, she'd splurge on a decent meal.

"Wasn't expecting a heat wave in November is all." Her voice was embarrassingly shaky.

"It's not like we have a dress code or anything. You can wear old jeans and T-shirts when it gets hot. And you'd be a sight cooler without a hat." Before she could react, he grabbed the bill of her vintage Texaco ball cap and peeled it off.

Her hair sprang around her face. Usually as soon as it hit her neck, she hacked it off. The monthly ritual seemed a penance she needed to pay for her past transgressions. Plus, it was all-around easier to handle when it was short. Since the beginning of summer though, she hadn't taken up scissors, and pieces waved around her face like new growth from a tree. A scraggly tree.

She'd given up her old life. Except for the name she shared with her grandmother, Wilhelmina, Willa for short. At the time she'd wanted something to hang on to, something to ground her.

But the hat and her given name aside, her hair had had to go. Wavy, thick, and chestnut colored, her hair had been her vanity and hacking it off had been symbolic. It had been what had attracted her ex, Derrick, also known as the worst mistake of her life. She wanted to leave the selfish, stupid girl she'd been behind.

Unfortunately, cutting it hadn't cut out the memories of her dad singing "Brown Eyed Girl" to her at night while stroking her long hair off her forehead. Her life hadn't been all bad—not even close in retrospect—and remembering the good hurt.

She finger-combed her hair behind her ears. It was all split ends and tangles and dulled color. She might be a greasy mechanic and his employee, but she was still a female standing in front of an attractive man. She didn't want Jackson seeing her with sweaty, gross hat head.

"Gimme that back." She grabbed the hat and mashed it on her head, tucking the ends of her hair that stuck out underneath as best she could. Her fingertips stopped to trace the unraveling embroidery on the front. The hat had been her father's. The last thing she'd ever stolen. Did he miss her?

Jackson had never looked at her the way he was looking at her right now. Was he suspicious? Curious? Either was bad. That was the nice thing about working with men, especially Jackson. He didn't gossip. He didn't ask questions unrelated to whatever projects were on the shop floor. He didn't care about where she was from or what had brought her to Cottonbloom. She needed it to stay that way.

"You sure you're okay? You're really pale," he said.

"I'm a-okay." She waved him off even though it was a lie. "What's your plan to handle Ford?"

His voice dropped as if talking to himself. "Can he be handled? I'm worried Mack and Ford are going to play chicken with the garage and then where will we be?"

Did he mean the garage might go under for real? The garage had been started by their father, Hobart Abbott, and had maintained a steady clientele and stellar reputation for more than forty years. Her heart accelerated from zero to one-twenty, bringing with it another wave of knee-weakening nausea. "Surely there's something you can do to stave off a disaster."

He muttered something unintelligible, ran a hand down

his face, and scratched at the dark stubble along his jaw. "We're talking more after work. I'll let you know."

He pivoted away and stalked toward the back door, maybe to join Wyatt in pounding his worries into the punching bag; or maybe he was seeking the privacy of the loft above the barn that he shared with Wyatt.

Turning back to the engine, all she could see was her tidy, small world disintegrating. That morning all she'd been focused on was making it to the end of the day when Mack would hand her the cash she'd worked her butt off for, and the barbeque plate from Rufus's Meat and Three she planned to devour for dinner.

But wasn't that the way of all natural disasters? Like the tornado that had peeled the roof off her rented trailer and let the rain in to soak her secondhand clothes and furniture. Thank God, she'd been at the shop with Jackson. They'd huddled in the closet full of cleaning supplies until it passed. He'd never made mention of the fact she'd reached for him during the worst of it. He'd let her hold on.

This disaster felt more like an earthquake, shaking the foundations of what she'd built in Cottonbloom. Could she get out before the fissures exposed her secrets?

Jackson exchanged a grunt with Wyatt, who was attempting to put his fist straight through the leather of the punching bag, and took the steps to their loft two at a time. He was glad to have a few minutes of solitude.

His usually orderly thoughts were like a mixed-up Rubik's Cube he couldn't solve. He gave the center support column a slap on his way to the kitchenette. Going against his rigid set of work rules, he grabbed a beer from the fridge, screwed off the top, and killed half before coming up for air. It was Friday, and everything on the shop floor could keep. He'd make up the time tomorrow. Not like he had any other weekend plans.

His thoughts still whirling, he walked to the windows along the back and braced a hand against the sill, taking more measured sips. Wyatt would be at the bag for at least another half hour. Jackson prayed Mack hadn't wrapped his truck around a tree somewhere out in the marshes. They all had their ways of coping.

Except for Ford. He was a runner. Even when they were kids, he spent more time avoiding his chores than it would have taken to just shut his mouth and get them done. Jackson had spent their youth trying to reason with him while Wyatt had preferred to try to punch some sense into him. Neither method had worked. Ford went on and did whatever the fuck he wanted to do, acting as if he thought because he was older, he was wiser.

Jackson emptied the bottle, tossed it into the recycle bin, and collapsed onto the overstuffed couch, closing his eyes. The image of Willa's pale face and huge brown eyes came into his mind. The mass of hair he'd released had given him his second shock of the day. The messy waves had framed and highlighted how delicately pretty she was with her thin nose, sharp chin, and heart-shaped face.

Of course, he was aware she was female. A girl. A *woman*. But for the last two years—really until the moment he'd pulled her ball cap off to cool her down and keep her from passing out—she'd first and foremost been a mechanic. And a damn good one. On her best day, she was better than either Mack or Wyatt, and almost as good as him. On her worst and blindfolded, she was better than Ford.

How old was she? He tried to recall if he'd ever asked. The day she'd come in with the want ad from the paper in her hand, he'd known she wasn't being a hundred percent upfront. The biggest red flag was her insistence on being paid only in cash. His pop had agreed. All of them had assumed she wouldn't last out the trial week anyway.

She'd not only stuck it out, but impressed the hell out of them. She'd become invaluable. But there was a dark, haunted look about her that spoke of secrets. As closely as they worked together day in and day out, he'd expected her to eventually crack and tell him the truth. Two years later and that day still hadn't come to pass.

Damn but she was pretty. Her enormous brown eyes and the dark arch of her brows were usually hidden or shadowed by the hat he'd assumed she wore twenty-four-seven. Didn't matter what she looked like, although it would have been a sight less disconcerting if she'd been hiding a few warts or hairy moles under her hat. He was basically her boss, and as such he stuffed any inappropriate thoughts back into the deep, dark recesses of his soul.

His frustration wasn't really about Willa anyway. He was pissed at Ford and the way he'd betrayed his blood. Even before he'd headed to LSU and gotten his degree, he'd acted as if he were too good for the garage even as he took his percentage of the profits. Their pop had been blind to Ford's lack of devotion to cars and the garage, and when he'd died unexpectedly last year, that blindness had incited a power struggle between Mack and Ford for the garage's future.

The clomp of boots sounded on the steps. Jackson opened his eyes, but otherwise didn't move. Still wearing his sparring gloves, Wyatt shot him a look, went to the fridge, uncapped two beers, and joined him on the couch. Jackson took the proffered bottle and sipped. Sweat rolled down Wyatt's face, and after pressing the cold bottle against his forehead, he chugged the beer.

They were fraternal twins, unlike in both temperament and looks, yet the ties that bound them were made of bullet-stopping Kevlar.

"If—and it's a big if—Ford is actually serious about selling, I think we should let things play out." Wyatt tossed his empty bottle toward the bin underhanded. It thumped the side, and rolled back and forth on the floor.

"I'm sorry, what?" Jackson had been sure that Wyatt would cast his vote for tracking Ford down and beating some sense into him.

"I know what you're thinking; Sutton has turned me into a wuss."

Jackson couldn't stop a chuckle from rising up and out. "You're definitely easier to get along with since you've been getting some on a regular basis." He sobered quickly. "What if Ford sells to some asshole out of spite?"

"Let me clarify. I don't propose we do nothing. Just not as in your face as I tend to favor. Sutton's already put out some feelers for information. Ford would have to contact a lawyer for the paperwork." Wyatt grimaced and looked toward the window and the woods beyond. "Considering Ford and Tarwater are golfing buddies, he would be the obvious choice."

"You okay with her talking to her ex like that?"

Wyatt and Sutton had met over a thong he discovered under the seat of Andrew Tarwater's Camaro. The Cottonbloom, Mississippi, lawyer had been Sutton's fiancé, and the scrap of lace had belonged to Sutton's best friend. Tarwater had not remained her fiancé for long. What Jackson had assumed was a simple rebound had turned into love, and Wyatt was indeed the definition of whipped.

But as long as Sutton made Wyatt happy, then Jackson would support her—and them—one hundred and ten percent. If she broke his brother's heart though, he would become her worst nightmare.

"I'm not worried about Sutton having second thoughts, if that's what you're getting at. Tarwater is a natural liar, so whether he'll even give up the truth is debatable. Plus, he's an asshat. If he says something to hurt her feelings, I'm not sure I won't get myself thrown in jail for assault."

"No worries, I'll bail you out." Jackson punched his arm and flashed a smile. "If you promise to clean my bay for the next month."

Their chuffing, slight laughter petered into a comfortable silence.

"It's a long shot, but Ford might actually do us a favor." Wyatt's tone was serious even though the sentiment sounded like a joke.

"Ford wouldn't cross the road to tell us the garage was on fire. He'd stand there and watch it burn for the insurance money. Him doing us a favor is more than a long shot."

"I don't know. He's lost weight and looks stressed. I'm worried about him."

The fact this assessment was coming from Wyatt held water considering their naturally adversarial relationship went back as far as Jackson could remember. "You think he's sick or something?"

"I don't know." Wyatt picked at the laces of his gloves, his voice vague but with an undercurrent of concern. "Let's look at the bright side. Anyone interested in buying his stake would be doing it because they love cars and restorations, and if they're rich, they might give the garage a leg up."

"That sounds like a moon shot."

"Maybe, but think about it. We'll never attract the kind of cars we need to build the restoration business. Not if we limit ourselves to Cottonbloom."

"You've made huge inroads over the river and brought in three cars in two months."

"The widow's walk of cars will dry up soon enough. Without some influence, this garage will stay small potatoes. We'll make a living, sure. But no matter how hard we bust our humps, we'll never get rich."

"Is that what you want? Money?"

Had Jackson stepped into *The Twilight Zone*? Wyatt was rock-solid dependable. Did his work without complaining. He never seemed to need or want money, unlike Jackson who had his racing to support. Hearing him now rocked the foundation not only of the garage, but of their already-skewed family dynamic.

"I want the freedom money can buy. We're twenty-nine. Haven't you ever wanted to take some time off to travel? See something besides the undercarriage of a car? Are you going to live up here forever? Don't you want to settle down with a good woman and maybe have kids?" Wyatt gestured around the loft and its mismatched furniture. The wall-mounted flat-screen TV had been their only splurge. "No offense, but I don't want to grow into a grizzled bachelor with you."

The questions whirred through his head like a misfiring engine. He hadn't thought about the future in those terms. He was focused on the day-to-day micro issues that arose with the cars under his care, not the macro issues of life in general. All he could do was shrug.

"How long has it been since you brought a woman back here?" Wyatt scrubbed the back of his neck, his dark hair in need of a trim and curling at the ends. "If we had more money, we could hire on more help, and you could work on occasionally getting laid."

A resentment that might have been tinged green with jealousy rose. "Just cuz you're settling down, doesn't mean everyone wants that. I prefer being alone. Love it, in fact."

An alarm that signaled a lie went off like a distant tornado warning. Truth was, since Wyatt had taken up with Sutton and spent a majority of his nights at her house instead of their loft, the quiet had become more burden than blessing.

"Your life is this damn garage." Wyatt linked his hands

behind his head and looked to the beamed ceiling. "Just like it was for Pop," he added softly.

The subtle admonishment drove a steel rod into Jackson's spine and tensed his shoulders. "What the hell does that mean?"

"It means the most meaningful relationship you have is with your car." The hint of a smile played around Wyatt's mouth. "And maybe Willa."

"Relationship? Willa and I work together. That's it." An echo of his earlier thoughts drove his knee-jerk defensiveness. It wasn't a lie, yet it didn't feel a hundred percent truthful either. He hated waffling through the gray area in between. Life was easier in absolutes. Black-and-white, right and wrong. One thing he could say with no qualms. "She's the best mechanic we've ever had."

"She's a goddamn prodigy, which brings up another point. We pay her next to nothing. As good as she is, she could make more money over the river in Mississippi changing oil at one of those quickie lube places. I don't know why she hasn't already quit."

"She wouldn't quit on me. *Us.* I mean us." He clenched his teeth together to corral his runaway tongue. If Wyatt's raised brows were any indication, he'd noticed Jackson's slip.

"I wouldn't be too sure about that. She asked for her pay and took off early. My guess is she has a job interview somewhere else. Might not even be back on Monday morning."

Jackson shot to his feet. Wyatt might be right. Something had been amiss with her for a couple of months now. A skittishness had marred their usual camaraderie, but he'd ignored it, hoping whatever was bothering her would work itself out. Ignoring problems was generally how he approached life and relationships. But he couldn't afford to ignore this one. He couldn't lose Willa.

Wyatt grabbed his forearm. "Hold up, we have bigger frogs to gig. Mack texted. He'll be back by five and wants to talk."

Jackson sank back down and wished for another beer or six, but he needed to keep his wits sharp, especially if he was going to drive later. Which he was.

"What is Mack thinking?"

"No clue. He doesn't tell me jack these days." Wyatt's voice reflected a wariness and worry that didn't sit well with Jackson. Wyatt was the most emotionally intuitive of all of them, even if that made him reckless and prone to acting impetuously.

Jackson looked out the window. Trees spanned all the way to the horizon. Their family had gone through upheavals and hard times in the past. His grandparents had been forced to give up cotton farming and sell the rich land. Tough years followed while his father built the garage. With money tight, it sat beside their family home out of necessity. The location outside of town hurt their business, but except for Ford, none of them wanted to pick up and move.

Memories of summers long gone echoed through the woods. Most of the leaves were gone, leaving green pines interspersed with bare branches. After their mother ran off and left them, the brothers had taken care of each other while their father had toiled away in the garage. Those days were harder, but they'd managed to have fun anyway. The resiliency of children.

Jackson had known he was destined to work in the garage from the time he could walk. He'd never wanted anything else. Fixing a car inside and out provided a simple joy. Yet, darker impulses drove him to the dirt track in search of an adrenaline rush behind the wheel. He couldn't explain the wildness that simmered under his general calm. Honestly, he did his best not to scrutinize the troublesome complexity of his moods.

Jackson usually confined his worries to his family and to the garage, but somehow Willa had gotten tangled up in his life without him noticing. All he knew was the thought of her moving on torqued his anxiety to new levels. Uncomfortable levels. He stood and held out a hand to haul Wyatt off the couch. "Let's get this over with. I have something to take care of."

Chapter Two

"I'll have a pork plate and sweet tea to go." Willa did a mental calculation for tax and pulled out two fives. More than she should spend, but her stomach vetoed any protest.

Now not only was she saving to fix her car, but she needed a cushion. If she had to move, money was a necessity. Any decent place required a deposit for rent. Not to mention utilities. And how long would it take her to find another job that didn't require her Social Security number or real name? The thought made her stomach hurt from something other than hunger.

"Make that two for here, Rufus, and I'm buying."

Willa spun around. Jackson Abbott's chest filled her vision. The animallike noises her stomach was making must have drowned out his approach.

"Sure thing, Jackson." Rufus favored them with a grin and turned to dole out barbeque, baked beans, and slaw.

She tucked her hair behind her ear, feeling intensely vulnerable without her steel-toed work boots, coveralls, and ball cap. Her flip-flops, worn-out jeans with a rip at one knee, and a black T-shirt with the emblem of a band she'd never listened to were from the thrift shop down the street.

"You don't have to pay." When she found her voice, it was breathy.

"I want to." His words were low and rumbly and sexy, and she resisted the urge to lay her cheek against his chest, desperate to have someone, anyone, to lean on, even for a moment. Obviously, hunger was impeding her mental faculties.

In the two years she'd lived in Cottonbloom, she'd never run into Jackson outside of the garage. Her forays to secretly watch him race didn't count since he'd never noticed her. The only place she was a regular was at the library, because it offered free Internet and entertainment—two things she couldn't afford to waste money on.

Her mental faculties slipped further away as she allowed her gaze to wander over his shoulders before rising. He'd showered, his damp hair darker than its usual rich brown, but hadn't shaved, his stubble even more pronounced from the afternoon. The scent of soap and clean laundry was mouthwatering in a different way than the barbeque was. The butterflies in her stomach did a slow bump and grind. God, she was hungry for so many things.

Rufus laid a tray with two plates and drinks on the counter. He and Jackson exchanged money. When she went to pick up the tray, he beat her to it, his fingers passing over hers. She hoped he didn't notice them tremble.

She didn't protest. Honestly, as weak and off balance as she felt from a combination of hunger and his presence, she might have accidentally dumped it on the floor. And, if she had, she wasn't sure she had the pride not to grab a fork and scrap off the top.

He unloaded the plates at a two-person table off to the side and nudged his chin toward the opposite chair. Now she was expected to eat across from him and hold a conversation when she wanted to bury her face in the barbeque and inhale it?

Still, he was basically her boss, and he had paid. Which meant she could eat a little better this week or put the extra money toward her escape fund or car repairs. She slid onto the vinyl seat and ripped the spork from its plastic bag. Luckily, he didn't attempt to engage her in conversation until she'd eaten all her pork and half her beans. She forced herself to go slow, yet he was only a quarter through his pork when she came up for air.

"How'd you end up in Cottonbloom, Willa? You got family 'round here?" he asked as she took a draw of tea.

She sputtered around the straw. Until this moment, the most personal question he'd ever posed involved a list of her ten favorite cars, make and model. "No family. Cottonbloom is a nice town."

That actually was the God's honest truth. Cottonbloom had been a pit stop on her way to Jackson, Mississippi. A place to grab something to eat and stretch her legs. She'd wandered down the streets on both sides of the river, window-shopping while enjoying an ice-cream cone she'd splurged on in the cutest little shop she'd ever seen.

At the time she hadn't realized they were actually two different towns. Cottonbloom, Mississippi, with the ice-cream shop and pizzeria and high-end stores on one side, and Cottonbloom, Louisiana, with the best barbeque in the South and antiques stores and secondhand shops on the other. Something about the river and vibe had drawn her. With an impulsiveness that had gotten her into trouble when she was a teenager, she'd bought a local paper and skimmed the want ads.

"Really?" He sat back in his chair. "You think Cottonbloom is nice?"

"You should know since you grew up here."

He studied her as if she were an engine with a valve or

two stuck, the intensity startling. "Most people think Cottonbloom is an odd place with our divide and rivalries."

"I think it's a special place." Breaking eye contact, she poked at the mound of slaw on her plate. She'd passed through more cities than she could name, some small, some big, all of them hard. Until she'd stumbled upon Cottonbloom and the Abbotts. Finding the ad for a mechanic placed by Abbott Garage had made everything seem fated. And she didn't even believe in fairy tales.

The sense of safety she'd cultivated was as immaterial as the fog that rolled off the marshes at night. She'd known it would eventually vanish. A couple of good years hadn't changed the way her luck ran—from bad to worse. She wouldn't complain or lament the turn. After all, it was no more than she deserved.

"If you think it's so odd, why hasn't a single Abbott brother moved on? Not even Ford." She shoved a sporkful of slaw in her mouth, savoring the flavors. It felt like her last meal before sentencing.

"I can't speak for the others, but I never considered it." He shrugged and looked toward a wall covered with autographed pictures of LSU football players. "I wasn't the best student, but I was good with my hands. Understood cars without trying. I never wanted anything else than to work in the garage with Pop."

"But he's gone." The words were out before she had a chance to stop them. She froze with the last of her slaw hovering midair.

"Yeah, he's gone." The only visible reaction was a tightening around his eyes, but his voice held a sadness he worked hard to hide even from his brothers. But she'd noticed.

"I'm sorry. I miss him too." Her apology and attempt at empathy sounded weak.

She did miss Mr. Hobart though. He had been nice to

her and given her a chance when not many others would. He'd been the glue that bound them all together and to the garage. Since his death, an uneasiness that felt vaguely selfish had niggled at her. A countdown had started, and now the end was in sight.

If she was going out, she might as well go out with a bang. Well, not a literal bang. That was out of the question. Although now the thought had been planted, she had a good idea what her dreams would entail that night.

Tentatively, she ran her fingertips over the back of his hand. He didn't flinch away from her touch. In fact, his fist loosened enough for her to tuck her fingers around his palm for a squeeze. It was like she'd plugged into an electric socket, the zip of energy raising the hairs on the back of her neck.

She'd touched him before of course. They passed tools back and forth with utilitarian expediency. This was different. Compassionate and tender. His hand was strong and the calluses spoke of hard work and expertise.

She let him go, trembling in the aftermath, and concentrated once more on getting food to her belly. She couldn't afford to think of Jackson like that, the cost too steep for her heart. Admiration from afar was her only option.

He pushed his half-finished plate to the side. Her gaze followed the food before returning to him. His eyes narrowed as he cast a look toward his plate and back to her. "I'm full. You want the rest of mine?"

Most people would demur and say no. Men didn't like women who ate like horses, did they? It shouldn't matter what Jackson thought of her. But it did. She battled her pride for all of two seconds before nodding, putting his plate on top of her empty one, and digging in.

She'd run away from home due to pride, fear, and a fair amount of immature stupidity. The intervening years had taught her pride didn't keep you warm or fed, and she'd

shed the useless trait. Fear was her ever-present compan-
ion, sometimes roaring, sometimes slumbering. But she
hoped she wasn't as stupid as she'd been back then.

Only since finding her footing at the garage had her
feelings of self-worth sprouted like buttercups pushing
through the ground after a long winter. This time around
she was more cautious. She did her best work at the garage every single day, but she understood there were more
important things than pride. Safety for one.

He was silent while she finished his food. Feeling like
a stuffed tick, she laid her napkin on top.

"You're long overdue for a raise. How about ten
percent?" he asked.

"Ten percent." Shock made her voice sound flat even to
her own ears.

"All right. Twenty. Do we have a deal?"

The food she'd relished churned in her stomach. He was
offering her a raise? Why?

"Jackson Abbott, just the man I needed to see."
Mr. Thatcher strolled over adjusting his suspenders over
his potbelly. Jackson half turned in his seat to exchange a
handshake and pleasantries.

But no smile. His smiles were rare and fleeting and precious. To her at least. She'd made it her mission to see the
dimples that carved furrows in his cheeks at least once a
day. Sometimes she succeeded, sometimes she failed, but
she never stopped trying.

"What can I do you for, Thatch?" Jackson asked.

"My wife's car threw a light and is chugging at idle.
She's due to drive down to New Orleans on Sunday for her
cousin's bridal shower. I know tomorrow's Saturday, but
could you take a gander?"

As quiet as a barn owl, Willa scooted out from under
the table as the two men discussed logistics. Jackson
wouldn't even notice. He never noticed her in the garage.

He grabbed her wrist. "Wait for me outside. I'll only be a sec."

He raised his brows and waited for her to answer even though he'd posed it like an order. Only when she nodded did he let her go, but his gaze heated her back the whole way out.

Jackson listened to Thatch ramble about his wife's car for two more minutes before impatience got the better of him. It was chance he'd been driving by and spotted Willa's car in front of Rufus's. He didn't want to press his luck. Escape was not an option.

He rose and clapped the other man on the shoulder. "You bring it by in the morning. We'll either get her fixed up or give you a loaner."

"Thanks, Jackson. Knew I could count on you boys."

Jackson waved two fingers over his head and quick-stepped to the door. Had she waited or hightailed it away? He stopped on the cracking sidewalk. She wasn't leaning against the bright yellow brick wall or window-shopping.

He scanned the other side of the river and the upscale shops of Cottonbloom, Mississippi. A figure limned by the setting sun stood in the middle of the footbridge that separated Cottonbloom, Louisiana, from Cottonbloom, Mississippi.

The tension across his shoulders flowed out, and his hands loosened from their tight fists. Willa Brown had been his right-hand woman in the shop for the last two years, and he'd taken her for granted. Treated her as if she were a high-end tool like his favorite socket wrench or air hammer. Always there and reliable. She was easy to be around, logical, sane. Funny even.

But now, for the first time, he recognized her as a flight risk. He couldn't lose her. She was too valuable to the shop. He put the tight clamp around his heart imagining her gone down to indigestion. Even though she'd eaten most of his food.

How could such a little thing eat so much? The hollow look as she'd eyed the heaping plates had given him pause. He did some quick math in his head. Even without the raise, she was making enough to at least feed, house, and clothe herself.

He cast back to that afternoon and her pale, clammy face. Had she nearly passed out from hunger? Maybe she had a parasitic boyfriend or a sick parent. Wyatt was right. He was more in tune with his car than the girl—woman— that had worked at his side for two years.

He crossed the street and walked next to the sparse flowers that were part of the beautification project for Cottonbloom, Louisiana. The cooler nights had sent everything but a few hardy black-eyed Susans dormant. Louisiana was fickle in the winter. Usually mild, she could pop out a few Indian-summer days even in November, then turn around and freeze everyone back into sweaters.

Willa hadn't seen him yet, and he slowed to a stroll. The last time he'd seen her out of coveralls had been the day she'd applied for the job. Her jeans were worn thin and molded hips that were curvier than the baggy gray coveralls had hinted at.

He blew out a long breath as he considered the way her tight T-shirt further emphasized her femininity. Her hair was a choppy mass of waves almost like she'd cut it herself—without a mirror. But the way she kept it tucked behind her ears was cute.

Most days he never thought about her being . . . well, a *her*. Like Wyatt said, she was a prodigy in the garage. He needed to focus on her skills and not on the way her ass filled her jeans as she stood on tiptoe to skip a rock in the water. But seeing her like this, outside of work and casual, skewed his perception. She wasn't just a female; she was a grown woman. Somehow the distinction seemed important.

"I wasn't sure you were going to wait." He cleared his throat after his voice came out low-pitched and too intimate.

"Yeah, well. It's not like I have any pressing social engagements." The familiar thread of self-deprecating humor set him at ease. Her next rock skipped three times before it sank.

"You feeling better than you were this afternoon? I was worried."

She shot him a look from under her lashes that would qualify as flirty from any other woman. This was Willa though. "Were you? I'm fine."

Her face had lost its pallor and her eyes were bright again. Rufus's barbeque had restored her. Why was she not eating regularly? He banked the question for later.

"What do you say about the raise?" He joined her, and she shifted to face him, propping her hip against the rail. He was going to catch hell from Mack for offering this raise without consulting him, but Wyatt would have his back on the spur-of-the-moment decision. He always did. And Mack would agree it was the right thing to do after he got over his sulk.

"Sounds too good to be true. What do you want in return?" The wariness in her voice and eyes threw him.

A normal reaction to a twenty percent raise would be happiness. Thankfulness. Relief, maybe. But she seemed suspicious. Fearful even. More questions arose about her history and how she'd landed in Cottonbloom.

"All I want is for you to keep up the good work in the garage."

"You need to buy Ford out. Why would you waste money on me?"

"Waste?" The word came out harsher than he intended,

and she took a step away from him. His breath caught with the thought she might be scared of him. "You deserve a raise, Willa. Don't fight me on this."

"All you want is for me to keep working like normal?"

"Keep working at the garage. That's it." A string of curses scrolled through his head. What had happened to her? And why was he just now asking himself these questions? He'd always prided himself on doing what was right, but he'd failed Willa. With everything that had happened in the past year, he'd become too self-absorbed.

Too many things hid behind her semisweet chocolatey eyes. Like a predator with prey, he considered other ways to flush out whatever demons chased her. He side-eyed her, an idea popping into his head. "And I'll need your Social Security number too."

She turned away from the water, her hands braced on the rail behind her as if she needed the support. "Why do you need that?"

"Mack's a stickler for the rules and wants everything aboveboard." A half-truth. Mack would prefer to follow the rules, but he'd be fine paying her under the table as long as she was willing to stay. She didn't need to know that though.

A look flashed over her face before she recovered to force her lips into the facsimile of a smile. A lie. "First thing Monday morning."

His heart accelerated. He'd overplayed his hand. Instincts told him she'd be gone. "Not necessary until the first of January."

"Two more months, then." She chewed on her bottom lip and turned back to face the river.

"That's when we'd need to file paperwork. No big deal." He rested his elbows on the rail and stared at the reeds bending to the water's will as it flowed south toward the Mighty Mississippi. "It's not a big deal, right?"

Her silence spoke volumes.

"Do you have a criminal record or something? It's not like we'd let you go over some youthful mistake."

"I don't have a record."

He heard nothing but truth in her voice, but maybe she was more adept at lying than he gave her credit for. She chafed her arms, looking smaller and more delicate in street clothes than the thick coveralls. He brushed the worries aside. No way was she a felon. Didn't mean she wasn't hiding from someone other than the law.

"Who are you running from? You got an ex out there wanting to hurt you?" Even the possibility shattered his usual calm, but he forced his voice into neutral anyway. Ever so slowly, he was peeling away to the heart of the matter, but one wrong move would scare her off.

She heaved a sigh. "It's complicated, and I don't want to discuss it any further if it's all the same to you."

It involved an ex. Her skirting of his question cinched it. He did want to discuss it further—including a name and address—but he understood. It was the way he felt about discussing his mother or father or Ford or anything of consequence. Cars were easy. Safe. Emotionless.

He was feeling anything but. A sense of vertigo swam through him and turned his stomach. Selfishly, he wanted to know more if only to settle his churning worry, but he wouldn't get any more out of her about her situation tonight.

He searched for a bland topic. Something safe like cars or the garage. "Like I said this afternoon, you can wear something besides coveralls to work. Something like what you're wearing now."

"Believe it not, but these are kind of my nice clothes. I wouldn't want them to get all greasy." She ran her hands over her hips and down her legs. He inhaled sharply.

Okay, unsafe topic. Very unsafe. Better to keep her in

coveralls at work. If she leaned over the hood of a car in those jeans, he wouldn't be able to not stare at her ass. Kind of like the way he was staring at her chest right now. He refocused his eyes on the writing across her bustline.

"So you're a big Outkast fan?" At her obvious confusion, he pointed at her chest. "Your shirt."

She looked down and splayed a hand over the band's emblem on the front. "Sure. They're really great."

"I didn't think they were together anymore."

"Oh well, this is an old shirt. I should toss it." She seemed flustered and fiddled with the hem as if trying to origami it into something different.

Hadn't she just told him these were her "good" clothes? Was he dealing with female insecurity? He needed a *Cosmo* or something as reference.

"Don't worry about it, you look seriously—" *Sexy.* The word popped into his head unbidden. His brain riffled for a more innocuous compliment. "Cute."

He looked to the water and scrubbed at the back of his head. A million other more appropriate words were available, and he'd picked *cute*? Okay, better choice than *sexy,* but what in the hell was wrong with him? His brain was misfiring and running on two cylinders.

A laugh spurted out of her. Her face lost its haunted, hunted look. This was the Willa he looked forward to seeing every day. The one he couldn't imagine *not* in his life.

"Gee, thanks. You usually reserve that kind of sweet talk for your car."

First Wyatt and now Willa? He needed to seriously re-evaluate his relationship with his Mustang. Right now though, he had more pressing worries.

"I'll see you Monday, right?" At her extended silence, he added softly. "If your past comes calling, I'll protect you. I promise. Don't quit on me, Willa."

He reached for her hand, much as she'd done in Rufus's. Her hand was softer than he'd expected considering the type of work she did day in and day out. He rubbed his thumb over the back.

Working side by side, they'd been physically close to each other plenty. Handing tools back and forth, dropping an engine back into a car with the hoist, working in the tight space of the pit together. But this was different in a way he couldn't quantify.

He stared into her eyes, trying to get a read on her, but too much flickered across her face. Finally, she broke eye contact and looked downriver as if plotting a course away from Cottonbloom. And him. "Of course I'll be there."

She was still contemplating running, but he prayed he'd convinced her to stay a while longer. He'd use the time to force her to accept his help. Their hands separated, and he drew his into a fist and tapped the rail, the moment veering into awkwardness.

"You need help with Thatch's car tomorrow?" she asked.

"Naw. I can handle it. Probably a sensor. You take the weekend off. Relax."

She gave him a slight nod. "See you Monday."

He left her, but after he slipped into the sleek leather seat of his Mustang, he waited. Her car was parked around the corner from his, the back end visible. It was a beat-up Honda, probably as old as she was. She walked from the bridge, stopping at the flowers to lean down and touch one, although she didn't snap it off. Orange light streaking the sky framed her.

She wasn't cute, goddammit, she was beautiful. Yet she was hiding underneath coveralls in their garage. She disappeared, and her car started with a puff of black smoke from the exhaust.

Hypersensitive to everything about her now, he evaluated her car like a doctor seeing a sick patient. The black smoke was an oil leak from an engine gasket. Not life threatening to the car yet, but her clutch was ready for hospice care. It could go any moment.

She drove away, and he considered following her. Where did she even live? He wanted to kick his own ass. Maybe Mack knew. She'd submitted paperwork her first week at the garage. Surely one of the fill-in-the-blanks had been her address.

His car started with a healthy growl. Usually, he relished the sound of the engine, and the way the car took his direction. Tonight, though, he drove back to the garage on autopilot, his thoughts centered on Willa and the fears that lurked behind the warmth of her eyes and smiles.

Chapter Three

Tugging the brim of her ball cap low, Willa sidled in the side door of the garage Monday morning half expecting Jackson to pounce on her with more questions. Everything looked wonderfully mundane for a Monday. Her tension eased, and she tipped her hat back so she wouldn't trip over the various parts being stored against the cement wall and signed the time sheet.

Mack and Wyatt chatted in front of the open hood of a Cutlass. Jackson was in the pit under Mr. Thatcher's car. The fix must have been more complicated than a sensor then. That was the way of things sometimes. A problem could sneak up on you. Everything would be running along smoothly, then *bam*—a catastrophe. One that ended up costing thousands of dollars.

Her problems had been like that. Her mother had died before any memories of her had had a chance to take shape. She hadn't missed what she'd never known. Her daddy had been the sun and moon and stars to her. She'd dogged his footsteps and soaked in all his attention and knowledge. She was a self-proclaimed daddy's girl.

Everything changed the year she'd turned fourteen. The owner of a Dodge Charger had stolen her daddy's heart.

Hindsight was an evil bitch, unlike her stepmother who had tried to be nice to Willa. The natural companions of fourteen, rebellion and angst, had filled the void left by what had felt like her father's defection. Looking back, Willa regretted the way she'd behaved. One of the many things she regretted.

Jackson had probed too close to a still-festering wound Friday night on the footbridge. She'd done a good job avoiding entanglements since she'd left home. If she'd sensed herself becoming too comfortable or attached, she moved on. She'd become too comfortable in Cottonbloom and *way* too attached to the Abbotts. Her mistake.

One she needed to rectify. She'd packed her meager belongings over the weekend. Looking at the two duffel bags that summed up her pitiful life had spiraled her into a crying fit. She couldn't face starting over again. Not yet. Anyway, she'd promised Jackson she'd be at work this morning. The way the shards of glassy green in his eyes had cut through her had made it impossible to deny him anything. Even if it would eventually lead to her downfall.

He was the most honorable, upstanding person she'd ever encountered. If he discovered what she'd been and done, he would hate her. And if her past caught up to her in Cottonbloom, he would find out. She was caught in a limbo of needing to leave but wanting to stay.

Two months. He'd given her a two-month reprieve. She would save and scrimp every penny. Repairs on her car would have to wait. Worst case, if her car died, she would move to a big city with public transportation. Abandoning the car would hurt, but would be a heck of a lot easier than leaving Jackson behind.

She caught Jackson's eye and he chucked his head in acknowledgment of her presence, both his hands buried in the undercarriage of the car. She should offer to help him.

Instead, she poured a cup of coffee and slipped back out the door, seeking thirty seconds of sunshine and peace.

She took a sip. Extra strong. Mack must have been the first one down. Jackson preferred his on the weak side. A Crown Victoria came into sight down the road, almost floating on its pillowy suspension. One or both of the Abbott aunts would be inside complaining of phantom noises and leaks. An excuse to check on their nephews. The car pulled up to one of the bay doors, and Hazel Abbott emerged from the driver's side.

Willa preferred Hyacinth, if only because she was funny and easygoing and lacked the laserlike perception of her twin. "Hello, Ms. Abbott. Pretty morning."

"Sure is." Hazel stepped over with a spring that belied her age even though she looked like an old biddy in her low-heeled pumps and Sunday dresses every day of the week. "How is everyone doing this morning?"

"Good. Everyone's good." Willa took another sip of coffee.

"I doubt that. I heard Ford has thrown a wrench in the gears, so to speak." A quick smile wrinkled the corners of her eyes like an accordion, but she turned serious again.

Willa's hand tightened on the Styrofoam cup. It was like watching one of Jackson's fleeting grins, although Ms. Hazel lacked dimples. "They had a meeting Friday. Ford is threatening to sell his stake."

"To whom?"

Willa worried she tread too close to gossip and thumbed over her shoulder. "I should get back. I already signed in."

"I trump Mack's time sheet." Hazel reminded Willa of her whip-smart, intimidating seventh-grade English teacher. "To whom?"

Willa stood up a little straighter. "Ford hasn't said, but the boys are worried."

"Does Mack have a plan?"

"You'll have to ask him, ma'am." She expected Hazel to march inside to turn her powers onto Mack, but instead she tucked her purse under her arm and continued to study Willa.

As a teenager her sole mission in life had been to upend everyone's expectations in the most attention-getting ways possible. That had changed. Now, her modus operandi was to imitate wallpaper. There doing its job, but no one really noticing. She never spoke up or caused a ruckus. To do so brought too much attention to her.

"You've been here a while, haven't you, Willa?"

She nodded slowly. "Couple of years now."

"What do you think about Ford?"

She tried to bite her tongue. Since she was leaving soon, she might as well start dropping some truth bombs on the way out. "I wouldn't trust him to work on my car." Considering the state of her car, the insult was a low blow.

Hazel's eyebrows bounced above the wire frame of her glasses.

"If you'll excuse me, ma'am, I really do need to be getting to work." Willa opened the door for Hazel and followed her inside.

Seeing his aunt, Mack called Willa over to take his place at Wyatt's side. Classic rock wove through the clang and occasional murmur as the four of them settled into their typical routines.

Except a new sort of tension hung over the garage. An expectation of change.

Wyatt was bent over, one hand somewhere around the air intake, the other reaching toward her making a grabby motion. "Socket wrench."

She placed it in his palm like a surgeon's scalpel.

"Heard Jackson gave you a raise." Wyatt twisted around

to send a grin in her direction. "'Bout time, I say. How much?"

Although he and Jackson weren't identical twins—Wyatt's black hair and gray eyes marked him as an anomaly among his brown-haired, hazel-eyed brothers—no one could mistake them for anything but kin. It was something about the way they held themselves, straight and strong and confident.

Their personalities, though, seemed almost the inverse of each other. Wyatt was the boyish, charming version of Jackson. Lighthearted. Easy to laugh, easy to anger. No broody silences. Yet he'd never fascinated her like Jackson.

"Twenty percent."

Wyatt made a scoffing sound and turned back to his work. "You should have asked for more. Jackson is desperate to keep you by his side."

His words jolted her even as her brain spun logic. Wyatt surely meant desperate to keep her at work in the garage, not literally by his side. Friday night had been the longest noncar-related conversation she and Jackson had ever had. And it had still mostly been about the garage. But he *had* called her cute. Without being able to stop herself, she glanced in his direction.

As if sensing her, his head tilted, his gaze snaring hers. She swallowed and kept staring. Weird. She'd spent the last two years studying him. Staring at him unawares. He'd never noticed her. Instead of old fruit-bowl-covered wallpaper, she felt like a centerpiece on display.

Breaking the odd connection, she forced herself to concentrate on the air hoses snaking through the engine compartment, checking their connections and marking the minutes by the music. Two songs played. She risked another glance in his direction. This time when their eyes met, she immediately whipped her gaze back on her work.

What was going on? It was like she'd lost her invisibility cape.

The day passed in fits and starts and crossed glances with Jackson that lasted too long for comfort. Somehow work managed to get done. By the time the afternoon rolled by, Mack and Jackson had buttoned up Mr. Thatcher's car and moved it from the bay to the parking lot, and she and Wyatt had finished connecting and testing the hoses. The Cutlass was almost finished.

Jackson joined her to look down at the finished engine. "Everything looks good."

He certainly did. His gray T-shirt and black work pants did amazing things for his butt. But her gaze got stuck on his strong forearms. Hair a few shades darker than the rich brown on his head dotted his naturally tanned skin.

"Yep. Real good." The words came out suggestively. Okay, yes, maybe in her head she'd been referring to his ridiculously attractive, muscled forearms. She'd admired them countless times before but had managed to keep her opinion to herself.

Her heart beat too fast and heat crept up her neck. Having been paid, she'd eaten well over the weekend and no weakness overcame her, but it was a good excuse to take a break in the AC, away from Jackson's sharp eyes.

"You want a Coke or anything?" She wiped her hands on a shop towel.

"Nah, I'm good." His stare was almost a physical touch.

She stopped inside the door of the break room to enjoy the slide of cool air along her neck and the sense of privacy. A counter along the back wall held a coffee maker and a bowl of snacks for waiting customers. She grabbed a Coke from the refrigerator tucked into the corner and grabbed a seat at the oval table in the middle of the room.

Extra chairs lined the far wall, but they rarely had more than one or two customers waiting at a time.

Her weekend of interrupted sleep was catching up with her. Old nightmares had been interspersed with dreams of Jackson. As expected, some had been intensely erotic, but most of them had been of the leaving variety. She'd woken with tears wetting her pillow.

She leaned her head against the back of the chair and closed her eyes. Air moved around her. She popped her eyes open to find a little girl staring at her from the seat catty-corner. The shock startled a yelp out of her.

The girl grinned, her two front teeth comically big for her delicate features. Her Afro was parted in the center and braided into two pigtails, ribbons trailing prettily. "Sorry 'bout that. Tried not to bother you, but Daddy told me to wait in here so I wouldn't mess up my dress."

"I shouldn't have closed my eyes. Thanks for the wake-up. You look very pretty."

The little girl made a face. "It was picture day at school. I do not normally dress like this."

"How do you normally dress?"

"Like a boy." The way she said it, so defiantly, piqued Willa's curiosity. The girl waved a finger from Willa's hat to her coveralls. "I like what you have on."

"Thanks, I guess." Willa muffled a laugh, not wanting to hurt the little girl's feelings. "Why do you dress like a boy?"

"'Cause I want to be president. Nash, the boy from my closet, said I could be anything I wanted." The girl folded her arms on the table.

Who was she to disagree with a little girl's imaginary friend? Maybe if Willa had had more imaginary friends telling her she could do great things instead of *real* friends getting her in trouble, things would have turned out differently. No, that wasn't fair. She only had herself to blame. She was the one who'd dated a drug-dealing jerk.

"You'll have my vote. What's your name?"

"Margaret, but everyone calls me Birdie. What's yours?" The girl offered a hand.

"Willa." Their shake was very adultlike.

"I'll have to use my real name when I decide to run, but Daddy says he'll call me Birdie even in the Oval Office." The slight exasperation in her voice was tempered by lots of affection.

"No matter how big you get, you'll always be his little girl." The past zoomed too close, and Willa's eyes turned watery. Her own father had said something like it to her every night before bed when she was young.

She couldn't remember exactly when he'd stopped tucking her in or kissing the top of her head or singing her to sleep. Maybe when he'd remarried. Or maybe their relationship had already fractured, allowing her stepmother to crowbar them even further apart. She fingered the fraying emblem of her ball cap.

The door to the break room opened and Mr. Thatcher stuck his head inside. "Let's go, Birdie."

The little girl hopped up. "Nice meeting you."

"You too."

Birdie was gone with a smile and a flash of her red skirt.

Would Willa ever see her father again? Would he remember that she was still his little girl?

"What is wrong with you, bro?" Mack's question pulled Jackson's attention away from the break-room door and back to the job. They were in the pit disassembling the exhaust of a car that had been towed to the shop that morning. "Is it Ford?"

The impending threat of Ford selling out wasn't Jackson's top worry. He glanced toward the break-room door in time to see his top worry slip out, adjust her ball cap, and join Wyatt at the Cutlass.

She wore the same ball cap every day. It dwarfed her delicate features. A man's cap. Now that he'd become attuned to her every move, he noticed the way she stroked the fraying threads of the emblem on the front. Absently. Habitually. The hat was her talisman.

But who had it belonged to? The ex she was hiding from or did some other man hold her affections?

"What's going on between you and Willa?" Humor and concern were in Mack's voice.

"Nothing's going on. Why do you think something's going on?" Jackson cursed the way the words shot out. Too telling for his brother to ignore after Jackson's morning confession of giving Willa a whopping twenty percent raise.

Mack straightened and dropped the tools in his hand into the proper drawers of the red metal toolbox one at a time, never taking his gaze off Jackson. The clang of each echoed in the pit.

"I only meant she seems even more skittish than usual this morning, and you can't seem to stop looking at her. Thought you got her settled back down by offering her a raise." Mack curled his hands around the frame of the car and tilted his head. "But now you've got me curious."

"Nothing like what your dirty mind can conjure up is going on." Jackson glanced toward the Cutlass to find Willa's gaze skimming them—him? She spun away and disappeared around the side. Was she hiding from him? "She put the address of the Driveway Motel on her application two years ago. Is that where she's been staying all this time?"

"Naw, she moved. Renting a trailer over in Country Aire last she told me."

She'd told Mack more than she'd ever told him. His

hand tightened on the grip of the wrench. Dammit. That thought didn't settle well.

Mack continued. "She made mention of her trailer being damaged during the tornado a while back. Had to replace a bunch of furniture apparently. And all her clothes."

"Why didn't she tell me that? Ask for help?"

Mack's eyebrows rose. "Willa Brown is the most independent woman—person—I've ever met. She would never dream of asking for help. She's a lot like you in that respect. Likes to keep to herself. I've always expected to come in one day to find her disappeared. Poof. No trace of her left."

Mack had put Jackson's fear into words. His stomach danced a jig. "I don't want her to go poof."

The sound of the air wrench as Jackson went to work put a pause on the conversation. Mack picked up where he'd left off as the noise faded. "Raise should keep her put. It was long overdue. Should have done it myself. I think she could use the money."

"Me too." More loud work ruled the next few minutes. "I asked for her Social by January so we could put her on the books."

Mack wiped his hands on a blue shop towel. "What'd she say?"

"Said okay, but she'll leave before she tells me. Us." Jackson lowered his voice even though through the music and ambient noise, no one could overhear them. "I searched for her online. Nothing."

"That's a good thing, right?"

"I mean, nothing as in, our Willa Brown doesn't seem to exist."

"I'm going to start calling you Sherlock." Mack looked in Willa's direction and chuffed a laugh. "Sherlock and Encyclopedia Brown."

Willa had earned the nickname because she knew a

little something about everything. All the reading she did in her off time, Jackson supposed.

Mack continued. "Pop never ran a background check as far as I know. His live-and-let-live attitude. I can't imagine she has an outstanding warrant out for her arrest."

She was back under the hood and on her tiptoes, reaching for something deep under the hood. Jackson wished she was in those worn-thin jeans instead of the thick coveralls. "Me either. She could have robbed us blind and run long ago."

"But you think she's hiding something," Mack said.

"Or hiding from someone." Jackson's tone darkened. "Told her we'd protect her if an ex came looking for her."

"Damn straight we will."

"Last thing I want is for her to disappear." When Mack's eyes narrowed on him, he added, "We'd never find anyone as good to replace her. And now that we're getting serious about restorations, we need her."

Mack focused again on his work, but his humming acknowledgment contained a fair amount of sarcasm. "Sounds like you've tried asking her outright. Maybe the best thing is to stick close to her. Earn her trust."

Jackson thought he'd done enough to earn her trust, but considering her evasions, he hadn't come close.

"Or you could sweet-talk Gloria down at the station to run her plates," Mack added.

Jackson turned his back to Willa as if she might sense the deception taking place behind her back. "Isn't that kind of underhanded?"

"Yep. Total dick move, but you'd be doing it for her own good, right? She can't hide from her past forever."

Was Mack right? He and Willa hadn't developed a real friendship. They were coworkers. And not even coworkers who chatted. Yet sneaking around and investigating her past without her blessing seemed like a betrayal. One she might not forgive him for. The thought was untenable.

The day ended with the Cutlass ready to be fired up. He'd drawn the stick to take her out for her first test run. No matter how many cars he'd taken apart and put back together, this was the most nerve-racking and exciting part of any restoration.

Jackson did one final check of hoses and connections before sliding into the driver's seat. The car had arrived with an immaculate interior. Well endowed with Cotton-bloom, Mississippi, old money, Ms. Carson, current owner of the Quilting Bee, had kept the car under a cover in her garage since her husband had passed a decade earlier.

The internals, however, had been a maze of rotting hoses and leaks. The parts now were a mixture of new, classic, and custom-made. Jackson loved the search to re-store things as close to the original as possible.

The Cutlass was a beauty. He didn't want to fail her. It took two tries for his trembling fingers to notch the key in the ignition. Blowing out a breath to manage his ner-vous energy, he cranked the ignition and pumped the gas pedal. The engine turned over several times before catch-ing with a roar.

Jackson couldn't hear anything over the rumble, but Mack and Wyatt high-fived while Willa smiled and gave him a double thumbs-up. The car sounded like a perfectly composed piece of music. He shut the driver's door and put it in gear, inching forward.

Wyatt opened the bay door, and Jackson coasted out into the setting sun, letting the car idle in the lot. He rolled down his window. "Might as well take her on a test-drive. Everything look good from out there?"

Mack walked around the entire car. "Looks perfect. No visible leaks. Keep an eye on the temperature gauge."

Jackson sent a "no shit, Mr. Obvious" look in Mack's

direction and inched forward a few more feet, spotting Willa backing away. He hollered out the window. "Why don't you ride along? You've put more hours in on her than anyone."

She glanced over her shoulder as if he could possibly be speaking to someone else. Jackson tensed, his hands tightening on the wheel, and waited. Finally, she skip-walked around the front of the car and slipped into the passenger side, her back not touching the seat.

Jackson tooted the horn as he pulled onto the parish road. He tried to focus his attention on the gauges and the way the engine sounded and not on the way Willa's fingers kept threading and unthreading on her lap.

"You didn't have a hot date or anything? Nowhere to be?" he asked.

"A date? What's that?"

Her sardonic tone made him smile.

"Come on now. You can't tell me the boys down at the Tavern aren't all over you."

"I don't hang out at the Tavern. And I'm not looking to date."

Her answer reaffirmed his questions. Just how bad had her ex burned her? "How old are you?"

"Twenty-five."

He almost brake-checked, which without seat belts might have sent them both into the windshield. Readjusting his hands on the steering wheel, he shot a sideways glance toward her. Physically, she struck him as younger than twenty-five, but something in her eyes pushed her toward ancient. It was a difference that was hard to resolve.

She grabbed his arm and an electric current buzzed through him. Her brown eyes were huge and flecked with gold toward the irises. How had he never noticed that? "We're overheating."

He shook himself. The car. She was talking about the

car. Sure enough, the gauge he was supposed to be watching had inched up. He rolled to a stop on the shoulder and turned the car off. After the growl of the engine, the silence was strange and awkward.

She tucked one leg up underneath the other, turned toward him, and said, "What now?"

Excellent question. In terms of the car, the answer was easy. A tow back to the shop and troubleshooting. In terms of her? Jackson wasn't sure how to answer. All he knew was something had fundamentally shifted between them, and he would do whatever it took to earn her trust. And maybe more.

Chapter Four

Darkness crept across the sky and the temperature had dropped noticeably. Yet Jackson hadn't made a move to call the garage for a tow. Willa threw him a sidelong look. The strange vibes that had ricocheted through the shop all day seemed to reverberate even louder in the confines of the car.

He faced front, his hands tightening and loosening on the wheel at regular intervals. Was he upset or angry? Neither response was like him. Car troubles generally didn't faze him. He would roll up his sleeves and get on with it, but this car was a big-visibility project. Ms. Carson planned to drive it and not auction it off. It would be priceless advertising.

"It's probably something minor," Willa said to break the tension. "A gasket. Or loose connection. I'll take a look underneath as soon as we get back to the garage. I can fix it, don't worry."

"I'm not worried about the car, Willa. I'm worried about you." He let go of the wheel and shifted toward her. "Why don't you trust me?"

She swallowed, the change from car talk to personal unwelcome. As she'd feared, their unplanned dinner together had been a tipping point. Nothing would be the same between them again. She hauled herself out of the low-slung seat and stalked down the shoulder back toward the shop.

A car door slammed and gravel crunched behind her. She upped her pace, but knew it was only a matter of time. Like her past, he was too big to outrun. The flames licked closer and closer.

He came up beside her and matched her stride, his hands stuffed into the pockets of his black pants. He didn't grab her and demand answers or make ultimatums.

"We walking all the way back, then?" he asked.

"I am. I don't care what you do." That wasn't strictly true. She cared too much.

"Pretty sunset." His voice was conversational, instead of confrontational. "This is my favorite time of year."

His attempt to normalize the situation settled her nerves somewhat. "Mine too."

"I like the stark trees and smell of burning leaves and homemade soup and football. What's your favorite part?"

She enjoyed fall because she wasn't sweltering in her trailer like in summer or shivering like in February when even Louisiana could turn frigid. Fall reminded her of making s'mores with her dad when she was a kid around the fire pit in her backyard. She couldn't admit any of that to Jackson.

"The same as you, I guess," she said.

His sigh struck her as disappointed and cast her back to high school where she'd never been in danger of being pegged a high achiever. But she wasn't that girl anymore. She'd dealt with far worse and come out the other side.

"I'm not a damn car." Anger heated her voice.

"I know that."

"Do you?" She stopped and he turned to face her. "You haven't spared a thought about how much you pay me or what I wear or why fall is my favorite season for two years."

"I know and that's my bad. I should have been paying more attention to you."

She made a scoffing sound. That's exactly what she didn't need. Everything depended on her staying under the radar. "You want to fix me like I'm some broken-down car. Or fix my problems or whatever. But that's not how people work. Maybe I'm unfixable."

Half his face was in shadows from the setting sun. Even in the best of times it was difficult to get a read on his mood, but the roughness in his voice was more pronounced than usual. "I don't want to fix you. I want to help you. I want you to trust me."

Part of her wanted to trust him. But she'd learned too many times that trust led to betrayal. It had started with her ex. He'd ripped her trust into tiny unmendable pieces. There was the time she'd trusted her roommate in Biloxi with the rent money. Instead, the girl had bought three painkillers off the streets, and they'd been evicted. Or the time one of her landlords wanted a different sort of payment than money. The list went on.

Accepting help led to being in someone's debt. And one never knew when or how any favor would be called in.

"I don't want your help. Don't need it. I want you to leave me alone and let me do my job." She resumed stalking back to the garage. How far would her hurt feelings and outrage carry her?

She didn't have to find out. Down the road a set of headlights cut through the gloaming, and she recognized the garage's tow truck. It slowed on the approach, stopping with a squeak of its brakes.

Wyatt stuck his head out the window, an easy half smile she couldn't return on his face. "Need a lift?"

Without a word, she hauled herself into the backseat of

the double cab and huddled against the far window, letting the brothers get the car situated. They troubleshot the problem with the Cutlass on the ride back. She didn't interject her opinion.

The past two years had lulled her into an idyll. Unlike Sleeping Beauty she was not waking to a handsome prince, but the field of thorns where the dragon lay in wait. In the darkness, she stared out the window and wiped a tear into her temple.

As soon as they arrived back at the garage, she grabbed her stuff and loaded into her crappy Honda with only murmured semipolite good-byes. Wyatt and Mack were focused on the Cutlass and didn't seem to notice. But, of course, Jackson did. He seemed to possess X-ray vision these days. Only when the garage was out of sight did she relax.

Country Aire trailer park wouldn't get a magazine spread unless it was in *Trailers and Trash,* but she'd lived in far worse places. When a tornado had taken off the roof and collapsed the wall of her first trailer, ruining her things in the process, she'd moved what was left into a smaller trailer at the back of the park. The rent was cheaper which helped defray the costs of replacing the couch, bedding, and most of her clothes.

She parked next to her front—and only—door. Sounding like a dying animal, her car engine spooled down as she got out. The relative quiet was filled with competing sounds. Muffled gunfire from an action flick on someone's TV warred with a loud telephone conversation. Several men gathered to drink outside like it was happy hour. Now that her time was growing short, nostalgia overcame her. She would miss the slice of freedom and solitude she'd carved out for herself here.

A whine grabbed her attention. She scanned the line

of pine trees beyond her trailer. The black-and-white mutt was back. It had been hanging around her trailer for the last couple of weeks, and she'd left out food every couple of days. Dumb of her considering she could barely take care of herself.

She stepped into the high grass between her and the dog. For its own good, she should shoo the dog away. She wouldn't be around to take care of it. But the decision to leave had left her feeling hollowed out and achingly lonely.

Instead of doing the responsible, smart thing, she crouched down and patted her legs. "Come here, boy. Or girl. Come on."

The dog crossed three-quarters of the field before stopping to pace a good dozen feet away, its attention fixed on her. She tried again, but only drew the dog forward a couple more feet. It crouched on the ground, its whine sounding like a cry for help.

"Good grief," she muttered and retreated to her trailer. She opened her fridge, seeing nothing that would tempt a dog. She checked her lean cabinets. The off-brand can of ravioli was supposed to be her dinner. She dumped the contents on a paper plate and grabbed a granola bar on her way back outside.

She sat cross-legged at the edge of the field, laid the plate of ravioli at her knee, and dug into the granola bar, taking small bites and chewing slowly. The trick didn't make the bar any more satisfying or make her feel more full. Its ears twitching, the dog raised its head and sniffed before slinking forward with its belly close to the ground.

The crinkle of the granola-bar wrapper froze the dog six feet away, and she set it on the ground, playing a solitary game of quiet mouse, still mouse.

The closer the dog came, the more ribs she could count along its side. Her chin wobbled, but she held the tears back. "Go on, baby. I won't hurt you. You can trust me. Promise."

That the words were too similar to what Jackson had said to her earlier tweaked her sense of irony. But she wasn't a stray dog. Or a car.

She coaxed the dog closer with soothing nonsense words. Never taking its eyes off Willa, it started to eat. She had never owned a dog, but she'd read enough to know not to touch one while it ate unless she wanted to lose some fingers.

After licking the plate clean of any remnants, the dog settled on its belly and looked up at her. Tentatively, Willa held out her hand. Once the dog had sniffed her fingers, she stroked its head. Although dirty, its fur was softer than she expected, and its eyes narrowed at her touch, seemingly content.

Had the dog, like her, once had a home? She set the plate to the side and inched closer. She ran her hand down its back, stopping to scratch its hindquarters. Black ringed one eye while the rest of its face was white, giving it a "boxer after a big-fight" look. A fight it had lost. The rest of its body was splotched with black on white. Willa wasn't familiar enough with breeds to make a guess as to its parentage.

Nothing except extreme hunger appeared to be wrong with it though. Maybe the dog just needed some luck to break its way. Willa could empathize.

She ran a hand around its neck, but there was no collar hiding in the fur. "Should we give you a name?"

The dog responded with a look that sent the hairs on her arms standing up. It was like it understood her.

"Okay. Since I don't know if you're a boy or girl, how about something middle-of-the-road like . . . River." It seemed appropriate considering how important the river was to Cottonbloom.

River tucked its head under her hand, and she smiled, resuming her gentle strokes along its head and soft ears. The temperature dropped faster now the sun was gone. She shivered and rose, her muscles stiffened from her long day and the cooler air.

The dog backed into the taller grass of the field. She patted her legs. "Come on. Don't you want to be warm and safe tonight?"

A bang came from the front part of the park, some idiot firing an air rifle. River ran to the line of pine trees and disappeared. It was for the best. The mutt probably had fleas. Still, she waited a few minutes, hoping the dog would return, but it didn't. Willa was well and truly alone.

Retreating to the trailer, she cleaned up in the lukewarm trickle that any respectable shower wouldn't associate with. Her double mattress took up most of the floor in the back room. It was comfortable, but more importantly, safe.

When she woke in the morning, it was to gritty eyes and the feeling she'd had terrible dreams. Only a sense of dread lingered. She pulled on her coveralls and stepped out into a crisp morning.

With River on her mind, she rounded her trailer and scanned the trees, squinting to see through the low-hanging fog. A furry head tucked itself under her hand and she startled. River sat next to her, looking out at the field as well.

She squatted down and gave the dog a thorough petting. If River hadn't smelled so bad, Willa might have given the dog a big hug. She went back inside, opened a can of chicken noodle soup, and poured it into a plastic container. She left River happily slurping at the soup.

The next few days passed as if a pause button had been pressed, leaving everything in limbo. She and Jackson resumed their usual working relationship, which consisted of Willa anticipating his needs with minimal discussion. By the time Friday rolled around, she had almost convinced herself things could revert to normal.

Except for the fact she'd caught Jackson looking at her with a worrisome expression, as if he were probing for weakness before he launched an attack. He could spend days troubleshooting an engine problem. He was too stubborn to give up untangling her secrets.

The shop floor was filled with the clang of equipment, but little conversation. Even Wyatt was unusually quiet. Attuned to Jackson's every move, she noted when he disappeared out the front door with Wyatt. Were they discussing her?

Not three minutes later, Wyatt busted in the front door. "Hey, Mack, give animal control a call. We've got a problem."

Mack strode toward his office. "Another rabid raccoon? Let me grab my gun."

"Stray dog acting like it wants to take Jackson's balls off."

Willa looked out the foggy window of the nearest bay. Her breath stuttered. There was no mistaking the black-eyed face of River.

She pushed past Wyatt and ran to the side yard. Jackson caught her arm on her way to River and pulled her into his side, putting himself between her and the perceived threat.

"Get behind me," he said close to her ear. "It might be rabid."

River's growling grew chestier and more menacing, and Willa peeked over Jackson's shoulder. River's dirty paws were planted wide, its focus on Jackson. He was the threat, and in a flash, she understood that the dog was trying to protect her.

She pivoted around to face Jackson and put her hand on his chest. His heart was thumping fast and hard. "The dog's looking for me."

"What do you mean?"

"It's been hanging out around the woods behind my place for a while now, and I've been feeding it."

The dog interspersed a few snappy barks between his growls, and Jackson's arm came up to block her, his hand around her upper arm. His movement escalated River's agitation.

Willa patted Jackson's arm and took a step, but Jackson didn't let go of her. She wasn't the one who needed protecting. "River thinks you're going to hurt me. Step back and let me calm it down."

"River?" A hint of amusement lightened his expression, although he kept his gaze fixed on the dog.

"Seemed appropriate. Go on. Back up." She gave him a little shove in the biceps, but like a stone statue he didn't move.

She didn't drop her hand. He transferred his attention to her, and she exhaled as if the intensity and fierce protectiveness in his eyes were a physical thing. He was magnetic, and she reacted as if she were made of metal. Before she could lean into him, he took a step back and then another.

She took a deep breath, crouched down, and held out her hand. "It's okay, River. Come on. No one here is going to hurt you, I promise."

River's chesty growls ceased, but the dog didn't move. Willa glanced over her shoulder to see all three brothers lined up like a gorgeous wall of muscle behind her. Jackson's hands were outstretched slightly as if he were ready to leap to pull her to safety.

"You have any of that beef jerky left, Wyatt?" she asked.

He fished a package from his pocket and handed over a piece.

"Okay, I need you guys to step off. You're frankly terrifying all lined up like that."

Wyatt and Mack retreated to the edge of the garage. Jackson only took two steps back. "I don't like this, Willa."

"Trust me." The irony of her asking for his trust didn't escape her in that moment, and by the flare of his eyes, it wasn't lost on him either. Nevertheless, he backed off.

Once he'd put a dozen feet between them, she turned back to River and waved the jerky around. "Come on, you know you want it."

Crouched low to the ground, River padded toward her like a stealth hunter and took the jerky out of her hand, settling in to gnaw on the leathery treat. Willa scratched behind its ears and patted its back, the spine still too prominent even with a week of relative plenty.

Jackson duck-walked over to join her. He offered the dog another, larger piece of jerky. The dog tensed, but accepted the offering, even deigning to let Jackson pat its head, although it never took its eyes off him.

"It must have followed me this morning. That's got to be five miles or more. It's a wonder it didn't get hit."

"Your dog is a girl, by the way. No dangling appendages."

"I should have checked her undercarriage, I guess. But she's not my dog." Her denial was weak considering she had been feeding it—her—the past week.

"She belonged to someone once upon a time." His voice was low and contemplative.

"What makes you think that?" Willa stroked dirt-roughed fur.

"No feral dog would tolerate us petting her, much less enjoy the attention. Look what she did to get to you. You showed her a little kindness, and she wants more."

"I gave her some off-brand ravioli is all."

"She's a pretty thing. Or will be once she's had a bath and gotten fattened up. Probably needs a good once-over at the vet too."

"I can't . . ." The lump in her throat grew to epic proportions. She could share her canned food with River, but no way could she afford a vet bill. Yet another living being she'd disappoint.

Now the dog had a little food in her belly, she put her head on her forelegs, her eyes heavy. She must be tuckered out from the journey.

"Let's get a water dish for her." Jackson stood and held out a hand.

She held on to River's ruff. "But—"

"This dog traveled miles to get to you. She's not going anywhere now she's found you."

She slipped her hand inside his, and without any effort at all, he pulled her up next to him, but didn't immediately release her. His thumb rubbed the back of her hand.

"Everything is going to be fine," he whispered.

He might have been referring to River, but it felt like his assurance encompassed more than the dog. He wasn't a soothsayer though. Bad things happened all the time to people who didn't deserve it.

"Sure it will." Not bothering to mask her sarcasm, she pulled her hand free and walked back to the shop floor.

Jackson made good on his promise, and as he'd predicted, River hovered around the door the rest of the afternoon. When she was ready to leave, she exchanged a glance with Jackson, but he didn't comment, only turned back to his work.

She loaded River into the passenger seat of her car and rolled down the windows to combat the strong dog smell. River rode with her head poked out the window, tongue lolling. Seeing her delight in spite of her near starvation and abandonment filled Willa with a welling hope that had taken a beating the last few weeks.

What if she gave Jackson her real Social? Did anyone out there even care where she was anymore? It had been five years since she'd run away from home. How long did memories last?

Chapter Five

Jackson turned into Country Aire Trailer and RV Park. The place was a total dump. A group of men gathered in lawn chairs at one of the first trailers. The smell of marijuana wafted through his car's vents. Heads swiveled toward his '69 Mustang as he drove by. He was used to getting attention for his ride, but this was the kind he didn't want. They looked like they had the knowledge to strip his car of anything valuable in under two minutes.

Dammit. He tightened his hands on the steering wheel. This place wasn't safe. It was a trailer park straight out of a movie. The kind tornados targeted in redneck jokes. The fact the park had actually been hit by a tornado only cemented the stereotype.

He circled the curve toward the back and spotted her beat-up car next to a narrow squat trailer with dingy formerly white siding, reflecting none of Willa's quirky personality. It wasn't a home. It was a place to live. He parked behind her and gathered his courage. She hadn't invited him or asked for help of any kind, and her reaction was sure to include a fair amount of annoyance.

But just because she hadn't asked for help didn't mean

she didn't need it. He grabbed the two sacks on his passenger seat and maneuvered out of the car. River gave a yip and trotted from somewhere around the back of the trailer. He dropped to one knee and greeted the dog. Her tail wagged. She had been treated kindly at some point or she wouldn't be this trusting.

Dusk was falling fast. A light shone through checked curtains in the front window. He had procrastinated long enough. Standing at the bottom of the metal, rickety-looking steps, he knocked. River settled on her haunches next to him.

The curtains ruffled. A few seconds later, she cracked open the door. He was eye level with a rainbow on the front of her white T-shirt, the fabric pulling taut over her breasts. He swallowed, gave himself a mental slap, and forced his eyes north.

Her feet and head were bare, and her hair was tucked behind her ears. Even with no makeup, her eyes dominated her face, her lashes long and dark. He was struck again by her innate femininity once out of her coveralls and hat.

"What are you doing here?" Suspicion was laced with mild panic in her voice.

Did she have a guy over? The thought made his body tense. The paper bags he cradled crinkled under the pressure. "I brought food and stuff for River. Are you busy?"

"I suppose not."

He took the first step up to her door, but she didn't back up, her reluctance palpable. River gave one bark. Her gaze bounced from him to the dog to his offering and she sighed. "Come on in."

He had to duck his head to clear the low door frame. The ceiling of the trailer was higher, but still low compared to the openness of his loft-style place above the barn. Claustrophobia enveloped him.

She took one of the bags out of his arms and set it on

the narrow counter of the tiny kitchen. He placed the other on a love seat wedged into the short wall at the end.

"Are you okay?" she asked.

"It's . . . cozy in here, isn't it?" His voice choked off.

For the first time all week, an impish smile quirked her lips. "That's a nice way to put it. I'd go with tiny. Cramped. Prisonlike." She opened the two windows, front and back, and pulled the curtains open.

"Better?" she asked.

He took a deep breath and nodded. Now that the cross flow of cooling air had alleviated his mild panic, he examined the space more thoroughly. It didn't take long. Beyond the small kitchen was a door he assumed led to a bathroom or closet. Beyond the narrow doorway at the far end, a mattress and bedding was visible on the floor. She didn't even have a proper bed. Yet he also noticed the multicolored rug on the floor and the fact the place was tidy and smelled faintly of lemon-scented cleaner.

Intellectually, he knew people lived in worse conditions around the world, but emotionally, he wanted to sweep Willa up and take her home with him. The implications only worsened his feeling of being trapped.

While he suppressed impulses she would battle with every scrap of her considerable pride, she unpacked the first bag and stacked the cans of dog food. The last thing she pulled out was a bottle of dog shampoo. She turned to him, her face tilted down toward the bottle she clutched at her waist.

"There's more food in the other bag and some treats." He scuffed his boot along the edge of the rug.

"I don't know what to say." Her voice wasn't much above a whisper.

He slipped a finger under her chin and forced her face up. Her chin wobbled and her eyes shone with tears. "I didn't mean to upset you," he said.

"It's been a long time since someone has done something nice for me." Her smile was in contrast to the tear that managed to escape.

He caught the errant sign of emotion with his thumb. The tear might as well have been a dunk in freezing water. He was awakened to everything about her. She could have used help before now, yet he'd been hell-bent on remaining cut off from everyone except his brothers. What once felt like proud independence now veered sharply selfish.

He'd never been good at expressing even the most straightforward emotion and what was churning inside him was complicated and set his internals at war, his heart leading the charge.

"What do you say we get River cleaned up?" He tried to force a normalish tone, but raw emotion made his voice sound like broken concrete. "Do you have a tub?"

"Yeah, a luxurious hot tub for eight in the back." Her laugh dried her tears. "I have a coffinlike stand-up shower. But it does have a wand we can maybe make work."

River balked at entering the trailer. Willa held her scruff, and he pushed at River's backside. She barked, but never tried to bite either of them. Once she was inside, the dog's agitation turned to curiosity, and she sniffed everything and anything.

Jackson rummaged through the bag on the couch and came up with bacon-flavored dog treats. As if River could smell them through the packaging, she stood at his feet, tail wagging and licking her chops.

"She knows what they are, doesn't she?" Willa asked.

"Looks that way." He ripped open the bag and pulled out a strip. "Sit, River."

The dog sat, and Jackson handed over the treat. She settled onto the rug to enjoy the bacony goodness.

"How could someone just abandon her?" A deep thread of emotion in her voice tugged him a step closer which in the small space put them only inches apart. Close enough to note the beautiful complexity of her eyes. What once he'd thought was a simple Crayola brown was actually all different shades.

When he felt himself slipping into a hypnotic state, he forced himself to look at River. "Maybe her family moved and couldn't take her. Or couldn't afford her."

"But to dump her . . ." She shook her head and chafed an arm.

"People can be cruel."

"They sure can," she said softly. Before he could question her further, she grabbed River's scruff. "Let's go, smelly dog. Gotta get you clean if you want to stay with me."

He helped herd River toward the bathroom. Coffinlike was an apt description of the shower. She turned on the water and got it warm before shoving the dog underneath the anemic spray. He wedged himself as close as possible and held on to River while Willa lathered her fur with a generous amount of shampoo.

River shook herself in the middle of a rinse, sending water in all directions. Jackson sputtered and ran a hand down his face. Willa's husky laugh set his nerve endings sizzling.

By the time she turned the water off, she was nearly as wet as the dog. Her white T-shirt clung to her body. Her nipples were peaked against the damp fabric, one covered by a rainbow, the other shadowing clearly through her bra.

His body surged, the ache in his groin matching the one in his chest. His interest wasn't friendly in the least. Neither was the compulsion to kiss her and strip the wet shirt off her body. The wall that had held his emotions at bay for so long teetered close to a total collapse. There was no containing his need now. His body was in mutiny.

River shot out of the bathroom and barked at the door.

"I'll let her out." He didn't even recognize his voice.

River shot out into the night and Jackson followed, watching her shake and lick at her fur. Willa's trailer backed up to an open field and a line of pine trees. The scene was tranquil if not particularly striking. He preferred the woods behind the barn, the river cutting a path through the trees. It teemed with life and memories.

Deep breaths of cool air calmed him, and by the time River came trotting back up, Jackson had marshaled his more basic needs and stuffed them back where they belonged, out of sight if not entirely out of mind. Until Willa trusted him, whatever brewed between them would never have a chance to boil.

He opened the trailer door, and this time, River took the steps without prompting. Willa had on a dry red oversized T-shirt. The change should have helped steady his sanity, but instead all he could focus on was the fact she didn't have a bra on under the looser shirt.

She opened a can of the dog food and upended it on a paper plate. River settled in to noisily eat. Willa turned to him with a smile he might classify as shy if he didn't know her better. "You want something to drink? I have Cokes."

He should leave. His lies, even if they were to himself, didn't sit well. Coming with supplies hadn't been a simple act of kindness. That damn rainbow T-shirt had exposed his ulterior motives like a pot of gold at the end. He ran his hands down his jeans and shuffled backward. The back of his legs hit the love seat, throwing him off balance. He plopped down.

Apparently taking his move as a *yes,* she grabbed two cans of Coke and joined him. The love seat sagged slightly in the middle, forcing them so close their shoulders touched. He took her offering automatically and popped the top. The burn of his first swallow didn't help settle him in the least, especially watching her take a delicate sip, as if the Coke were something to be savored.

How had he never noticed her lips, full and a dark pink, the top slightly fuller than the bottom? His hand tightened and dented the sides of the can. Blowing out a slow breath, he scanned the trailer, searching out clues about her.

He didn't see a TV anywhere. His too brief glance into her bedroom had revealed a stack of books and a tarnished brass lamp on the floor next to the mattress. More books were stacked on the window ledge next to him. A hardback with library letters and numbers on the spine was on top. *Jane Eyre*. He picked it up and flipped through the pages.

"Sorry, champ, all words and no pictures."

He suppressed a smile at her tart jab. "What's it about?"

"An orphaned girl is sent off to a charity school. Once she's grown, she takes a post teaching a girl at a secluded estate where she meets a man. They fall in love, but he's got some skeletons in his attic. She runs away, inherits money, a big fire scars him, but love overcomes. It's a classic. I can't believe you haven't read it." She set her can down and took the book out of his hands. "I've read it four times now."

"Not sure I've even read a book since high school. Unless car manuals count." He flashed her a smile. "You must have been a great student."

She didn't return his smile. In fact, she shifted to put her back into the corner of the love seat as if his compliment were an insult. "Why would you think that?"

He scrubbed a hand along the stubble of his jaw to his nape. "All the books? The way you talk sometimes. We don't call you Encyclopedia Brown for nothing."

"Actually, I didn't start reading until I . . . left home. No TV. I'm not into smoking and drinking with my neighbors, so yeah, I read." The way she brushed down the spine of the book with her finger was like a caress.

What would her hand feel like on him? The thought popped into his head before he could squash it. To cover his confusion, he picked up the next book. It was a spy novel that sounded vaguely familiar. "I've seen this movie."

"Book is always better." Her voice had lost some of the strain. She bent at the waist and stroked River's ears. "I was a terrible student, actually. Only made it through because my best friend pushed and helped me."

"I thought about dropping out. Didn't see the point. All I wanted was to work in the garage with Pop, but he made me stick it out." Even over a year after his pop had died of a massive heart attack on the shop floor, the emptiness of the loss was vast.

She straightened and brushed his hand with hers, the touch feather light. "I miss him too. He was so nice to me. Not like some I've worked for."

His rising aggression smothered the sadness and he welcomed it. "What does that mean? What did they do?"

"You know how it is." She stood, but he grabbed her forearm and pulled her back down.

"No, I don't. Why don't you tell me how it is?"

"Most people aren't decent like you and your family, Jackson. I've been on my own for a while now. I look young, which some people—men especially—equate with weakness, and they think that means they can take things I'm unwilling to give."

He couldn't help the harshness of his voice. "And did they take it?"

"I was never raped, if that's what you're asking. But I've been groped plenty."

He wasn't sure which kick in the gut took more of his breath away, the confession itself or the matter-of-factness of her voice. "Did you go to the police?"

Her laugh sliced at his heart like a million paper cuts. "Like they would believe me? I'm a nobody. It was easier to pack up and move on. Until Cottonbloom," she added in a whisper.

He loosened his grip and stroked the soft inside of her forearm with his thumb. She didn't pull away. "I'm sorry you had to deal with crap like that all by yourself."

"I'm used to it."

That any woman got used to being treated like that was all kinds of wrong, but the fact it was Willa made him want a list of her past employers. He'd make certain they never treated another woman disrespectfully again, even if it meant literally busting balls.

A shadow of the violence in his heart must have shown on his face, because she said, "You can't change the world, Jackson." A hint of tease softened the moment.

He might not be able to change the world, but he could damn well make hers a better place. That kind of announcement wouldn't sit well with either of them. Even thinking it was scary enough.

Dogs made for safe, warm, fuzzy subjects, right? "I'll make a vet appointment for River in the morning."

"She looks healthy enough to me."

"She might have heartworms, and she'll need her shots. Plus, if you plan to let her inside, you'll need medicine to keep the fleas and ticks off. A good once-over is probably all she needs."

"I can't afford a vet bill." She chewed on her bottom lip and flipped the book around in her hands, her voice akin to confessing a high crime. Her pride was a rock wall that would take time to scale.

"I'll cover it. Consider it a loan." A loan he'd never call.

"What do you want in return?" It was the same question she'd asked when he'd offered her the raise. She vibrated with agitation.

"Nothing. Except for you to stick around."

"I don't know. I don't like being in debt to anyone." The uncertainty in her voice set him on edge.

But he wasn't just anyone, was he? Not only had he violated his code by lying to himself, but now he recognized the manipulative shade of his "unselfish act." He'd hoped the dog might bind her to Cottonbloom. And him. "What are you running from, Willa?"

She stood so abruptly, River growled and jumped to attention. "Thanks for the dog food and stuff. I'll see you later."

Time. He needed more time to earn her trust. If he pushed her too hard, she would disappear. With a sigh, he heaved himself off the love seat, set his coke can down on the narrow kitchen counter, and cracked the door open. "I'll set up something for the morning."

"I have plans in the morning."

His eyes narrowed on her, not sure if she was telling the truth or pushing his buttons. "Afternoon then."

"Fine." She shrugged, her gaze skating off to the side. River jumped past him and streaked around the side of the trailer.

Willa clambered out and stood at the edge of the field. The wind had picked up, and the grass wavered. River was gone.

"River!" The plaintive note in her voice bordered on desperation.

"She'll be back," he said with more conviction than he felt.

Goose bumps rose on her arms. The wind had switched directions throughout the day and was now blowing cool from the north. "Maybe she can't stay. Maybe she's too afraid of what might happen."

He took a sharp breath. Her profile was strong and stoic, but her narrow shoulders had rounded as if she needed to protect herself at all times. Everyone needed someone to lean on. What would he have done without Mack and Wyatt?

"She has more courage than you give her credit for." He reached out to touch Willa's shoulder, but thought better of it. Stuffing his hands into his pockets, he backed away and slipped into his car. His headlights illuminated her slight figure at the edge of the field. She didn't turn.

He didn't know what was going on between them, but it felt important. Monumental even. Unfortunately, the secrets separating them seemed almost as big.

Chapter Six

Willa peeked out past her curtains, half expecting Jackson to have returned sometime during the night to stake her out. He seemed determined to keep tabs on her. The fact he was digging and would continue to dig until he hit truth should make her want to throw everything she owned in the back of her Honda and lay rubber out of town. Not that her tires had any rubber to spare.

A million reasons to leave circled in her head, but one really good one to stay outweighed them by around two hundred well-muscled pounds. It was the first time another soul had been in her trailer, and Jackson seemed to stretch the space to the point of snapping bolts and popping nails. It had been both disconcerting and comforting.

Seeing no one outside, she followed River down the portable metal steps, juggling an armful of books. River had scratched at the door an hour after Jackson left, and Willa had been so relieved, she'd allowed River to sleep in her bed. Waking next to a warm body had been a new experience, and not an unpleasant one.

But, in the brief time between dreams and reality, she'd imagined a different warm body. One with rumpled brown hair and greenish hazel eyes with a flashing, lazy smile and hands that were rough from hard work but knew how to be gentle with her. She'd woken with an ache in her belly and heart.

She waved good-bye to River as if the dog were a person and headed across the river into Mississippi. She hadn't lied to Jackson. She had a standing Saturday-morning date with stacks and stacks of books at the Cottonbloom Library.

She drove across the steel-girded bridge into Cottonbloom, Mississippi, and to the library on autopilot, her mind back in Louisiana with Jackson. She had a blueprint to handle curious men who wanted more than she could give.

The problem was she did want to give Jackson more. Everything. Confessions had threatened to leak out—like the fact she'd let her best friend down in the most earth-shattering way possible—but the leaks would turn into a torrent and eventually the dam she'd built to protect herself would collapse. Already she was plugging holes like the little Dutch boy.

She parked in front of the library and took the steps two at a time. The library occupied an old mansion that had been gifted to the town by an old-maid recluse. Upon her death, officials had found boxes upon boxes of books. In a stroke of genius, the house had been converted into a library. A sizable extension had been added to the back, but it did nothing to detract from the street-side charm of the white columns and marbled porch.

Willa could spend hours wandering the different rooms, each with their own theme and treasures, but her favorite was a large upstairs room that housed the historical fiction. Something about stepping into the past and living someone else's life for a few hours helped her bear the thought of the years stretching out in front of her.

"Figured I'd find you up here." Marigold Dunlap pushed

a cart of books into the room. She was the head librarian, middle-aged, thick around the middle from her self-proclaimed addiction to peach cobbler, and the nicest woman Willa had ever met. With curly red hair and dark blue eyes, she crackled as if an electrical current gave her endless energy.

Willa had discovered the sanctuary a library could provide during her six months living in Baton Rouge. The anonymity and quiet of the huge marbled public space was a balm to the chaos of her days spent scrabbling together enough money to live and avoiding trouble on the streets. The peace came with the added perk of free computer use.

She would pretend to read to avoid being accused of loitering. The pretend reading had soon turned into real reading. One of the first things she did after settling in Cottonbloom was to find the closest library.

Marigold wasn't like the shushing, aloof librarians she'd encountered at other libraries. She had a loud laugh that traveled from the first to the second floor, an open, inquisitive nature, and good heart. Still, it had taken more than a handful of Saturdays for Willa to respond to the other woman's overtures.

"How was *Jane Eyre* this time? Was Rochester still a secretive, lying bastard?" Marigold's laugh made Willa giggle in return.

"Hasn't changed a bit, but I can't stay away from him." Willa turned back to the row of books. "Recommend something new for me."

"Want gothic and romantic and chilling?"

"Sounds right up my alley," Willa said.

Marigold went deeper into the rows and came out with three books. "Try these."

Willa clutched them to her chest, not bothering to examine them. Marigold's seal of approval was good enough. "How did the football team do last night?"

"Lost. We're out of the play-offs, but we beat Cotton-bloom Parish, so the season is still a rousing success."

"How's Dave feeling?"

"Fair to middling. Chemo is a real bitch."

"I'm so sorry." Willa reached for Marigold's hand and gave it a squeeze.

Tears shimmered, but Marigold blinked them away. "Prognosis is good, so I'm hanging on to that."

Her husband was a general contractor which meant Marigold was now the family's sole provider. The stress of the financial and emotional burden had carved deeper furrows across her forehead and bruised her eyes. With her own situation tenuous, all Willa could offer were optimistic platitudes, which wouldn't be fair. The worst might indeed happen and often did.

"Is there anything I can do?" As the offer came out, she realized it was as useless as a platitude. Marigold would never ask for help.

Sure enough, she smiled even though her eyes showed the trace of tears. "Introducing you to my favorite books brightens my day."

Willa forced her lips into an answering smile. "I can't wait to dive into these. I'd better check out. Do you mind?"

"Of course, come on." Because Willa didn't live in Mississippi and couldn't provide identification, Marigold checked out books on her account for Willa. At first it had been awkward, but Marigold had a gift of putting people at ease and earning their trust. Even Willa to some extent. In return, she guarded the books with her life.

The most heart-wrenching loss when the tornado had blown through hadn't been her clothes or furniture or trailer, but the six library books. She'd tried to pay for them, but Marigold had waved off her attempt.

They descended the staircase side by side. "I may have adopted a dog," Willa said.

Marigold gasped and gave a little clap. "That's wonderful. I worry about you in that trailer all by yourself."

"I'm hardly by myself." At least twenty of the trailers were filled at the moment. Private conversations drifted through thin walls and open windows. It qualified as too much togetherness in her opinion.

"Exactly. You're surrounded by ne'er-do-wells."

Some troublemakers roamed the park, but most of the residents were like her. Trying to survive. They might not be the friendliest bunch, but they all understood an aspect of life Marigold had never faced.

"I can take care of myself, but it is nice to have some company, even if our conversations are generally one-sided."

"Generally?" Marigold chuckled and Willa joined her.

"I'm supposed to take her to the vet this afternoon. Jackson Abbott has offered to pay. Should I let him?" Willa chewed on the inside of her mouth.

"Of course you should," Marigold said breezily.

"But what if he—I don't know—wants something in return."

Marigold took her upper arm, stopping halfway down the steps. "I don't know what all happened to you before you landed in Cottonbloom, but one thing I do know . . . those Abbott brothers are good men. Honest and fair-dealing. Dave helped the twins fix up their loft."

Had she been that transparent? "I may—" She cleared her throat when the words came out choked. "I may have to move on soon."

Worry clouded the vibrant blue of Marigold's eyes. "I'm sorry to hear that. I'd certainly miss you. But you'll still be around for Christmas, won't you? I'm counting on you for dinner Christmas Day."

Willa had the urge to throw herself at the older woman

for a hug. She was the closest thing Willa had to a real friend.

"I don't know. Nothing is for sure."

"Nothing is ever for sure, darlin'. That's one thing I've learned the hard way this year." Marigold's voice was even and knowing. Not waiting for a show of sympathy, she led them onto the busier first floor. "You need a computer this morning too?"

Willa glanced toward the bank of free-use computers along the back wall. "Maybe I'll read the headlines right quick while you check me out."

"The books will be ready when you are. Take your time." Marigold headed to the front desk.

Willa slipped onto the hard plastic chair at one of the terminals and pulled up the online site of her hometown newspaper, scanning for any mention of her father or his garage. Nothing in the most recent articles, but an ad placement on the side drew her attention.

Her father stood in front of his garage with a half-dozen employees lined up behind him. He looked uncomfortable in the way of men not used to or desiring attention. Across the bottom was written *The Best Mechanics at the Best Prices. Come see us at Buck's*. The ad must have been her stepmother Carol's idea.

She enlarged the picture, but it pixelated before she could tell if the look in his eyes was happy or sad. Next she typed the name of her ex-boyfriend in the search bar. The hits were all old and familiar. He either wasn't out of jail or was staying under the radar. The lack of information should make her feel better, but with her own fortunes teetering on change, the anticipation of something bad happening built her apprehension.

Derrick blamed her for ruining his life. Granted, he wouldn't have gotten in trouble with the drug dealers from

Memphis if she hadn't buried his huge stash of heroin and meth in the state park right outside of town. But he would have ended up in jail one way or another.

Willa shouldered a heavy dose of blame herself. Her naïveté knew no bounds. Derrick had been the first boy to pay her any attention, blinding her to logic. Or maybe that had been her hormones. A year had passed before she'd figured out he had a side business as a small-town drug dealer. The humiliation and shame had the power to churn her stomach this many years later.

Marigold waved and pointed to the stack of books on the circulation desk before heading back up the stairs. After one more look at her dad, Willa closed the browser, grabbed her books, and headed back to her place.

She was surprised but not shocked to see Jackson's Mustang parked in her usual spot. She found him behind her trailer at the edge of the field on his haunches talking in his low gravelly voice to River while he scratched behind her ears. She looked mesmerized by him. Willa couldn't blame the poor dog. She often felt that way around him.

What would it be like to be the recipient of the single-minded attention and care he was currently directing toward River? The stab of jealousy was as real as it was ridiculous.

She stayed at the corner, adopting her usual observation stance. His hair was longer than usual, the ends curling at his collar. Unlike Wyatt, Jackson kept his hair short and his shirts tucked. Speaking of, his shoulders and back stretched his long-sleeved black T-shirt taut. His squat highlighted the curve of his butt and muscular thighs. Between working in the shop and the rounds he went with the punching bag in the barn, he was in phenomenal shape. That, added to his hard-line view of right and wrong, meant he would have done well in the military.

"Are you ready?" His rough voice penetrated her examination of his stellar butt.

Her gaze shot up to meet his. How long had he been watching her watch him? He rose and turned toward her, never taking his eyes off her, the movement full of power and grace. Amusement blunted the intensity of his stare, and flames licked up her body.

Embarrassment, yes, but also the new awareness that had marked the last week. Not on her end. She'd always experienced a tingly curious warmth around him. It was the sudden return of interest that had her sniffing the air like a dog in heat.

He approached with River on his heels, a new collar and leash giving her little choice in the matter. She trotted ahead to lick Willa's hand.

Willa rubbed the top of her head. The olive-green collar matched the dog's eyes. "Did she hassle you over the collar and leash?"

"Nope. Seemed happy to wear it, in fact." His voice dropped into another timbre. "Another sign she belonged to someone at some point. She wants to belong to you now."

Like fleas, invisible yet biting, guilt had her turning away from the trusting eyes of the dog. Her life was too complicated to make promises. While they were at the vet, she'd make inquiries about a shelter that would take River in and find her a home.

"Since I know dog hair all over your interior will make you stroke out, I'll drive." She headed to her Honda, trying to shed the guilt through humor. "Unless you can't stomach being seen in a Honda."

"I'll scrunch down in the seat if I see anyone I know." He might be mostly teasing, but he hadn't protested her offer to keep his car free of dog hair either.

River stationed herself in the backseat, her head between

their shoulders, her doggy breath rank. Willa cranked the engine and gave a silent prayer. The Honda coughed its way to running. The squeal it made on reverse was reminiscent of a rejected opera singer.

"Your clutch could go at any minute."

"You don't say," she muttered dryly. Hopefully, he wouldn't look behind them and see the plume of black smoke.

"Why don't you talk to Mack and get on the schedule so we can fix her up?"

"Because I know what the garage charges for labor, and I can't even afford myself."

"We can work something out." He acted like it wasn't a big deal. And, Lord knows, the brothers had a constant rotation of project cars they worked on and took to auction. The side business satisfied their obsession and brought in extra cash.

The difference was they owned the garage, and she was an employee. This vet visit was bad enough. She couldn't afford to get further into debt with Jackson. It would only bind her tighter to him. "Don't worry about it. I've got it handled."

"Okay." He drew out the word.

The car did not help her cause when it shuddered as if entering its death throes on her shift from second to third gear. She gave the accelerator a pump, and it settled into its usual sickly cough.

The vet's office was set several streets away from River Street on the Louisiana side of Cottonbloom. Willa had seen the sign go up, but hadn't given the place much thought otherwise.

With River between them and Willa holding on to her leash, they stepped inside the double doors. The place smelled of antiseptic and bleach with an underlying scent of wet fur and something earthier that reminded her of a farm.

"I'll check us in." He nudged his chin toward the bank of chairs against the wall. A TV was mounted in the corner and set to a cartoon.

Jackson and the receptionist spoke in voices too low for her to hear. She tapped her foot, nervous on River's account even though the dog seemed more curious than anything.

A woman poked her head out of a door beyond the receptionist's desk. "River?"

Willa popped up and wiped her free hand down the leg of her jeans. River trotted toward the woman who'd called her name and the leash slipped out of Willa's grip. How had the dog learned her name in so short a time?

Jackson scooped up the leash and Willa followed him into a small examination room. The vet was younger than she expected. Maybe thirty or a little beyond. Tall and striking and blond. Considering her line of work, she was smart too.

The vet was dressed in a blue-and-white-striped cotton blouse, slacks, and flats, casual yet with an air of sophistication. She and Jackson looked great together. Willa pulled on the fraying hem of her secondhand T-shirt.

"I'm Isabel Mercier." She offered a hand to them both, and introductions were made.

Willa tried to gauge Jackson's interest in the pretty vet, but his expression was as bland and stoic as ever.

"A stray, huh?" Isabel squatted down and reached out. With the door shut and escape not an option, River scrambled back a few feet, her ears pricked and her chest rumbling.

Willa got down on her knees and put her arm around the dog, leaning in to speak comforting nonsense close to her ear. With Willa at her side, River submitted to the vet's examination and the series of vaccines, although the low rumble was like constant thunder and her eyes followed every movement. Isabel passed a small handheld device over River's scruff.

"What's that do?" Willa asked.

"A chip reader. It's becoming more common for owners to implant a chip that contains contact information, but River doesn't have one." Isabel looked River over, her expression serious. "She's had a litter of pups in the past but is spayed now. She either belonged to someone or spent some time in a shelter. I'd guess she's around three years of age."

"Is she healthy?" Willa's hands tightened in the dog's fur.

"Malnourished, but I expect that will change." Isabel smiled, making her even prettier. "We'll have her blood work back in a couple of days, but yes, healthy as far as I can tell. I assume you and Mr. Abbott will be adopting her?"

Willa's gaze shot up to Jackson. "Not together. I mean, we're not together. It would be me. Alone."

Was that a flash of amusement on Jackson's face? It was gone too fast to tell. "Willa and I are just coworkers."

Just coworkers. The qualifier hurt even though Willa couldn't argue the point. The dry, barren fact didn't dampen the longing for something so far out of her grasp it hurt to reach for it.

She buried her face in River's fur and took a deep breath. "What if I can't keep her? Do you have any suggestions? A no-kill shelter? Or a family with kids maybe?"

"Sure," Isabel said slowly. She grabbed a flyer from a drawer and handed it over. It was for a shelter in the next parish over. "It's not no-kill, but they try their best to find good homes."

She followed Isabel out of the room and to the front

desk. Isabel and Jackson chatted about ordinary things like where he worked and how she came to be in Cottonbloom. The small talk was drowned out by the dollar amount the receptionist reeled off. Jackson handed over his credit card.

She'd planned to repay him a little at a time, but the amount constituted her rent for a month. Her only other option was to dip into the money she had saved for her next move or car repairs.

Something he said made Isabel laugh and throw him a flirty look under her lashes. Willa clenched her hands into fists to keep from grabbing Jackson and calling dibs.

When they were outside, she said, "That was expensive."

"'Bout what I expected." His tone was unconcerned.

"I don't have that kind of money, Jackson." Even though her lack of means wasn't his fault, and he was doing something ridiculously nice for her and River, she was annoyed. She put her hands on her hips and closed the distance between them.

"I told you once already that I don't expect you to pay me back."

"But then I'll owe you." A cool gust of wind sent fallen leaves swirling around their feet. River pulled on the leash and snapped at the moving targets.

"It bothers you that much?" He matched her challenging stance.

"We're *just* coworkers." She hadn't meant to throw his words back at him with such virulence.

"Are we?" His voice changed, soft and rough and comforting like a pair of well-worn corduroys. "I thought we were friends too."

Were they? Her friendship with Marigold was simple and straightforward and easy to label. Whatever bonded her to Jackson was none of those things. It was complicated and tangled and an unknown entity.

"I guess we're sort of friends." More than a smidge of uncertainty hitched her words.

"Friends help each other. Let me help you." His tentativeness was unexpected. He was usually Mr. Confident.

It was a repeat of his offer on the side of the road when the Cutlass overheated, and she wanted to slingshot her standard answer back. But the truth was, she did need his help. Or rather, River did. Willa's hand tightened on the leash.

Unable to actually say yes, she nodded. Once they were back in her car and headed to her trailer, an awkward silence descended. What was he thinking? Even after hours and hours of study, he remained a mystery.

"You going to ask Dr. Mercier out on a date?" She couldn't believe the question popped out, much less with claws drawn in her voice. When he didn't answer right away, she muttered, "Forget I asked."

"No." The word cleaved the tension in the car.

With her eyes trained on the road, she tightened her hands on the wheel. "Don't forget I asked?"

"No. I mean, no, I won't be asking Dr. Mercier out on a date."

"Why not?" She risked a glance in his direction to find him staring at her, his expression darkening with intensity. Her face heated as if he had Superman's powers to incinerate.

"Not my type."

She harrumphed. "She's beautiful and smart and totally into you. If that's not your type, then what is?"

He smiled. Not a flash, but one where he showed his straight white teeth and eye crinkles and dimples. It was like a shooting star or an eclipse. An event so rare she was mesmerized.

The wheel jerked. She had steered them onto the narrow shoulder of the parish road. After righting them, she dared not look at him again. His smile sent oxygen rushing through her, fanning the embers of hope not even the last five years of hiding could completely extinguish.

More than anything, she wanted to be with someone like Jackson. No, not true. Not someone like him. Him and no one else. Underneath his gruffness, innate kindness and integrity knitted together to form the man. Which was why she couldn't trust him with her secrets. If he turned away from her, those embers of hope would be doused with a fire hose.

Country Aire was in sight, and she made it to her trailer without plowing into anything or anyone. River had curled up on the backseat but jumped like she'd been Tasered when the car rolled to a stop. She bolted into the field as soon as Willa opened the door.

"I hope she's not traumatized. She'll be back, right?" Willa hugged herself and stared over the swaying golden grass of the field.

"You've got to have faith she'll understand you only want to help her." His rumbly voice was like a caress. He stared out into the field as well. "Don't give her up."

"I might not have a choice."

"Of course you do."

She bit the inside of her mouth until the metallic taste of blood made her ease up. Her past choices overshadowed her current ones. Her dad was still out there and vulnerable. If Derrick tracked her down, then everyone she cared about would be at risk too. Jackson included.

"I'm racing tonight. Why don't you come down to the track?" His voice had lost some of its intensity.

Her face heated as if he could read her mind. Did he know how often she found herself at the track on Saturday nights? She generally bypassed the ticket booth and crowds and watched from outside the fence on a small rise. The excitement of the races was offset by anxiety over his safety. Jackson drove with an abandon that was both awe-inspiring and terrifying and very unlike his typical deliberateness.

She snuck a glance. He raised his brows, the corners of his mouth quirked up slightly. A challenge had been issued.

Forcing a vague tone, she said, "Maybe I will."

His smile deepened and his dimples made a brief appearance before going into hiding once more. "I'll be on the lookout." He drove away, his Mustang's engine sounding like a virtuoso in an orchestra.

Chapter Seven

Jackson scanned the crowd and cursed under his breath. Because of the LSU football bye weekend, more people were in the stands and milling around than usual. No sign of Willa though. He'd been sure the twinkle in her eye had been an acceptance even though her answer had been wishy-washy.

His worry over her well-being was totally logical. If she were at the track, it meant she hadn't hightailed it out of Cottonbloom. It meant she was safe. That whatever she was running from hadn't caught up with her yet. But logic couldn't explain away the tightness in his chest and the agitation that had him pacing next to his race car.

Dammit. He turned and kicked the rear tire. The image of Willa's huge expressive brown eyes wouldn't get out of his head. Her full lips and curves had imprinted themselves in his brain so when he closed his eyes at night, she was all he could see. Even her chopped-off hair held its appeal, waving around her face and tucked behind her ears.

She'd always been there beside him in the garage, but only with the threat of losing her looming, did he actually see her. Something important, possibly vital, flared between them.

He wasn't the most outgoing of men. When things were being divvied up in the womb, his twin brother had gotten the majority of the charm. What he'd been gifted with was an unshakable steadfastness to his family and friends and the garage. And somewhere along the way, without realizing it, the umbrella had expanded to include Willa.

His emotions were better kept compartmentalized. His pop's death had been gut-wrenching, but the easiest way to deal with it was to ignore the feelings altogether. He was handling Ford's threats about selling his share in the garage in much the same way. But when the anger or frustration or grief got to be too much, the track always provided an outlet. Although winning was a perk, it was the cleansing rush of adrenaline he was after.

Whatever was brewing this time, however, seemed explosive, and he wasn't sure if a single race could defuse it.

"You're up next, Jackson." The race coordinator hollered over the engine and crowd noise.

Jackson took one last look around. Disappointed, he climbed through the window of his old-school Monte Carlo. The doors were welded shut, and the inside stripped of everything except the essentials. The car was a beater, but with his modifications, it was faster than most of the cars on the track, and he was always the best driver.

He pulled on his racing helmet and maneuvered to the start. Five racers tonight. The track would be crowded. He needed to get out first to avoid being caught up in traffic. His focus narrowed to the start signal, and his foot hovered over the gas.

The green lit up. Tires spun, and the noise of engines was deafening. The car next to him clipped his bumper, but he kept moving. He took the lead and hugged the left of the track, forcing the other cars behind him.

Keeping the car on the edge of control and chaos was a physical endeavor. Plotting moves and staying ahead of the competition required him to evaluate the landscape like a chessboard. The crowd was a blur of color in his periphery on their first lap.

A red Ford Mustang moved up on his right. The car housed the only man who stood a chance against Jackson. Max was in his early fifties, mean as a copperhead, and a hell of a good driver. On the next turn, the Mustang grazed the side of Jackson's car. Jackson gritted his teeth and leaned his car into the rub.

They made two more passes around the track side by side. Jackson would make his move on the final lap and leave Max eating his exhaust.

Jackson couldn't say what drew his single-minded attention away from the track the moment he hit the back straightaway. But it landed on a figure on the far side of the fence, fifty or more yards away. A tingle went down the back of his neck. Aunt Hyacinth would say someone just walked over his grave.

He blinked and turned his focus back to battling two thousand pounds of metal. The adrenaline pulsing through his body took on a different flavor and had the opposite effect from what it usually did, shattering his steellike concentration. The hesitation cost him half a car length to the Mustang. He hit the gas on the next turn to make up ground and the back end of his car swung around too fast for him to maintain control. A rookie mistake.

Everything blurring, he went with the spin, hoping momentum would push him far enough to the outside of the track to avoid getting nailed by another car.

The impact was swift and hard enough to send his head knocking into the roll bar. He closed his eyes. His car came to a stop, the engine dead, the crowd noise like ocean waves. A few minutes passed, enough time to string together a world record in cursing. He'd never caused a wreck.

A knock sounded. In orange reflective vests, two members of the safety crew peered into his window. He gave them a thumbs-up and climbed out. The race was over, and so was his car. Totaled.

He pulled off his helmet and tossed it onto the front seat. The hit had taken out his rear bumper and crumpled the back end. The frame was bent. He might be able to salvage the engine.

The car that hit him was being hooked up to the tow truck. Steam hissed from the hood. Jackson muttered a curse when he saw the number on the side. It belonged to the most volatile driver on the circuit. "Is Don all right?"

"He's fine. His engine block is damaged, and he's mad as hell, but he could have avoided you if he'd backed off. What happened? Car have a problem?" Randall asked. He'd been buddies with his pop. His grizzled beard made him look older than his years.

"I screwed up."

Randall's eyebrows rose. He didn't need to say anything else. Jackson did not screw up on the race track. He wasn't hotheaded. Except a glimpse of someone who may or may not have been Willa had disintegrated his legendary discipline as easily as the track clay crumbled under his boots.

A second tow truck lumbered out to move his car off the track. He wouldn't be back racing until after the new year. He walked back to the pit area where the drivers congregated. Don was on him before he could peel his leather jacket off.

"My car's a wreck, dude. What the fuck?"

Jackson shrugged. They all knew the risks and rewards of dirt track racing.

"Jackson? Jackson!" An achingly familiar voice called his name and he whirled around.

Willa threw herself into him. The impact knocked her baseball cap off, and he couldn't see her face buried in his neck, but her arms were tight around him, her hands roving over his back.

"Are you okay? Tell me you're not hurt." Her voice was muffled against his skin.

He wrapped an arm around her, dropped his face into her hair, and inhaled deeply. She was literally a breath of fresh air in the middle of fried foods and sweaty drivers.

"Nothing hurt but my pride."

She pulled back. Her gaze roamed over his face and torso, her worry palpable. "Concussion?"

His internal organs sizzled under her gaze. "I'm fine. Promise."

Her mouth thinned, and she slapped his arm. "You scared me to death. You've never lost control like that."

"Hey, we're not done." Don shoved his shoulder from behind. "You're going to pay for the damage to my car, hotshot."

Jackson turned, trying to keep Willa behind him, but she stepped out to stand at his side, hands on her hips.

"You know how this works," Jackson said in a low voice with more than a hint of threat.

"But it was your fault." A whine entered Don's voice. The man was a bully with the heart of a coward.

Willa piped up, her voice snappy. "You had plenty of opportunity to drop back and avoid hitting him. You need to practice on an empty track before they let you in another race, *hotshot*." The last word dripped with acidic mockery.

"Shut up, bitch."

Already on edge, Jackson's control took a leap off the cliff. Whatever had been brewing all night boiled over. With the expletive still ringing in the air, Jackson launched himself at Don and took him to the ground.

Don had two inches and a good twenty-five pounds on Jackson, but it was mostly fat. Plus, Don hadn't grown up with three brothers who preferred to solve problems by taking it behind the barn. The asshole didn't stand a chance.

They rolled twice, and Don got in a glancing elbow to Jackson's cheekbone. The left side of his face went momentarily numb. His fury stoked hotter. On their next roll, Jackson came up on top, straddled the other man, and got in two quick jabs. Blood spurted out of Don's nose. He cupped his hands over his face and rocked side to side with a pitiful-sounding high-pitched moan. Jackson hopped to his feet, massaging his knuckles.

Willa grabbed his biceps and tugged. "Come on. Let's get out of here."

He resisted, too much dynamic energy still pulsing through his body. "That all you got? Get up."

Don stayed down. Jackson glanced around. Everyone was quiet and watching. He felt like someone else was inhabiting his skin.

"Please, Jackson. Let's go. What if the police come?" Willa pulled harder, her hands biting.

The threat of the police didn't budge him. What did was the soft, pleading look and worry in her eyes. For him.

He took a step, and she slipped her hand all the way down his arm to weave her fingers with his. He didn't resist this time and let her lead him away. She scooped up her hat on the way out of the tent. Licking heat spread from his hand, up his arm, and into his chest. He was a nuclear plant in the middle of a meltdown.

The chill in the air didn't do much to cool him off. They slipped out of the front gate of the racetrack and into the dark parking lot. Trucks and cars were jumbled together in a free-for-all. The farther they got from the track, the less frantic Willa seemed, and in turn, the threat of a meltdown receded. Her run-walk slowed to a stalk and her grip eased enough for blood flow to resume to his hand.

"Are you crazy?" Her voice was hoarse.

His equilibrium was not fully restored. Between the wreck and the punch, his behavior had been erratic and completely unlike him. He took a couple of deep breaths. "Possibly."

She made a harrumphing sound, and he could imagine her rolling her eyes as she tended to do when confronted with the absurd. A step ahead of him, she pulled him along on the shoulder of the road.

Her hat was back on her head, and she was in the same pair of jeans from that morning, but a different color T-shirt and an olive-green cotton jacket. Her hips swayed as her legs ate up the distance.

He'd watched her work more times than he could count, in awe of the nimble gracefulness of her hands. Now he was aware that trait wasn't exclusive to one body part. Her every move contained a dash of sensuality and strength. It was potent.

"Are we walking home?" He might as well have been talking to the whippoorwill calling in the tree they passed under. She was pissed.

And how could he blame her? The night had gone to hell. It wasn't the first time he'd been involved in a crash, but it was the first time he'd been the cause of one. He'd jumped Don and maybe broken his nose. Don could press charges if he really wanted to be a jerk. Jackson's cheek throbbed, and his left eye was swelling.

So why did he feel like whistling?

The chaos continued to spin his head and set his heart to beating faster. Even though they were well away, she kept hold of his hand. The gesture seemed more than expedient; she was protecting him. Their relationship took another turn, this time on two wheels and slightly out of control.

Something she'd said tickled his memory. "You said I'd never lost control like that. How would you know?"

She disentangled their hands, her pace picking up. "An assumption. You're Mr. Control Freak in the garage."

He didn't allow her to escape, grasping her wrist and pulling her to a stop. "Have you been to the track before?"

"No." She rubbed her nose and looked toward the line of dark trees across the road. He waited. "Maybe," she whispered.

"To watch me?"

"Maybe," she repeated even softer.

How had he never seen her? The same question could be applied to the last two years in the garage. Because he hadn't been looking. Had he feared the consequences if he'd allowed himself to care about her before now? But that was the rub. He'd cared for her long before now, even if he couldn't put a time stamp on when it had happened.

Tonight had knocked the breath out of him. Not the wreck, although that had been the start. He didn't pick fights and bust faces. His control was broken, and there was not enough duct tape in Cottonbloom to put it back together. A wild impetuousness reared from somewhere in the confusion she'd unleashed. As ill-advised and danger-ous and stupid as it was, he wanted to kiss Willa.

Her mouth was parted as if in invitation. He leaned for-ward but before he got close to his destination, she gasped and laid her hand along his cheek.

"Your face!"

"What about it?"

"You look terrible." The way she said it, half worried, half exasperated, made him laugh, even though his cheek pulled painfully. She didn't join him.

Her wrist was too narrow and delicate to exhibit the strength he observed daily in the garage.

"Not like I'm the good-looking twin." It was an old joke

between him and Wyatt. Jackson was two minutes older—and wiser—but Wyatt was better looking. Truth was, Jackson got plenty of attention—usually more than he was comfortable with—from the opposite sex. Dr. Mercier had made it clear at the vet's office she would welcome a call from him not involving animals. Yet his interest in the pretty vet hovered at subzero.

She made a huffy sound that registered as disbelief. "Seriously?"

"Seriously, what? You don't think Wyatt is good-looking?" He wanted to tease a smile out of her.

"Sutton thinks so and that's all that matters." The corners of her mouth ticked up slightly. Maybe she wasn't so mad. "You're not bad either. When you're not grossly swollen and turning blue, that is."

He hadn't been looking for any affirmations, but her assessment stole a portion of his oxygen. He stifled the urge to fist pump.

"Come on. I'll drive you back to your place." She tilted her head and gestured behind her. The bumper of her car was visible twenty feet down the road. She dropped her hand from his cheek, but her fingertips glanced over his jaw, the touch feather light.

He forced his fingers around her wrist to uncurl. He didn't want to let her go, so he tangled his fingers with hers. It should have been strange, yet felt completely natural.

They broke apart when they reached her car, and he folded himself into the passenger seat for the second time that day. The Honda coughed like a lifelong smoker that needed an oxygen tank. The side mirror reflected the plume of black smoke trailing behind them.

He had a feeling if he brought up helping pay for repairs again, Willa would clam up and shut the door on whatever brave new world he'd stepped into. Anyway, he was curious about something else entirely.

"I saw you," he said.

"Huh?" She tossed him a glance but in the darkness of the cab and with her hat, he couldn't tell if she was being intentionally obtuse.

"Up on the hill, outside the fence. I saw you as I headed into that final turn."

"Are you blaming me for your wreck?" Her voice was as dry as his throat.

He avoided answering, because she was to blame. Even before he'd spotted her, his head hadn't been in the race. She had infected him like a virus. Probably not the kind of pretty words a woman wanted to hear.

Racing a car around a half-mile dirt track with the threat of an accident looming at any second didn't scare him. She did though. Not only had she shown up tonight, but she'd been coming to the track to watch him for some time. He didn't like uncertainty. He preferred to know the odds before taking a chance.

She parked on the side of the garage like she normally did even though no customers took up the spots out front.

He laid his head against the back of the seat and did something he rarely did—lied. "I'm not feeling great actually. My head hurts"—not a total lie, although he'd had worse hangovers—"and I'm a little wobbly." Total lie.

"Is it a concussion? Do I need to take you to the hospital?" Her hand went back to the ignition, ready to pump life back into the car.

Had he overplayed his hand? "Not a concussion. Just my cheek."

"Hang on and I'll come around." Worry threaded her voice and in the brief amount of time it took her to make it to his door, guilt made his headache worse. When she offered a hand and then notched herself under his arm to offer support he didn't need, his body's clamor for more drowned out any impulses to confess.

He leaned into her, and her arm tightened around his waist. She was soft in all the right places. They made their way through the barn and trudged awkwardly up the stairs to the loft side by side. He flipped the light on. She stopped short and looked around.

"Yep. Exactly what I pictured."

She'd never seen the loft even though they'd spent countless hours together in the shop next door. The second revelation that landed on his head like an anvil was her insinuation that she'd thought about where he lived. Did it mean anything?

The skylights gave the loft an openness and charm counteracted by the utilitarian furniture. A worn couch and coffee table faced the wall with a flat-screen TV. At least the place was neat and orderly. Mostly because Wyatt had been spending his nights at Sutton's. As much as he complained about his brother's messiness, Jackson missed having him close at night like when they were kids.

"You pictured this cold, lonely place?" Why had he said that? Maybe he had hit his head hard enough to give him a concussion.

She hitched toward him, but between their height difference and her hat, he couldn't see her face. He grabbed the bill, pulled her hat off, and tossed it toward the couch.

"Hey, you can't keep doing that." She ran a hand through her hair and ruffled the back.

"You look better without it."

She kept smoothing her hand over the top of her hair until he stopped her, grabbing her wrist and pulling her hand away.

"You don't have to be nice. My hair looks terrible," she said softly.

"I'm not being nice." He ignored the ironic bent to the declaration. Nice wasn't on the spectrum of what he was feeling. He fingered the end of one wave at her nape. Her hair was soft but thick. "I'll bet it would be even prettier long."

She touched the ends, her fingers close to his. "It used to be long. I cut it."

"Why?"

Her brows drew in and her gaze shifted. "To leave the old me behind, I guess."

He'd expected a trite answer and cocked his head. Was this an opening to push for more information or would she turn tail and run like a fox? Unwilling to risk it, he pasted his lips together and practiced patience.

Why had she let that little nugget slip out? He was examining her as if she were a damaged engine to be flagged for either renovation or the junkyard. What he thought was important to her. Her sanity would be safer if it wasn't.

"It could use some evening out, but it's cute. I like it short," he said.

"Do you?" Her long hair had been her vanity. She'd spent countless hours at the mirror primping to attract attention. Derrick, her first and only boyfriend and destroyer of dreams, had loved it and that was a big reason she'd hacked it all off.

"Short hair suits you. It's—" He looked to the ceiling for a moment before dropping his gaze back to hers. "Spunky. Unique."

Spunky? It made her think of an annoying, precocious child. The expression on her face must have been obvious.

His laugh rumbled like the leading edge of a storm, still miles away with plenty of time to take shelter. Yet all she wanted was to stand still and wait for the onslaught.

"Okay, how about tough and sexy?"

Sexy? The assessment was like a lightning bolt. Sizzling and scary. She had a difficult time coordinating her throat muscles. Her ability to handle men and attraction had been stunted at nineteen, and she felt her inexperience keenly. Her goal the past five years had been to hide her sexy.

And she'd done it. Alone. Having learned her lesson, she'd denied herself any meaningful contact with men, and appearing as unattractive as possible had made that easier. Could Jackson really see past her chopped-off hair and secondhand clothes?

He was good-looking and confident and could have his pick of the prettiest women in Cottonbloom. Even the casual linking of Jackson's name with a woman's had made her insides cramp. It would be a game of which one was not like the others if you threw Willa in with the other women he'd dated.

She put a few feet between them and crossed her arms under her breasts. "You don't have to be mean."

His brows twitched, which according to the reference book her brain had compiled over the past two years meant he was annoyed. Although she had no idea why. Facts were facts, and all things being equal, she was the one with the strongest claim to annoyance.

She plowed on. "I know I'm not like the other women you've stepped out with. Not like Dr. Mercier at the vet office. Not like Sutton. You should see if she can hook you up with one of her friends. Or call the vet. She was definitely interested." Throwing other women in his path was the last thing she wanted, yet she couldn't stop her word vomit.

"I told you once already, I'm not interested in Dr. Mercier." He took a step toward her. She took one backward.

"Why not?" She took another step, this one even bigger, but he matched her retreat with his advance.

"Because I'm interested in someone else."

Two more steps and her back hit the wall with nowhere else to go. He caged her in, his hands flat next to her shoulders. She trailed her gaze from one of his big, callused hands up his roped forearm and the bulge of his biceps to his eyes.

She might be naïve and in denial, but she wasn't dumb. The last two weeks of dancing around one another had led her to one startling and unexpected conclusion. Finally, Jackson saw her as a woman and wanted her. It was the stuff of her dreams and nightmares.

"We shouldn't," she said weakly, unable to keep her hand from touching his chest. The muscle jumped under her fingertips, his heart strong and steady and pounding fast. Not as fast as hers though. Her head was swimmy with nerves and anticipation and dread.

"Why not?" He tossed her question back with a smile big enough to showcase his dimples. When he smiled like that, worries and responsibilities sloughed off like rust and revealed a younger, impossibly handsome man.

Her irritation morphed into something else entirely. Something that made her want to bite his bottom lip until he pushed her up against the wall with his body. It was probably good he didn't smile more often or the female population in a twenty-mile radius would be a constant puddle of hormones.

Things she hadn't allowed herself to feel in years came back in a flood. No, a flood implied a slow rise. This was a tsunami. One that called for a blaring alarm and a frantic escape.

She tried again. "I don't want to."

Except her other hand rose to join the first and curl around the thick muscle of his side. Stupid hands.

"I can tell you don't want to at all." His gravelly voice rushed through her as he leaned closer.

"Damn straight I don't." She pulled him closer until their lips were inches apart.

He ran a hand down her arm to her wrist, his fingers stroking the soft skin over her thrumming pulse. He maneuvered their hands until they were pressed palm to palm. His hand was so much bigger than hers. Capable. Confident. Strong.

She wanted to burrow in his arms. But even more than the physical closeness, she longed to lay her troubles on his broad shoulders and unflappable spirit. She wanted to confess everything from the moment she'd met Derrick to the reasons she was still hiding. But he would hate her weakness and lies.

"You don't really know me." Her small truth whispered between them.

"I might not know anything about your past, but that doesn't mean I don't know you, Willa Brown."

The fact he didn't even know her real name was a deep cut on her heart. He deserved honesty, which was the one thing she couldn't give him. She took a breath to tell him just that. Before she got a word out, his lips silenced her.

She didn't fight the kiss, which only underscored her selfish weakness. To save them both future heartache, she should push him away, but instead, she tipped closer to him, her free hand skimming up his chest to pull at his neck. He wrapped his arm around her waist and fused their bodies from chest to hips.

As if he sensed her uncertainty, his lips were gentle on hers, giving and not demanding anything in return. She squeezed her eyes shut. What if she allowed herself this one fantasy come true? A memory to hold on to when times got bad. It was only a kiss.

The justifications blurred the line between right and wrong. She touched her tongue to his bottom lip. A rumbly groan vibrated his chest against hers, and her breasts grew achy and sensitive.

He pushed her back against the wall and lodged his thigh between her legs. A kiss. She could only allow herself a kiss. The rest of her body ignored the order.

Heat cascaded through her, centering between her legs. She squirmed, but instead of relief, the emptiness grew acute. The evidence of his arousal pressed into her belly. Her knees wobbled and more of her weight fell onto his hard thigh, only magnifying what she really wanted.

She drew in a deep breath. His scent was a combination of cars and clean laundry with the earthy hint of adrenaline-fueled sweat. It was good. No, better than good. It should be bottled and sold, except she wanted to keep him to herself like a greedy miser.

On an exhale, he touched his tongue to the seam of her lips, and like whispering the magic word, her lips parted for him. *Just a kiss.* The words were a mantra. She wouldn't let it go any further.

Except she had imagined countless times what it would be like to be with Jackson. Would he be gentle or rough? Would he talk to her or take her in a flurry of silence? Would he hold her afterward or leave?

The reality was here and more intense than she'd ever imagined. He pressed their joined hands over her head, she played in the hair at his nape with her other hand. How many days had she stared at the back of his neck wanting to lean in to lay a kiss where his hair flipped up at the ends when he let it get too long? How many days had she wanted to stroke a finger over his stubbled jaw?

Their tongues danced, stroking and seducing the doubts from her head, until the word scrolling was *more, more, more.* A sound came from her throat. One she didn't recognize that fell between frustration and a plea.

She wasn't completely inexperienced, but one thing became starkly clear. Her experience was that of a teenaged girl enthralled with her first boyfriend. Whatever was happening between her and Jackson was on a different level. A level that she'd never come close to touching much less had a chance to explore.

He ground himself against her. Instinct had her rotating her hips against his thigh. Slanting his mouth over hers, he raised the stakes, the friction of their lips and tongues and bodies stoking a wildfire. His expertise both frightened and excited her. She clutched him closer and arched her back to try to satisfy the ache growing through her body like a sickness with only one cure.

If she gave in, what would happen in the morning? A sliver of logic infused her sex-charged body. The lies between them were living, breathing entities, haunting her.

"No," she said against his mouth. With difficulty she turned her head, breaking the kiss.

He lifted a few scant inches and brought their joined hands down next to her head. Staring at their linked fingers, she fought a wave of despair. They could have sex, but they could never be together. She had ruined any chance of that five years ago, and her lies since only compounded the impossibility.

"What's wrong?"

"I don't want this."

An eternity of silence passed. She opened her hand and tugged. The tendons along his hand tensed, but he released her. She took a step to the side, freeing herself from the gravitational pull he had on her, her hand still tingling.

He scrubbed his hands over his face and didn't speak. What was he thinking? Nothing from her constant examination of him gave her a clue. Was he mad? Hurt? Maybe he thought she was a tease or playing games. Was there a game called smashed hearts and lies? Because she was winning.

Instead of facing the consequences, she did what she did best. Cowardice heaped with a healthy dollop of self-preservation sent her running out of his loft and to her car. A glance over her shoulder revealed no one. He hadn't given chase. Why would he? She wasn't worth it.

Was he like the other men who'd preyed on her because she was in their power and seemingly weak? She tried to summon righteous anger, but none came. He wasn't like any man she'd ever met.

Once she was on the road back to her trailer, she touched her lips. No matter what happened, at least she had the memory of their kiss.

Chapter Eight

Monday morning, Jackson kept his eye on the door, waiting for Willa to make an appearance. If she didn't show in the next five minutes, he was going to hunt her down and make her talk to him.

He'd spent fruitless, frustrating hours replaying their kiss. As kisses went, it had knocked his world into a new trajectory. One that seemed to be spinning faster. He wasn't sure what the kiss or what her running had meant.

He should have followed her. He muttered a curse. His body had been at war with his mind and his doubts had won.

Jackson stared at the hunk of metal under the hood of his aunts' Crown Victoria. He normally tried to avoid working on their car, not because he didn't love his aunts Hyacinth and Hazel, but the car posed no challenge. They brought it in on a regular basis for fluid changes or to report nonexistent noises under the hood.

It was a thin ploy to keep tabs on all the brothers. The aunts had stepped in after their mother ran off when Jackson and Wyatt were still in diapers. Since Ford had up and vanished a few weeks earlier, the aunts had been in more often.

Wyatt strolled over, cleaning a socket wrench with a blue shop towel. "Why didn't you tell me you wrecked Saturday night? I had to hear it from Randall."

"I forgot."

"You forgot that for the first time ever you screwed up on the track?" The sarcasm was thicker than the air on a July day.

Why hadn't he mentioned it? Embarrassment, but also the knowledge that Wyatt wouldn't be able to let it go.

"Frame's bent, but I think I'll be able to salvage the engine." Jackson checked the clock and glanced over his shoulder at the door.

"We can take the truck and tow it home after work if you want."

"Yeah, that'd be great."

"I would've come picked you up. Who'd you get a ride home with?" Wyatt's overly casual tone drew Jackson's attention, but his brother's face was blank.

Dammit. He knew already. No use in avoiding the truth or outright lying. "Willa gave me a lift."

"You broke Don's nose."

The drawback to living in a small town was everyone knew everyone else's business. "Good."

A smile played through the surprise on Wyatt's face. "I didn't believe Randall at first, but all the boys at Rufus's backed him up. He must have pissed you off something fierce."

"He did." Jackson ignored Wyatt's obvious curiosity and glanced at the clock. Willa was ten minutes late. She was never late. "Where the heck is Willa?"

"She'll be here."

"I'm not so sure." Jackson put his hands on the raised hood and stared at the tangle of hoses as if he could divine the future, like reading the lines on someone's palm. "I might have wrecked things with her too."

"What happened?" Wyatt sat on the edge and leaned back enough to make eye contact with Jackson.

Wyatt was settled and happy with Sutton Mize, but it hadn't been an easy trek for either of them. As hard as it was to believe, Wyatt might actually have acquired some wisdom he could share. Anyway, sooner or later, Wyatt would drill down to the truth.

"I kissed her," he whispered.

"Punching Don. Kissing Willa. Not like you at all, bro." Wyatt whistled and shook his head. "But about damn time, I'd say."

Jackson's hands dropped to his sides. "Why do you say that?"

"I'd bet my share of the garage on the fact Willa's had a crush on you since day one. She never wants to work with either me or Mack. You two have some weird chemistry under the hood. Only a matter of time until it spilled over and exploded."

Jackson's body tingled. "Except she ran off like I had suddenly developed a highly contagious case of the cooties."

Wyatt's lips twitched, but settled into a thoughtful line. "What did she say?"

"Told me to stop. Said she didn't want me and ran."

"You didn't go after her?"

"I was confused and physically incapable of running."

"That good, huh?"

Jackson never thought he'd be one to kiss and tell. "Amazing. Now, tell me what I did wrong."

"I'm assuming you're not talking technique." Wyatt snickered. "You didn't shove your tongue down her throat, did you?"

Jackson knuckle-punched Wyatt's arm, but there was no anger in the move.

Wyatt continued. "Let's look at things from her point

of view. She's nurtured a crush on you for a while, and all of a sudden, you start to pay attention to her. She's obviously desperate."

Wyatt brushed off Jackson's knee-jerk "Hey."

"I mean she's desperate for this job. She's running from something or someone and doesn't feel comfortable asking for help. I've gathered through basic chitchat that some of her previous jobs have involved scumbag bosses. Could be she got scared that you were taking advantage of her."

"What do you mean?"

"You know, screw me or you're fired. No matter how cute she thinks you are, that's not a good position."

Wyatt's conclusion was like a fist around his heart. The last thing he wanted was to add to whatever troubles Willa carried around. "I would never take advantage of her like that." His voice came out on a croak.

"From her perspective, if things go bad, who's the one that will get fired? Not you."

Jackson rubbed his nape. His skin was ablaze while his insides felt frozen. "You're right. I shouldn't have touched her."

"Now, hold up, I didn't say that."

"You're confusing me. Spit it out in black-and-white."

"You need to decide what you want. If it's a quick screw to satisfy your curiosity, then don't be a selfish dick and leave her alone. If it's something more, then make sure she understands it isn't about the garage."

"It's going to be complicated."

Wyatt's smile was commiserating. Jackson hadn't even needed to think about what he wanted. Whatever was happening between him and Willa definitely wasn't a one-night thing.

"Complicated is what we Abbotts seem to do best."

"I'm worried I've run her off."

"Then go—" The door creaked open. "There's your girl."

His girl. Yep, that sounded good.

Willa sidled in as if she were trying to blend into the cement wall. In her gray coveralls and with her ball cap pulled low, she was making a decent job of it. He let Wyatt's assessment roll around in his head. Had she had a crush on him for two years? Had he been that blind? The answers were, he damn well hoped so and yes, he had been that blind.

He had never considered getting serious with a woman. The loss of his mother had been an abstract but biting loss. The memories of her were so faint that he wasn't sure what was real and what was imagined. But one indisputable fact was clear; he had been abandoned.

Add to that the Abbott curse. None of the twins born throughout the generations had ever married. Jackson had assumed he and Wyatt would grow into grizzled bachelors together. In fact, he'd counted on it. But with Sutton and Wyatt getting more serious by the minute, that possibility faded and a new future hovered, indistinct and unsure yet tantalizing.

"What are you going to do?" Wyatt asked.

"Find a time to talk to her." Talking was out of Jackson's comfort zone, but he would try his best for her.

Wyatt gave him a nod and returned to the truck that had come in over the weekend. While they worked on getting the restoration portion of their business built up, they took on regular mechanical jobs for the easy cash. Plus, many of their customers had been coming to Abbott's since their pop had started the business. It was a community of family and friends.

Willa didn't look in Jackson's direction, and instead approached Mack who was in the third bay with a Trans

Am they'd been tasked to restore into a *Smokey and the Bandit* replica. Jackson tapped his fingers on the Crown Vic and tried to remember what his aunts had complained about this time around.

He glanced toward the third bay. Gesturing at something under the hood, Willa stood shoulder to shoulder with Mack who had bent his head over to hear what she was saying. Jackson was jealous. Not because he was worried about Mack and Willa together, but for the simple fact she had picked Mack over him.

Jackson wanted Willa by his side. He felt like he was missing a sock or a glove or the left ventricle of his heart because it seemed to be acting funny.

The morning passed with Willa ignoring him. His worries amped up. Had she assumed he'd been using her? The passing minutes and hours tangled his tongue.

Mack busted in a side door. "That mutt is back."

Willa dropped the air wrench, quickstepped over, and pushed past Mack. Jackson followed her.

She dropped to her knees, ran her hands over River's body, and muttered, "Silly dog. Are you okay?"

River didn't look injured but she did look exhausted. Her tongue lolled and her sides heaved. She was clean, and her ribs seemed less prominent. Without asking or being asked, he went to the barn and came back with two plastic bowls, one full of kibble, the other water. He'd bought more food. In the back of his mind it had been an excuse to drop by her trailer.

"Thanks," she mumbled, still refusing to look up at him.

River drank until she hit bottom before moving to the kibble. Jackson, Wyatt, and Mack stood in a loose semi-circle around Willa and River.

"You might as well start bringing the dog to work with you," Mack said. "I'd hate to find out she was hit by a car trying to follow you."

Willa's face was pale and her eyes huge under the brim of her cap. "That would be great. She won't be a bother, I promise."

"She could become our official mascot," Wyatt said brightly. "Actually . . . what if she becomes the official mascot of Abbott Brothers Garage and Restoration?"

Jackson recognized the sudden zeal in Wyatt and shifted until the brothers were facing each other. "You got an idea?"

"We could put her on T-shirts or mugs and hand them out at auctions. Good way for people to remember us." Wyatt's voice had turned contemplative. "People love dogs. Especially dogs with a story."

Jackson looked from Willa and the dog to Mack. "That's a helluva good idea."

Mack ran a finger over his lips and stared at River. "She's a unique-looking dog, I'll say that. But this is up to Willa since she owns her. What do you think?"

Willa stood, but avoided eye contact with Jackson. "Sure, why not."

"We'd pay you." Jackson wasn't sure where the words came from, but as soon as they were out, they felt right.

Her gaze darted to his and then away. Not long enough for him to get a read on what emotions lurked beneath. Her usual boldness was muted, and instead of sarcasm, her voice was leery. "You paid her vet bill and bought her food. How about we call it even?"

Wyatt clapped his hands once and rubbed them together. "Excellent. I'll ask around and see who has experience creating logos. Sutton might know someone. Or maybe we can get a student up at Cottonbloom College to do it on the cheap."

Wyatt tugged Mack away and gave Jackson a pointed look. Jackson waited until they disappeared into the garage. River stood in front of Willa, never taking her gaze off Jackson. He had no doubt the dog would protect her against all comers—even him.

The longer he let the implications of their kiss linger, the more awkward it would become. "Listen, about the other night—"

"Forget about it." She moved so quickly to get away that River barked.

He followed. "Look, I'm not sure what you thought—"

"I'm trying my best not to think about it. Trust me, it won't happen again." Willa pulled the door open with such force, it bounced on its hinges and nearly took his face off.

River had slipped inside with her, leaving Jackson alone. He slapped the cement brick wall wishing he could kick his own ass. Her suggestion that they were now "even" only confirmed his fears.

She was freaked out and thought he had been taking advantage of her position in the garage. Her last statement rang through his head. *Trust me, it won't happen again.* He wasn't sure he could live with that.

Willa kept her head down and made straight toward the third bay and her assignment for the day. With each step, the curses and admonishments became more colorful. She was the biggest idiot this side of the river. No, on both sides of the river, maybe even south of the Mason-Dixon Line.

The heat in her face edged up to inferno levels. After their panty-disintegrating kiss, she'd spent all day Sunday battling embarrassment and disgust. She was the kind of heroine she cursed in books. Wishy-washy and full of mixed signals. She'd kissed him one minute and told him she didn't want him the next.

Problem was, this wasn't a story with a guaranteed happy ending. She *did* want him, but eventually, he would find out the truth. Her fantasies would be transformed into nightmares. If they had sex, it would be on a bed of her lies.

The melodramatic turn of her thoughts brought her back to earth and injected some much-needed humor, even if it was black. What would a bed of lies be made of? Porcupine quills? Or maybe old diapers because she was full of you-know-what.

What had he been about to say before she cut him off? What had he assumed she thought about the kiss? Now she wished she'd been able to control her mouth and hear him out.

She risked a glance across the garage. He was back, and as if he had supernatural powers, he turned and his gaze snared her. A new sort of tension coiled between them like a rubber band ready to snap.

One thing was clear. There was no returning to the way things had been. Normal didn't exist in her world and hadn't for a long time, but she'd been safe. In a few weeks, the Abbotts would come asking for her Social Security number. The hourglass was running empty.

"Good Lord, why don't you and Jackson just do it already?" Wyatt's voice spun her around. His expression was a combination of tease and serious inquiry.

"How is it any of your business? Where'd Mack go? I was supposed to be working with him today." Was there an internal setting past inferno, because that's where she was headed fast. She pushed the brim of her cap up and dabbed a shop towel over her forehead.

"Spreadsheets to stare at. Now, what's going on?"

"What did Jackson tell you?"

"He didn't have to tell me anything. He's my twin brother." He leaned over and jiggled a hose. "Broken clamp. Could you get me a new one?"

Willa took longer than necessary to comb through a

drawer filled with parts and return with a replacement. She handed it over, and he picked up the conversation. "Look, I know you've had a thing for him since day one."

She opened her mouth to protest, but the raised eyebrows he aimed in her direction transformed her outright lie into a qualification. "I admire his skills under the hood."

He cleared his throat, but humor still snaked into his voice. "I'm gonna assume that wasn't a euphemism. By the way, that's almost exactly what he says about you."

She shrugged. "Well, it's true. I am a really great mechanic."

Wyatt's big belly laugh made it impossible to be annoyed with him for long. If she'd had a lick of sense, she'd have crushed on Wyatt. He was nearly as good-looking as his twin, easier to be around, and *way* less complicated, but it had always been Jackson and always would be.

"I love my brother, and you've become like a little sister. I want both of you to be happy, even better if that's together. So what's the problem?"

"How long do you have?" She kept the sourness in her voice to a twist.

"How long are you going to keep running?" Wyatt was bent over the car testing hoses, and she was thankful, sure that her expression would have given her away.

"What do you mean?" Her lips felt rubbery.

His sigh echoed against the metal. "We'd have your back."

"You can't promise that because you don't know."

He turned and half sat on the edge of the car, polishing a socket wrench, but looking at her from the corners of his eyes. "I know the person you are now. The kind that's funny and nice and takes in stray dogs."

The last thing she could handle was any of the Abbotts, but especially Jackson, turning their backs on her. That's why she'd always turned her back first.

"Let it go, Wyatt. We have work to do." She hadn't had to use the hard, take-no-shit tone since she'd come to Cottonbloom, and it grated like squealing brakes.

Even though she'd been firm with Wyatt, doubts assailed her when she was trying to sleep or drive or generally function like a normal human. *Was* she going to run the rest of her life? If so, what was the point of living? The questions haunted her over the next days.

Another Thanksgiving without her dad came and went. Even though Marigold and Ms. Hazel had invited her for dinner at their respective houses, she'd declined both. Marigold already had enough going on with her sick husband to bother with hostess duties. And sitting across from Jackson surrounded by his family would only remind her of what she was losing. She had heated up a turkey-and-dressing frozen dinner and shared a can of cranberry sauce with River.

The unusually warm November had been kicked aside by a cold December. Willa took River out the side door of the garage for a potty break and chafed her arms. The sun on her face was offset by a chill from the north. Even the thick coveralls couldn't keep fingers of wind from creeping down her neck and up her sleeves.

Her sleep of late had been rocky. The wind and cold seeped through the gaps around windows and doors of her trailer, but she was afraid to run her kerosene heater while she slept. Horror stories of fires or carbon monoxide poisoning made the rounds through the park every winter without fail.

She propped her shoulder on the cement wall, tucked her chin into the collar of her coveralls, and closed her eyes.

River's chesty growl pulled her from a slight doze to full wakefulness in two seconds flat. A man stood not more than a dozen feet away, staring at her. If he was a customer, she needed to tell River to stand down immediately. She was supposed to be a mascot not a menace.

Instinct rooted Willa to the spot. The man took two steps toward her. River's growl increased in both fervor and level, the hair along her back standing up. The man stopped, looking from the dog to Willa and back again.

The danger and threat in the man's eyes and in the tight pull of his mouth was familiar, but she didn't recognize him in particular. Instead, she recognized the type. Derrick had once seduced her with the excitement of danger. This man wasn't here to get his car worked on. He was here for a shakedown.

"What do you want?" She cursed the tremble in her voice. She'd once been able to bluff and bluster her way through confrontations like this one. That was when she'd had nothing to lose.

"I want my money." The man's voice was rough but lilted with a Cajun accent.

Her day of reckoning was here, and it was not at all like she'd imagined it. She'd expected Derrick himself would come to exact his pound of flesh and then some.

"How much?" She took heart in having River close. No way would the man get close enough to touch her. Unless he had a gun. She shuffled sideways toward the door, but stopped herself. If he followed her, then Jackson or one of the boys could get hurt.

"Forty thousand."

She nearly choked on a gulp of air. It was more than she'd imagined even in her worst-case scenarios. "Did Derrick send you?"

The man's mouth opened and closed before he finally said, "I don't know who the fuck Derrick is. I was told his brothers would cough up the money."

She attempted to channel the rush of kneecap-dissolving relief into logic. Think. She needed to think.

Jackson rounded the corner of the garage and stopped short, his gaze pinging between her and the man. "What's going on?" His naturally rough voice had the power to intimidate even without the thunderous expression on his face.

"I'm here for my money." The man shifted toward Jackson, but kept a keen eye on River.

Jackson put himself between Willa and the man. United in their common goal of protecting her, River moved to his side, her growl never wavering.

"And who are you?" Jackson asked.

"You one of Ford's brothers?"

"What's this got to do with Ford?"

"He's gotten himself into a pickle. A forty-K pickle."

A few beats of silence passed. "Gambling?"

The man nodded once. "Betting on games. Football. Basketball. You name it. Now he owes me."

"Where is he?"

"I'm his bookie, not his babysitter."

"Did Ford send you here to collect?"

"Not exactly, but certain people told me you'd cover his debts or . . ." The man's smile was like an arctic breeze down her spine.

Willa had never considered Ford part of the garage. He flitted in and out between his trips to auctions and car shows to drum up business, too highfalutin' to get his hands dirty. He was the only brother with a college degree and lorded the fact over his brothers. But he was still an Abbott.

Jackson turned his head enough so she could see his profile. "You all right?"

Her insides were still jockeying for their textbook positions and the scare had shifted something fundamental inside of her, yet her words came out almost chirpy sounding. "I'm fine."

"Let's talk inside." It was obvious by his tone Jackson had turned his attention back to the bookie.

Jackson stepped closer to the man. River crouched and added a cutting bark to her growl. Willa called the dog back to her as Jackson led the man around to the front and into the garage. She stayed outside, crouched beside River, her face buried in fur.

When she'd thought the man had been sent by Derrick or the drug dealers he had worked for, one thought rose above all others. She hadn't wanted to run away. She'd wanted to stay and fight.

Tears brought on by the collision of past and present and relief trickled into River's fur. A rough tongue flicked against her cheek and Willa laughed. River had been ready to protect her at all costs. Was Wyatt right? Could she count on Jackson and the Abbotts to do the same? Was it even fair to ask it of them?

She sidled in the door, half expecting to see a fight in progress, but the garage floor was empty and only muffled voices snuck out of the waiting room.

She returned to the Trans Am, although she gave up after five minutes of staring at the closed door of the waiting room. The crunch of gravel signaled an arrival. She wasn't the one who usually greeted customers, but she was loath to interrupt whatever was happening behind closed doors. She checked out the window. It was Sutton Mize.

Sutton stepped into the garage. Her preppy pink and gray diamond-patterned sweater, crisp gray slacks, and high heels made Willa feel even more unkempt than usual. She adjusted her ball cap.

Pushing her sunglasses to the top of her head, Sutton swept her gaze around the garage and picked her way around parts and tools toward Willa. "What are the boys up to?"

Normally, Willa would keep her mouth shut, but

Sutton would know everything soon enough. She and Wyatt shared their secrets.

"Man showed up wanting money to cover Ford's gambling debts. They're all hashing things out in the waiting room."

Sutton performed a literal pearl clutch. "Oh no. I wondered if he might be in trouble. Last time I saw him he looked stressed. Have you noticed?"

Willa shrugged. "He hasn't been by the garage in weeks."

"I'm worried."

"For who?" Willa asked.

"For everyone." Sutton's tone was darker and more serious than her sunny disposition hinted at. "Changes are coming."

Willa's breath stalled in her chest. Sutton was right, Willa could feel the changes lurking outside their door. The question was whether they were sharp-toothed wolves or warm fuzzy sheep. Her experience was of the wolf variety.

"Do you think they'll pay the man off?"

"How much was it?"

"Forty K."

"Goodness. Poor Ford." Sutton fiddled with her strand of pearls and stared at the closed door for a moment before turning her attention back to Willa, a slight smile curling her lips.

The silence stretched to the point of uncomfortableness. Why was Sutton still here?

"What are you doing New Year's Eve?" Sutton finally asked, her perfectly plucked eyebrows rising.

"I don't know."

"My parents are throwing a party."

Willa made a throaty sound of fake encouragement, not good at this kind of small talk.

"I want to officially extend an invitation."

Willa was nonplussed. While she and Sutton were on superficial speaking terms, they didn't qualify as anything resembling friends. At least not how she remembered friendship.

"I'm going to be . . . busy that night."

Willa almost said *working,* which would have been laughable considering the garage would be closed, and Sutton knew it.

"Doing what?"

Reading was a lame excuse, although the truth. A string of nonsensical *um*s and *ah*s emerged from her brain.

"So, that's settled, you're coming." Sutton's grin was so easy and infectious Willa had a hard time nurturing even a nugget of resentment about the manipulation.

"Seriously, I can't. I don't have anything nice to wear." It hurt to admit as much, but she guessed that Sutton's party would be nothing like a high-school kegger or the parties her ex had thrown. No jeans and T-shirts allowed.

Sutton cocked her head, her smile turning calculating. "I'd love to make you a dress."

"Why?" Willa curled in on herself and fiddled with the hair poking out of her hat. Meeting kindness with suspicion was a natural response not even her two years in Cottonbloom had been able to shake.

"Because you must be tired of coveralls. And selfishly, designing makes me happy. You'll be doing me a favor."

Wyatt had bragged that Sutton's skill with a sewing machine was as impressive as his skill under the hood of a car.

"I'm not really a dress person." Actually, it had been so long since Willa had worn one she wasn't sure anymore. She'd used to love to wear pretty dresses to church. And later she enjoyed the attention she received from the male sex in her short skirts. A shame only slightly dulled by the years rose.

"I'll make sure you're comfortable and look good."

"Don't waste your time on me." Willa's voice invited no argument. "Speaking of wasting time, I need to get back to work."

"Sorry to be a distraction." Sutton walked away, but said over her shoulder, "The offer stands if you change your mind."

"I won't," Willa muttered to herself and meant it.

Sutton planted herself in Mack's office to wait. The meeting broke up less than five minutes later. The bookie came out of the waiting room first. He turned and held a hand out for a shake, but Mack ignored the gesture.

Willa was too far away to hear what passed between them, but the visual of the three brothers lined up, Mack in the middle, and facing the smaller man, was arresting. The bookie took several steps backward, keeping his eyes on the brothers, before he turned and hightailed it out the door. A wise move.

The brothers gathered in a semicircle. Willa sidled close enough to hear, but not close enough to be noticed. Sutton was attempting the same in the doorway of the office.

"Ford's been MIA for weeks. Anyone have an idea how we can find him?" Mack asked. He'd grown out his winter beard, dark and wiry, and with his tall, broad frame he reminded Willa of a bear. The anger and agitation radiating from him brought to mind the old saying, don't poke a sleeping bear. Mack was awake and ready to take someone's head off.

Wyatt's attention was focused on scuffing his boot along a groove in the floor. "He might be at our mother's."

The beat of silence was like the last tick before a bomb exploded. An impressive string of curses left Mack before he gritted his teeth and scrubbed a hand over his beard. "You know where she is?"

"I don't, but Aunt Hazel does." Wyatt shot a look toward Jackson. "And I think Jackson should be the one to track Ford down."

Willa sucked in a breath and tried to get a read on Jackson. Nothing but a twitching muscle in his jaw changed his expression, but she could sense his tension and shock.

"No way is that happening," Jackson said almost too quietly to hear from her vantage point. "You do it. You're the one who's all gung ho to find her and make nice."

"What in hell is going on?" Mack threw his hands up.

Wyatt made a noise between resignation and frustration and looked to the ceiling. "A couple of months ago, Aunt Hazel told me she could pass our mother's info along. I can't deny that I've considered contacting her, but if we call and Ford's there, he'll run. If I show up and Ford's there, I'd bust his pretty face in. You'd probably maim him, Mack. Jackson's the only one who could pull this off."

Jackson backed away, shaking his head. "Hell, no. Get someone else. Send Hazel if you have to."

"While I would enjoy seeing Hazel try to put Ford over her knee, it has to be one of us," Wyatt said.

"Make it anyone but me." Jackson turned his back on them and slammed the door on his way out back.

Willa took a step toward where he disappeared, but stopped herself. The last thing she needed at this point was to entangle herself further in his life.

Chapter Nine

It had been days since the bookie's visit. Mack and Jackson had been quieter than usual, which meant they'd been close to silent. Perhaps because Wyatt had been the one to drop the bomb about their mother, he seemed the least shell-shocked.

"Hey, Willa, Aunt Hazel is bringing the Crown Vic in again. You mind looking under the hood and jiggling some hoses?" Wyatt winked in her direction, his hands occupied with dashboard wiring.

"Sure. No problem." She kept one eye out for Hazel's arrival and one eye on Jackson. She'd been assigned to work with Wyatt on the Trans Am every day that week. Was it the natural work flow or deliberate avoidance on Jackson's part? She spent half her time wanting to pretend the kiss never happened and the other mad because *he* was pretending the kiss never happened.

For the umpteenth time, she relived the kiss, second by second. For her, it had been amazing and scary and eye-opening. But maybe the kiss had been run-of-the-mill for a normal person. There was no one she could ask.

A familiar engine knock cleared her mental fog and brought her out from under the Trans Am. Jackson inched her Honda into the first bay. She dropped the socket wrench and stalked over, catching him by the arm as he slipped out of her car.

"What do you think you're doing?" Her voice came out high-pitched and echoed off the concrete. She tried to push him aside to reach the driver's seat, but he blocked her and wrapped his hand around her wrist.

"I'm replacing your clutch."

"No you're not."

"I am." His face was stony. "Get back to work."

She sucked in a breath. He'd never used that tone with her before. They'd always been closer to partners than boss-employee. "Is that an order?"

Emotion flared in him like a match thrown onto gasoline, but the evenness of his voice doused it. "I bought a clutch last week."

"Return it." She didn't break eye contact.

"Let me do this for you." His voice was softer now.

"You've done enough already. I've almost got enough saved to—"

"Use that money on something else. Like tires."

Dammit. She did need new tires. "But—"

"Willa." The way he said her name was full of frustration, but also something sweeter she couldn't identify. Although his grip on her wrist was firm, his thumb rubbing slow circles on her pulse point was soft. The tremble started somewhere in her chest but spread outward until she was sure he could feel it too.

She couldn't put words to what passed between them in those moments, but it filled her with a heat that wasn't embarrassment or anger or even resentment. Those were easy emotions. Childish even. What both bound and repelled them was more complicated.

"Let me go," she whispered.

He did. She turned away to hide her confusion, rubbing

her wrist, not because he'd hurt her, but because she could still feel his touch like a brand. Wyatt whistled. Her attention flew to the window in time to see the Abbott aunts' Crown Victoria stop with a jerk across the front of the bay doors.

Okay, she had to keep it together. Her knees somehow supported her weight. She wiped her still trembling hands on a shop towel, adjusted her hat, and went outside.

Hazel slipped out of the passenger door with a natural grace while Hyacinth unfolded her tall, lanky frame from behind the steering wheel.

"Hiya there, young lady," Hyacinth said.

"Hello, Ms. Hy. The bays are full and the boys are inside working. They sent me out to take a look. Is the weird noise under the hood back?" If Hyacinth noticed Willa's voice was strained and close to breaking, she didn't comment.

Hyacinth had a loud, unladylike laugh and easy way about her that Wyatt had inherited. "It's not like that's the only reason we bring the old girl in." Some of the bravado went out of her stance, and she examined her fingernails. "The weird noise is in the back end. Underneath. I might have hit something."

Willa took a deep breath, regaining some control now she was out of Jackson's orbit, but the sooner she was alone the better. "I'll do a thorough check. Promise."

"Thanks." Hyacinth made her way to the door, the fabric of her track suit swishing.

Hazel lingered.

"A fresh pot of coffee is brewing," Willa said, hoping Hazel would leave her alone.

No matter how polite and nice Hazel was, she intimidated the tar out of Willa. Something in her stare seemed to flay open any secrets, no matter how well hidden.

"I'm not the coffee addict my sister is."

When that was all she said, Willa squatted down to inspect the muffler. There was a chance they weren't playing possum this time. "Any idea what she hit?"

"I don't think she hit anything. This time, at least."

"You didn't hear the noise?"

Hazel's sardonic look ended the game.

To say she'd done it, Willa reached underneath and wiggled the exhaust, protecting her hand with the towel. It didn't move. She stood up and tucked the towel in her back pocket. "I guess everything is fine, then." The pitch of her voice made it sound more like a question than a statement.

"I suppose you're jealous of Sutton Mize." Hazel's head tilted and her gaze was like the first cut of a knife, sharp and digging.

The unexpected question sent her reeling. There were many reasons she could be jealous of Sutton. She was pretty by anyone's standards and always dressed like she'd stepped out of a magazine. Based on Wyatt's asides to Jackson, she was also funny and good in bed. And the invitation to her family's New Year's Eve Party only solidified the fact she was nice too. The whole package.

"Because of her clothes?" Willa tugged on her shapeless coveralls.

"No, because she's with Wyatt." Hazel's eyes narrowed.

"Why would that bother me?"

"I was under the impression you and Wyatt are close. And he is charming and very good-looking."

The matter-of-fact way she said it made Willa bow up. "Not as good-looking as Jackson."

Hazel's smile reminded her of River right after Willa had given in and shared her dinner the night before—self-satisfied. The old lady had played her like a mandolin. "I find your opinion very interesting indeed."

"Why do you care what I think?"

"Because I care about what my nephews care about."

Hazel blinked, her eyes magnified behind her glasses. She and Jackson shared more than eye color. The same depth of feeling and intelligence hid behind an outward show of cool regard.

The implication gave Willa pause. "Nothing can happen."

"Why not?"

"Because it's complicated and . . . and . . . none of your business." Willa clamped her mouth shut. She was being unbelievably rude to a woman who could drop a word in Mack's ear and probably have her fired.

"Of course it's none of my business, but cut me a break. I'm old and nosy and love those boys like they're my own. I worry about them and Jackson most of all."

"Why Jackson?"

"Because he's too like his father. Tends to wall himself off when things go bad. Since Hobart died, he's been looking too much inward. I noticed things had changed recently and wondered if you had something to do with it."

Willa opened and closed her mouth, at a loss for a response.

"Goodness, I'm getting chilly. I think I will warm up with a cup of coffee." Hazel shuffled toward the door.

Willa caught the door handle before Hazel could open it, their hands overlapping. "Wait. A good change or bad?"

"Most definitely good."

Her heart fired off a flare. "How can you be sure it's because of me?"

"I'm an old spinster, but can I give you some advice?"

Willa felt a little like she'd crossed into an alternate universe. Besides Marigold, she wasn't used to other women taking an interest in her. And now in a matter of days both Sutton and Hazel were reaching out like she was almost part of a real family again. She nodded.

"Tell him how you feel."

"I can't." She croaked out the words through a dry, tight throat.

"I don't know what brought you to Cottonbloom, but my guess is your life hasn't been easy and you have a difficult time trusting people. Am I right?"

"Maybe?" Her questioning lilt broadcast the truth behind the word.

"You can trust Jackson. In fact, I'd go so far as to say you could trust all the Abbotts. Me included."

Willa wanted to throw her arms around the woman. Would she smell like cold cream and lotion, things she associated with her own grandmother? Instead of acting on the foolish urge, she dropped her hand from the door and stepped back.

Hazel's final glance was one Willa recognized and hated even if it was tinged with kindness. Pity.

She cracked the door and called for River. The dog shot out and danced around her legs. Willa scooped up a stick on their way to the magnolia tree for a few rounds of fetch. River's simple joy in the game despite her less-than-kind past was a comfort.

Over the past few days Willa had gone from inconspicuous to exposed, and it wasn't a comfortable place to be. Everyone from Wyatt to Sutton to Hazel to Jackson were examining her. Like a scab picked off a wound, a rawness had been uncovered and she wasn't sure if it would heal or fester.

Hazel sidled closer to where Jackson was working, holding two cups of steaming coffee. "Coffee break?"

If it had been Aunt Hy, he would expect small talk and gossip, but he and Hazel were too similar to play those sorts of games. He wrapped a hand around the mug and sipped. "Did Wyatt send you over to talk about our mother and Ford?"

"No. But if you're looking for my opinion, I think you should go. Might be healthy for you boys to reconnect with her."

"We're grown. Don't need a mama." Jackson eyed her under his lashes. "We have you and Aunt Hy for that."

Hazel's smile was affectionate but wistful. "Always." She sipped her coffee and studied him.

"Was there something the matter with the car?" Reading Hazel was like trying to decipher a different language. He might recognize a word here or there, but the context made little sense.

"I expect not." She took another sip and swept her gaze over the garage. "It's brighter in here. Cleaner. You boys have done a good job transforming the place. I don't know why Hobart was hesitant to take a chance on restorations."

"Mack deserves the credit." The garage did look more prosperous and professional since Mack had effectively taken charge. "Pop was waiting and hoping Ford would come around."

"Hobart could be blind." Hazel's gaze cut to him over the rim of her cup. "Do you take after him?"

"What do you mean?"

"Willa is still outside. Alone. Maybe you should check on her." Hazel didn't smile or wink or offer any hints.

He peeled off his mechanic's gloves and slapped them against his palm, his gaze down. "Am I that obvious?"

"You'll be waiting forever if you wait for her to come to you. She's unsure of herself, but not of you."

"Did she say something?" Suddenly he wanted to pump his aunt for as much intel as she could provide on Willa.

"Go ask her yourself."

"Maybe I will," he said with more confidence than he could muster inside. An apology had been brewing since their disastrous kiss, but Aunt Hazel had tempered his guilt with a drop of hope.

He went out the front door, but she wasn't with the Crown Vic. A happy bark turned his attention to the magnolia tree. She bent over to give River's head a rub, then tossed a stick end over end. The dog jumped to try to catch it midair, but missed. River's happiness didn't seem diminished by her failure.

River noticed him first, veering toward him with the stick in her mouth. She dropped it at his feet, and he threw it farther than Willa's toss. She stood framed by the glossy green leaves of the giant magnolia.

The tree had been his favorite place as a kid. In the summer it was covered in blooms as big as his hand and the scent called forth bittersweet memories. He'd climb up into its lower branches when he needed to escape his family and think. Being a twin meant never being lonely, but sometimes he craved solitude. Wyatt had never seemed to need the same.

He stuffed his hands into his pockets and took a deep breath. "Aunt Hazel said that you—"

"She told you? I mean, it's true, but none of her business." She gestured with her hand over him like a model selling a high-end car. "It has nothing to do with you and me or what happened or didn't happen or . . . whatever."

Her eyes darted from side to side in a panicky way, and he was pretty sure her cheeks hadn't been that red when he'd walked up. He grabbed the nearest branch of the magnolia, his emotional balance disturbed.

"I'm not following. Were you and Aunt Hazel talking about me?"

She closed her eyes and muttered a few choice words before staring somewhere in the vicinity of his neck. "She didn't tell you anything, did she?"

"Only that I should get my head out of my ass and come talk to you."

Her laugh eased the tension. Damn, he'd missed her

laugh. It had been days since he'd heard it ring out in the garage.

"I cannot imagine Ms. Hazel cursing. Ms. Hyacinth, maybe. Did lightning strike?"

"I might be paraphrasing slightly, but that was the gist." River returned, but when it became clear the game was over, she settled at their feet and chewed on the end of the stick. Seeking a moment to gather his thoughts, he leaned over to give the dog a pat, then straightened, forcing himself to look in Willa's eyes. "You should know something. I kissed you because I wanted to. And, I hope you kissed me back for the same reason and not because you felt obliged to."

"Obliged to?" The genuine confusion on her face gave him the courage to continue despite the fact his stomach was using his heart as a punching bag.

"Because you work here and I'm part owner. I'm not that kind of guy. If you think what we did was a mistake and don't ever want me to talk to you again, then I'll make sure we're assigned to different projects for now until . . . forever. But I hope that's not what you want." He swallowed, trying to even out his voice. "Because it's not what I want."

During his halting speech, her expression changed to something he wasn't able to read. He waited, mental preparations under way for soul-crushing rejection.

Which is why he was wholly unprepared for her to pop up on her toes and mash her lips against his. He blinked, her face blurry. She pulled his bottom lip between her teeth and bit down hard enough to prod him into action.

He wrapped his arms around her and lifted her off the ground with a chesty rumble. River barked and nipped at his ankles.

"Tell her you want this. Want me." He wasn't sure if he or River needed assuring more.

She pulled away and addressed the dog in a breathy voice. "River. Stop. It's fine." She looked back at Jackson. "I want this."

"Not because I'm your boss?"

Her half smile was teasing in the sexiest way possible. "You'll never be the boss of me, Jackson Abbott."

Screw the ribbing he would receive from his brothers and the disapproving looks from his aunts, he was going full-on caveman and dragging her back to the loft to finish what they'd started.

A whistle sounded from the side door. Willa shot out of his arms and squatted down next to River. Wyatt made a come-on gesture with two fingers, his customary smile nowhere in sight.

"We're not done." Jackson shuffled backward toward the shop door, keeping his eyes on her.

"We're not?" Her face was hidden in River's ruff, and her noncommittal tone sent him veering into confusion. Again. Why couldn't women come with an instruction manual like a car?

"Don't leave today without seeing me."

She raised her face to fix him with a stare that did not settle his nerves. "That sounds like an order from my boss. Is it?"

A big part of him wanted to say yes. Anything to get her alone and talking to him. "It's a request from a friend."

She stood, but her guard was up, the soft look in her eyes gone. "Didn't Mack tell you? I already set up to leave early today. And I'm taking tomorrow off."

"Why?" When one corner of her mouth pulled back and her eyes narrowed, he tempered his voice. "Anything I can help with?"

"Nope. I'm doing a favor for Marigold. Can you get my car done in time?"

The fact he couldn't decipher truth from lie scared him.

She only offered brief glimpses behind her brick-and-mortared wall. The rest of the time he was in the dark stumbling around searching for a way through. She slammed the door on him once more.

"It'll be done in two hours, but I'm not going to let this go."

"Fine." There was defiance but also a challenge in the word.

He retreated, conceding the skirmish, but not willing to surrender the battle.

Chapter Ten

Willa wandered the Louisiana side of downtown Cotton-bloom. Two city workers were talking football while stringing Christmas lights around the trunks of denuded crepe myrtles that lined the road. Ignoring Christmas was hard around Cottonbloom. Both sides of downtown looked like elves had barfed tinsel and lights and red bows on everything, living or dead. She'd even seen a dog with reindeer antlers on its head. It was three days before the dreaded holiday and the rare chance of snow in the forecast had sent the Christmas meter to obnoxious.

With Dave too sick to even get out of bed, Marigold had asked Willa to help construct a curtained stage for the library to use for puppet shows. While she wasn't an expert carpenter, Willa had been happy to be able to pay back a fraction of the kindness Marigold had shown her. It had taken longer than she'd anticipated, but she and Marigold had shared some laughs and the result had made her proud. At least if she had to disappear from Cottonbloom, something tangible and worthwhile would remain.

With the project completed, she'd headed back to her trailer to wash off the paint as best she could. Shivering in the plummeting temperatures, she left River curled up on her bed and headed to town for a hot lunch. At the crossroads, she'd pumped her brakes, almost giving in to an impulse to head to the garage. And Jackson. The unfinished way they'd left things had her afraid to be alone with him. Not because of what he might do, but because of her impulse to jump his bones. An all-around bad idea.

She stepped into Rufus's Meat and Three, the smells and warmth an instant mood lifter. Clayton Preston was manning the counter. It was early yet for lunch and only one other customer, an older man reading the paper with a cup of coffee, was inside.

"What can I get you, Willa?" Clayton asked.

Clayton was brother to the Cottonbloom, Mississippi, police chief and a recent parolee from the state penitentiary. His forearms were covered in tattoos and his eyes reflected experiences that belied his physical age. When she looked at him, in some ways, she saw herself.

"A pork plate, please."

He doled out the food, and she paid in exact change. After a moment's consideration, she dropped two pennies in the "give a penny, take a penny" tray. She was painfully aware there were people worse off than she was. Before she'd landed in Cottonbloom, she'd been one.

She took her plate and sweet tea to a table facing the window. With only her cold trailer and River waiting and her self-control to stay away from the garage in tatters, she ate slowly. Clayton approached with a steaming cup of coffee.

"Like some company? I'm tired of talking to myself."

She nudged her chin toward the chair across from her. "Sure. What about old man Morrison?"

"He forgot his hearing aid." Clayton's smile lifted a decade or more off his shoulders. "Taking his order was a trial of patience."

"Seems like you've settled into Cottonbloom well."

Like her, Clayton was a transplant, although his path had originated in New Orleans and taken a detour through jail.

"Cottonbloom is a nice town. There's some that don't like or trust me because of my past, but nothing will change that except time. And maybe not even that." He took a sip of coffee.

Willa stabbed the slaw with her spork, his words resonating. "Do you wish you could go back and do things differently? I dream about it all the time."

Clayton set his elbows on the table and turned the coffee cup in his hands. "One thing I had to come to terms with in prison was the futility of wishing for the impossible. Reality is what it is. You can choose to confront it or run away."

Willa dropped her spork, rubbed her hands down the legs of her jeans, and met his gaze. "What is your reality?" She was asking a lot, but he didn't shy away.

"I had to own up to what I'd done and live with the consequences."

The question that had been stewing since she'd met him popped out. "What were you put away for?"

"Stealing cars and dealing drugs." He didn't seem embarrassed or offended at her curiosity.

The longer she stared into his eyes the more familiar the road he'd traveled seemed. The stops along the way might have been different, but the scenery was the same.

"What if something really bad happened to someone you cared about? And what if it was your fault but it's too late to fix things?" She braced herself for laughter or dismissal at her vagueness.

"It's never too late to apologize."

She swallowed and pushed her plate to the side, her appetite turning to nausea. "She's dead."

He didn't gasp or turn away. "And you hold yourself responsible?"

"My best friend OD'ed on heroin she bought from my ex-boyfriend."

"Did you know she was using?" No accusation shaded his voice. In fact, he sounded as impersonal as the policeman who'd questioned her afterward.

"It started with pot. Didn't seem like a big deal. Then, things happened after we graduated high school, and I wasn't the kind of friend I should have been. She shot smack one night at a party."

"She got hooked."

"Yeah. I didn't realize how serious it was until it was too late."

"Look, I've seen more than my share of addicts. There's nothing you or anyone else can do if someone's set on using."

She picked at her thumbnail, the sting centering her and keeping her from flashing back to the past. "But I introduced her to my scummy boyfriend. Brought her around his house, his parties. If I hadn't—"

"Stop." He took her wrist, his grip firm. "What-ifs are useless. All you can do now is live your life."

"That's what you're doing?"

"I'm tryin'. My brother and his girl, Sadie, have my back. I'm doing my best to mend what I can and leave the rest behind." His smile this time was tinged with a sweet bitterness. "Not gonna lie, it's tough, but people make it better."

The bell over the door tinkled and a family of four walked in, their spirits high and their hands full of bags with wrapped presents. The children shoved each other as their parents herded them toward the counter.

Clayton stood and rapped his knuckles on the table.

"You take care, Willa. I'll be working through the holidays if you want to talk more."

She turned in her seat to watch Clayton take the family's order. She'd done so much looking behind her that she never considered the distant future. She'd only concerned herself with the next meal, the next month's rent money, the next town. But being in Cottonbloom and around Jackson had her looking beyond her immediate needs to what she wanted.

The family took the table on the other side of the restaurant, chattering about Christmas and the likelihood of snow. Confronted with their normalcy and ease together, her insides jostled. It didn't feel as simple as jealousy though. It was akin to longing.

If she told Jackson the truth and he turned away, at least she'd know. She wouldn't be living in this hellish in-between, waiting for her execution papers. Her heart felt sore from overuse, like a muscle she hadn't exercised in too long.

She forced herself to finish her food. Making full use of what was in front of her was a hard-learned lesson. After dumping her empty plate, she stepped outside. Her layers of flannel shirt, sweatshirt, and hoodie kept out most of the cold.

She walked across the footbridge toward the Mississippi side of town and window-shopped at the Quilting Bee, laughing to herself at the thought of hanging a picture or lighting a scented candle in her trailer. But the quilts along the walls drew her closer to the window, and she cupped her hands against the glass to look. They were intricate and lovely and warm-looking. Probably expensive too. She moved on.

Standing outside Abigail's Boutique, she stomped her feet to get her chilled blood flowing. The mannequin in the window wore a fancy off-the-shoulder gown in black. It was pretty enough but how did a woman raise her arms in the darn thing? So impractical. Willa shook her head.

She took a side step toward the footbridge, ready to huddle in front of her kerosene heater for the foreseeable future. The door to the boutique opened with a jangle, and Sutton popped her head out. "I thought that was you. I'm so glad you changed your mind."

"What? No, I didn't—"

Sutton grabbed her arm and pulled her inside the shop. "God, it's frigid out. Can you believe they're talking about snow showers? I can't even remember the last time it snowed in Cottonbloom."

Willa paused, feeling like Dorothy escaping black-and-white Kansas and landing in Technicolor Oz. Racks of clothes, some arranged by color, and headless mannequins in beautiful clothes peppered the floor. The smell was light and feminine, starkly opposite the grease-and-metal manliness of the shop.

Willa had never been inside the high-end clothing store. The only new clothes Willa splurged on were underwear. Apparently, the line she wouldn't cross in the name of poverty was buying used panties.

Sutton continued to chatter about Christmas in Cottonbloom. The Santa had showed up to the parade rip-roaring drunk and the Girl Scouts and Boy Scouts had gotten into a fight about whose float would go first.

While her ears were focused on Sutton, the warmth and smells and the racks of clothes overwhelmed her other senses. Zigzagging through the racks, Willa reached out and skimmed her fingers along the sleeve of a silky white blouse that was as thin and airy as gauze.

Sutton stopped in the back of the store next to a display of scarves and jewelry. She set her hands on her hips and examined Willa like a pinned bug. "You look like the marshmallow man. How many layers are you wearing?"

"Three or four. It's cold out." Defensiveness crept into her voice.

"And that hat." Distaste made the word sound like an epitaph. "Will you take it off?"

"It keeps my head warm." She didn't make a move to remove it.

"We're inside, and it's plenty warm in here."

Willa gave in, mostly because her scalp was tingling with sweat, although it was due more to embarrassment than temperature. Pulling the hat off, she caught sight of the two of them in one of the six-foot mirrors mounted on the wall. She ruffled her hair and looked away, the comparison too depressing.

"To be clear, I'm not here to take you up on your offer of a dress," Willa said.

"Weren't you? I think subconsciously that's exactly why you were standing outside my shop." Sutton moved around the back of the cabinet and came out with a tape measure. "I need to get your measurements."

Was she right? Willa wasn't a fan of fairy tales, and Cinderella happened to be her least favorite of them all. Cinderella never took charge of her destiny. She let a fairy godmother and a prince save her. That's one reason why she loved *Jane Eyre*. Jane took charge of her life, and it had been her choice to return to Rochester at the end.

Willa held her hands up to ward off Sutton and her tape measure. "Look, I don't need a damn fairy godmother."

"How about a friend, then? Everyone could use more of those." Sutton's smile was so genuine and her eyes were so full of understanding that Willa had to blink back a rise of tearful emotion, her breathing turning ragged.

"Are you doing this because of Wyatt?" Her voice was wobbly.

"Him but mostly Jackson. Underneath all his frowns

and the loner vibes is a pretty special guy. Wyatt and I might not be together if it wasn't for him."

"Jackson and I aren't . . . I mean, you don't think . . . there's nothing going on." Willa flapped the front of her hoodie and wondered if it was possible to spontaneously combust.

One corner of Sutton's mouth rose along with her eyebrows and her *uh-huh* was definitely sarcastic. "You can't tell me you and Jackson haven't kissed or anything. I see the way you two look at each other."

"How's that?" Her voice had acquired a weird squeak.

"Like you're the chocolate to his peanut butter. So have you kissed him or what?" Sutton tugged the hem of the hoodie up, and Willa raised her arms like a toddler and allowed her to slip it off.

Clayton's advice rang in her head. She wanted a friend, maybe even needed one, and it wasn't like Sutton was a stranger. She was Wyatt's girlfriend which gave her extra marks. Willa peeled the sweatshirt off by herself, leaving her in a baggy red plaid flannel shirt.

"Okay, so we've kind of kissed. The first time—"

"The *first* time? Way to go."

"Yeah, well, I ran off and he thought I was mad at him for taking advantage of me because he's sort of my boss."

"But you weren't mad?"

"I was embarrassed. And a little wigged out."

"But you do like him?"

Willa sighed and rolled her eyes. "Yes. Although I'd prefer to be the peanut butter in any potential relationship. Crunchy and not smooth."

Sutton's laugh pealed through the store. "Crunchy peanut butter, it is. Have you got anything on under that shirt?"

"A bra."

"Come on back here." Sutton led her into a spacious changing room. "Off with it."

Willa squeezed her eyes almost shut to block out the three-sixty view of the two of them, slipped the shirt off, and crossed her arms over her chest more to hide the ratty bra than her boobs. Next Sutton tugged Willa's pants low on her hips.

"Arms up."

When Sutton didn't tease her about the sorry state of her underwear, Willa complied, and Sutton efficiently took several measurements, mumbling the numbers under her breath as she jotted them down.

"You have a gorgeous figure. I'm jealous." Sutton tossed her the flannel shirt, and Willa held it over her chest.

The compliment unfurled in her chest like the beauty of spring's first buttercup. "I'm too busty."

"I have a feeling 99.9 percent of men would disagree with that assessment." Sutton shot her a smiling sidelong glance before leaving her to get dressed.

It wasn't her habit to spend much—or any—time in front of a mirror. But with her reflection unescapable, she forced her shoulders back and her hands to her sides and really looked. The physical work in the garage plus her skipped meals had left her stomach flat and her arms taut. Even so, her body had filled out since she'd left home. Curves that she hid under her coveralls were on display.

What would Jackson think of her body? She yanked her pants up and shoved her arms into the sleeves of her flannel shirt, fumbling with the buttons. Getting naked was a far cry from a couple of kisses. Not going to happen. But now the thought was planted, it grew roots and flowered. Heat in her lower belly made her ache like a fever was coming on. Or maybe the stomach flu. She actually felt sick with desire.

When she emerged from the changing room, Sutton

was sitting on a stool behind the counter with a white sketch pad in front of her, her bottom lip caught between her teeth, as a pencil flew across the page.

Without looking up, Sutton said, "I'm thinking something simple. Not black. Too stark for you. Maybe a blue. No lace or ruffles or fringe. Not your style. A classic old-Hollywood silhouette that will highlight your amazing bod."

Willa stepped forward, hypnotized by the lines and curves taking shape. The sparsely drawn figure even looked a little bit like her, with short hair and a pointed face. The dress was something a heroine out of one of Willa's books might wear. If the actual creation was even half as pretty as Sutton's drawing, Willa would be in awe.

"You like it?" Sutton's tone and Cheshire cat grin made it clear that Willa's face already bore the answer.

"You know it's beautiful, but I'm not sure I'll feel comfortable wearing it."

"Comfort, schmum-fort. You think these bad boys are comfortable?" Sutton came around from behind the counter and kicked up her foot, showcasing her red high heel. "Newsflash—they're not."

Willa couldn't help it, she laughed along with the other woman. Still, the camaraderie was slightly nerve-racking after so many years without. "I'd better head. River will be whining for her dinner."

"I'll have something for you to try on soon after Christmas. I'm going to get started tonight." Sutton walked her to the door and leaned in the gap after Willa hit the sidewalk. "I'm closing up early and headed back to the garage. I'm giving Wyatt his Christmas present. You going to be around?"

"No." Again the impulse to see Jackson was like a chant in her head. "No," she said more firmly. "I'm headed back to my place."

"How about we keep this dress business between us and surprise Jackson?" Sutton raised her eyebrows.

"Sure." Probably smart in case Sutton didn't follow through or Willa decided not to go to the party. Sutton took a step back. As the door was closing, Willa grabbed it before she had a chance to stop herself. She swallowed. "I just wanted to say 'thanks.' This was unexpected, but really nice."

Sutton's smile didn't disappear but morphed into a surprised delight. Willa partly meant the offer of a dress, but mostly she'd meant the offer of friendship, even if Willa couldn't take her up on it. Before Sutton could say anything else, Willa mashed her cap on her head and ran-walked back across the river.

Chapter Eleven

Jackson slipped back inside the garage after watching Sutton present Wyatt with his Christmas present—his dream car, a 1970 V8 Plymouth Hemi Cuda. Jackson had helped Sutton locate one that wasn't too expensive or too beat up. Wyatt would relish the chance to lovingly restore it. As much as Jackson wanted an up close look-see at the car, he knew better than to interrupt the two lovers.

As happy as Jackson was for his twin—and he was— a peculiar loneliness spread through his chest and compressed his heart. Wyatt would always be a huge part of his life, but everything was changing and changing fast.

Since his memories began, his life and times had revolved around the garage. One day had blurred into the next with nothing of great significance standing out until the day his pop collapsed. Jackson had pumped his chest while Wyatt had blown his own breath into their pop's lungs, but he'd still died.

Jackson glanced over at the spot in the first bay. Since that day, chaos had stalked him. He didn't like chaos. Maybe no one was comfortable with chaos and change, but Wyatt seemed to roll with it easier than Jackson did.

He trudged up the stairs to the loft. Wyatt was moving

his stuff little by little to Sutton's house. Ford was still MIA, and the bookie was breathing down their necks for the money or else. Jackson wasn't sure what the *or else* consisted of, but probably not a fruitcake.

Snowflakes drifted from the gray sky, swirling in cross winds. A childlike wonder pushed away the encroaching worries and vast solitude. What was Willa doing? Was she sitting outside her trailer with River watching the snow fall over the fallow field?

A more practical thought followed. It was literally below freezing outside and Jackson didn't recall seeing anything more than a space heater in her trailer. How did she keep warm? Maybe she didn't. The thought of Willa alone and shivering left his insides flayed and raw.

He glanced over at the present he'd bought her. A handsewn quilt from the Quilting Bee. It had been mocking him for days, but the opportunity to give it to her without looking weird hadn't presented itself. And probably never would.

Her secrets still hung between them, but damned if he could sleep while she suffered. Her pride and independence wouldn't keep her warm through the coldest nights Louisiana had seen in a decade. He considered taking the quilt to her, but decided to bring her to the quilt.

With the decision made, he pulled onto the parish road two minutes later, the back end of his Mustang fishtailing as the melting snow slicked the roads. Her car was parked next to the trailer, white dusting the roof and hood.

He knocked on the door and heard a bark from inside. Willa cracked the door open, the layers of clothes making her appear a foot bigger all the way around. A hoodie was drawn tight so a framed oval of her face was all that was visible.

"What are you doing here?" The fact there was no anger, only surprise, in her voice counted as a win.

"Checking on you."

"I'm fine." She cast her gaze over his head. "Oh my goodness, it's snowing."

"Yep, and it's cold. Supposed to get down into the teens tonight."

An anxious look flashed before she forced a tight smile. "River and I will have to cuddle up then."

"You can't stay here. Come back to my place. Please."

Nothing about her softened. "I told you once already I don't need saving."

An anger usually reserved for the racetrack welled up inside of him like a geyser he was unable to cap. "I'm not trying to save you; I'm trying to help you." His voice roughened and rose until he ended on a near shout. "That's what you do when you care about someone, dammit."

Her eyes went wide and her lips parted. "What do you mean?"

He was as shocked as she was that he'd said it aloud. But the truthfulness organized the mess in his chest into something manageable, and he plowed forward. "I mean that's why I fixed your clutch. And helped with River. And why I'm here. I'm not great with talking about"—he ran a hand through his hair, damp from snow—"my *feelings*."

"What do you want from me, Jackson?"

Were those tears in her eyes? His hands twitched. He wanted to draw her close and hold her until she smiled her crooked, teasing little smile.

He considered the loaded question. If he asked for everything swirling around in his head, she would slam the door in his face. "I want to sit in a warm room, watch it snow, and share a beer. I want you to grab a few things and stay at my place tonight. You can have my room, and I'll take the couch or Wyatt's bed. That's it."

She stared at him for a long time, her breath puffing

white between them. With a sharp exhale, she asked with a warning in her voice, "Just for tonight?"

"For as long as you need."

She stared at him for a long moment before nodding and shutting the door. Relief had him blowing out a breath that turned white in the air. He stomped his feet. He'd left so fast, he hadn't grabbed a jacket.

Not five minutes later, she stepped out, holding a toiletry case and two plastic grocery bags, one with books and the other with clothes. River brushed past her to snuffle around his legs and notch her head in his hand for a pet.

She took a step toward her car, but he grabbed her. He couldn't even feel her arm under the bulk of her layers. "Roads were already a little slick and your tires are balder than a baby's butt."

Her lips twitched. "You okay with massive amounts of dog hair in the Mustang?"

"I'm capable of vacuuming." Before Willa and River, he would have never let an animal into his car.

Once they were on the road, he pointed to the bag on her lap. "Are you expecting to be so bored you need to read?"

"Library books. In the event of a natural disaster, I don't want to leave them in the trailer. Several got ruined when the tornado rolled through a while back."

"Doesn't the library have an act-of-God forgiveness policy?"

"Marigold cut me a break." She shifted to look out the window.

So many questions fought to escape, but he forced an even tone. "Marigold is a sweetheart. How's Dave? I stopped by last week but he was too sick to talk."

"You went to see him?" She turned back to him.

"Why are you surprised? Dave helped us convert the loft."

"Yeah, Marigold told me that. I guess I don't picture you having many friends. You're always alone."

"Seriously? Kettle meet pot."

The sound of her laugh filled the car. It did nothing to heat the interior, but a place inside of him warmed, and he smiled.

"We're a good match then." Her laughter trailed into silence. Her expression was frozen into what he guessed was horror.

But the slip of her tongue bolstered his confidence. "We are. That's why we work so well together."

Her relief was palpable, and she relaxed into the seat, clutching the books to her chest. They arrived at the loft, and he ushered her and River up the stairs ahead of him, discreetly upping the thermostat so she would be more comfortable.

While she set the bag of books on the coffee table, he did a walk-through of his bedroom. Unlike Wyatt, he kept things tidy by habit. The bathroom wasn't a disaster either. He set out a clean towel and washcloth. When he returned, she stood at the picture window, still wearing all her layers, but she'd pushed off the hoodie. Her hair stuck out like the spring growth from a bush.

She was chaos incarnate with her secretive, messy past and equally unconventional present. Chaos was unpredictable and scary and to be avoided. So why didn't he want to run like hell? He stepped closer.

"I can't remember the last time it snowed here," he said softly, afraid to spook her. "Too bad it'll melt tomorrow."

"Then we'd better enjoy it while it lasts, huh?" The smile she aimed in his direction was wistful.

A clarity had risen from the seismic shifts of recent

events and put him on alert. Was she referring to the weather or them?

"Did you see snow as a kid?" It was a first volley to try to hammer past her formidable defenses.

She chafed her arms even though the room was warm and she had on enough clothes to insulate an arctic explorer. "A few times. Enough to build a tiny snowman once."

That meant farther north, but not too far. He doubted the years had chipped away her accent. Mississippi? Arkansas? Maybe even north Louisiana.

"What were your parents like?"

An internal debate seemed to be taking place. Finally, she said, "My mom died right after I was born. An aneurysm. It was just me and my dad." She cast him a glance through her lashes. "He owned a garage."

"Just like us." The similarities between their childhoods were startling, yet somewhere along the way their paths had diverged, leaving Willa alone.

"Mr. Hobart reminded me of my dad so much. Your pop was a real special guy."

"Is your dad dead?"

She shook her head, but didn't speak.

"Is he looking for you?"

"I don't think so. Not anymore." Her voice cracked, and like a whip flaying his heart open, he bled for her.

No longer caring about the implications or whether or not it was a good idea, he stepped behind her and wrapped his arms around her. She tensed before her weight fell against his chest, her head resting against his shoulder.

"It wasn't his fault. None of it was his fault. He's a good man." She trembled.

"I have a hard time believing whatever happened was all your fault either." He would bet she'd long ago atoned for whatever sins she'd committed when she was young.

"I don't know anymore." Her voice was small and forlorn, but her words lit hope inside of him. He was close to earning her secrets. "I could really use a hot shower. I'm still cold and probably smell like a wet dog."

She cleared her throat and stepped away. He let her go. They were in a constant dance of coming together then pulling apart.

River lifted her head where she was curled up in the corner of his couch. Willa went over, scratched under her chin, and dropped a kiss on her furry head. River licked her cheek and settled her head back on her paws.

"You hungry? I could rustle up some soup and crackers. Maybe a grilled cheese?" he asked.

"I'm *always* hungry." She gave a little ironic smile.

Behind the smile lurked depressing implications. How many nights had she gone to bed hungry? Or cold? How many nights had she gone to bed scared or lonely or desperate?

"I left a towel in the bathroom. Make yourself at home," he said even though there were a million other things swirling in his head. A million other things he wanted to offer her besides food and a hot shower.

She disappeared into the bathroom with one of her bags and the toiletry case. He stood and listened to the sound of the water for a few minutes. It was a small comfort knowing she was here and safe for now. He heated up canned chicken noodle soup and buttered bread for grilled cheese. The smell never failed to invoke his childhood.

They'd lived on soup and grilled cheese as kids when their pop had been too busy working to fix dinner, which was most nights. The aunts had brought over casseroles once or twice a week, but food didn't survive long with four boys in the house.

The self-sufficiency and independence he'd gained had carried into adulthood. If the accusations of his few girlfriends were any indication, he was *too* self-sufficient and independent. He'd never needed them like they seemed to need him.

Willa was the opposite. She fought needing anyone—especially him. Was the compulsion a defensive habit or was that how she really wanted to live?

River sat up and Jackson stopped stirring to stare at the bathroom door. She stepped out in yoga pants and a T-shirt that read CAT HAIR IS LONELY PEOPLE GLITTER with an uneven scattering of sequins.

Without the hundred layers and with her damp hair tamed and tucked behind her ears, she looked so pretty his breath shuddered out. How had he gone nearly two years with blinders on where she was concerned? Maybe it had to do with self-preservation. Willa was a force of nature when he was used to living on placid waters.

"Smells good." Unable to endure his examination a moment longer, Willa cracked the silence.

"You don't have a cat." The weirdly domestic sight of him cooking offset the rough, sexy edge of his voice.

"No, but I assume whoever dropped it off at the second-hand shop did." She touched the rough sequins on her shirt with an eye roll, but her gaze streaked to his to assess his reaction. "After the tornado, most of my stuff was ruined, and I didn't have the funds to jaunt off to the mall."

Instead of reacting with pity or sympathy, he laughed. "Things are starting to make more sense."

Her stomach felt like it was being dragged across river rocks. The dig at her wardrobe stung more than it should have. "I know I'm not fashionable like Sutton, but—"

"Not that." He waved her over to a small stereo and handed her a CD.

It was Outkast. She shrugged and handed it back. "So?"

"You were wearing an Outkast T-shirt at Rufus's. You said it was your favorite band. Are they really?"

She'd forgotten about that. A giggle escaped. A *giggle*? She stifled it immediately. "No. I do have a fading smidge of pride left. I didn't want to admit where I bought it. Are they any good?" She handed him the case back.

"Not bad, but not my style. I was trying to figure out what *you* liked about them."

The significance of his admission hit her like a slap upside her head. He had listened to Outkast to try to understand her. Who did that? No one she'd ever met before.

"That was really sweet of you, Jackson." Where had that wobble in her voice come from?

Thankfully, he didn't call her on it. "Soup and sandwiches are ready."

While he doled out two bowls, she located silverware on the second try and set the table. He plopped down a box of crackers between them and sat down across from her. It was . . . homey and nice. Really nice. Like "she could get used to it real quick" nice.

Before she could panic, he asked, "If it's not Outkast, who is your favorite band?"

The small talk calmed her impulses, and she dipped the corner of her grilled cheese into the soup. "Music isn't really my thing. I like the classic rock that you guys play in the shop okay. The radio in the Honda was broken when I . . . got it." She stumbled over the words, not quite a lie, but not the truth either. She forced a smile. "I guess you're a big Eagles fan?"

"They're all right. Pop liked the classic stuff. It would be weird to hear anything else in the garage. Around here, I listen mostly to country. Some Southern rock. I'm a simple man with simple tastes." He smiled and his dimples flashed.

Simple, her butt. He was the most complicated of all the brothers. "You keep telling yourself that, stud."

The shift in mood was immediate and tangible. Even though she'd said it with a certain amount of tease, there was no denying the sexual undertones. Or overtones. All sorts of tones were blaring like tornado warnings. She concentrated on her soup as a potent silence spread.

"I wish you'd told me your trailer got trashed during the tornado." His voice was low and rumbly. "I would have helped."

That day was imprinted on her memories, but not because of the loss of her trailer. The time she'd spent huddled in the back storage room of the garage with Jackson had cemented her infatuation with him. She hadn't been working at the garage more than a couple of months, still feeling out the brothers and Mr. Hobart and always on guard in case one of them got any ideas.

The roaring wind overhead had forced her to abandon her position of aloofness. The fear was raw and primal and acute. Different from the gnawing anxiety she grappled with on a daily basis. She had latched on to him, the one warm solid thing in her existence at the time. He'd been stoic and calm and exactly what she'd needed in the dark.

"I hadn't been working at the garage long and my experience with people—men in particular—is that help isn't free and the price is usually more than I'm willing to pay." She kept her voice light, but his expression turned stormy.

"I'm not like that. None of us Abbotts are." He shrugged, and his face cleared of most of the darkness. "Except for Ford. He probably would expect something."

"Yep. He's one reason I tried to stick with you at work at the beginning." She grabbed a cracker and stuffed it into her mouth. The defense mechanisms that kept her silent had obviously been shorted out by the snow. At this rate, she'd spill her life story before the soup got cold.

"And here I thought it was because of how good-looking I am." The self-deprecating edge to his voice made her want to crawl into his lap and do things she'd only dreamed about.

Yes, he enriched her fantasy life, but no way was she going to confess that. Instead, she forced a tease into her voice. "Well, you are the pick of the litter, but that's not why I like working with you."

"Then it's my extraordinary skill under the hood?"

That was true too, and at his side, her expertise had grown leaps and bounds. She could certainly claim his mechanic prowess as the reason she preferred working with him over his brothers. But, in this at least, she could offer a partial truth.

"After the tornado, I felt safe with you. Wyatt and Mack are nice and all, but they're not . . ." *special.* Her brain finally clamped off her mouth.

"Willa." The way he said her name was both heartbreaking and hopeful.

The longer they stared, the more fractured her breathing became. When she couldn't take it anymore, she stood. "I'll clean up."

"Not a chance." He took the bowl out of her hands, stacked it on top of his own, and put them both in the sink. "Dishes will keep. How about I make some hot chocolate and we enjoy the snow while it lasts?"

Thankful for the chance to escape for even a few minutes to compose herself, she retreated to the window. The flurries had lightened, but enough had already fallen to dust the ground and decorate the trees as if Mother Nature had sifted powdered sugar over Cottonbloom.

Her reflection wavered indistinctly in the window, as if

she were a ghost. And wasn't she close? She was living a half-life between past and present, truth and lie. She was tired. Tired of being strong and silent. The loneliness was like hauling around chains that added links every year.

Jackson joined her and handed over a mug with a few floating marshmallows. His reflection somehow seemed more solid than hers. She took a sip, the rich sweetness recalling the simplicity of her childhood.

"That hat you wear. For a long time, I assumed it was an ex-boyfriend's, but it's your dad's, isn't it?" he asked.

"Yeah, it's his." Both good and bad memories were connected to the hat. "He was straightforward and honest. Taught me everything he knew. I worked in the garage from the time I became useful. Worked the register at first, but he had always let me tinker. Bought me an old engine when I was ten and taught me how to take it apart and put it back together."

"You must have enjoyed it."

"I did. Plus, I got to hang out with him, which sounds totally geeky, I know. When I got on up in high school, things changed." One of her biggest regrets. If she'd spent her spare hours at the shop fixing cars instead of trying to fit in, would everything have worked out differently?

"How so?"

"He remarried." It was an old story. The wicked stepmother. Except she hadn't been. Not really.

The snow petered out as they stood and watched darkness stretch across the sky. The world was preternaturally quiet. She felt like one of the kids from the Narnia books after they'd stepped out of the wardrobe into an enchanted land.

He slipped the mug from her hands and set it down on the coffee table. She kept her gaze on his reflection as he paused behind her, not touching her but close enough for his heat to radiate.

After a near eternity, he wrapped his arms around her from behind, one low on her waist, the other heavy and solid over her chest. She should step away and distance herself from the spiderweb of entanglements. Instead, the elephant-sized weight on her heart ambled to the corner of the room, not gone but ignored.

She leaned back into his chest and reveled in his strength, both physical and emotional. Was it so wrong to take comfort in his arms? She wouldn't let it go too far.

His heat was near incinerating. She would never be cold in his arms. To someone who'd spent more than her fair share of nights shivering in a ball under scant covers, it mattered. She turned her head and nuzzled her forehead into his neck, the stubble at his jaw rasping across her skin. Shivers erupted.

She took hold of his arm across her chest. His forearm was a thing of beauty. A part of his body worthy of being sculpted by a famous artist. Now instead of visually admiring it, she took her time exploring the crisp hair, the soft skin of the underside, and muscled ridges with both hands.

He coasted his lips along the shell of her ear to her jaw and tightened his arm around her waist, fitting them together. Good thing, as her knees wobbled and weakness flooded her system. Or was the heavy, sugared feeling pure arousal?

Her experience with men varied from quick teenaged grappling in the back of cars with Derrick to pinches and grabs inflicted when she least expected it. Whatever tender alchemy Jackson performed was foreign and intoxicating.

She turned her head enough to detour his wandering lips to hers. A gaspy moan escaped her when his mouth found hers. She didn't have time to get embarrassed. Urgency thrummed, and he bypassed the coaxing preliminaries of their last kiss. His tongue pressed for entrance, and she didn't hesitate to open for him.

His grip on her hip had a slight bite, but in concert with his tongue and lips, it only fed her arousal. Heat coiled in her lower belly. She arched her back and pressed her bottom into his pelvis, trepidation and excitement warring.

He switched his hold and scooped her into his arms, moving so fast her head swam. She squeezed her eyes even tighter, wanting to stay in her semidream state. Any light behind her eyelids was snuffed out and she peeked. They were in his bedroom, the king-sized bed against the wall getting closer. His profile was unreadable in the darkness. She leaned forward to press kisses along his jaw.

The world tipped again as she made contact with the mattress. A portion of his weight settled over her, but he held himself over her on his elbows. He speared his fingers into her hair and held her still while he resumed dominating her senses with his lips.

He rocked his hips slightly, and her legs spread to accommodate him without an order from her brain. His erection ground against her. After so many years of forcing her desires dormant, her body was slick and begging.

She slipped her hands under his shirt and explored his back with fingertips and nails. He hissed in a breath and arched into her touch. Power zinged through her like a lit fuse. She moved her hands ever higher. He propped himself up, grabbed the back of his shirt with one hand, and jerked it off in a less-than-graceful motion.

Instead of coming back over her, he slid his hand under the hem of her T-shirt and stroked the bare skin of her stomach. Her muscles flexed in response. He lifted the edge of her shirt, and between the two of them, her shirt joined his on the floor.

She wrapped her hands around his biceps and tried to

pull him back over her so he wouldn't have time to evaluate and judge her cheap white very nonsexy bra.

"You're amazing. Everything I've dreamed about," he whispered.

The words shot ice into her veins. He brushed his lips over hers, but she was frozen and unable to respond with an answering fire. She wasn't amazing. She was a liar and had lived a nightmare, not a dream.

She pushed at his chest and scooched backward on the bed, hitting the mass of pillows and trapping herself in the corner.

"What's wrong?" He knelt on the bed, sitting back on his heels. His voice had gone wonky in her ears as her heart pumped furiously.

"I've been lying to you. To all of you." Her conscience tried to soothe her frazzled nerves. Omission of the truth wasn't as bad as outright lying, was it?

"I figured." He moved toward her, but she held up a hand and he stopped. "Why don't you tell me?"

"What if you hate me?"

"I won't." He said it with such certainty that she almost believed him. Almost.

She drew in a shaky breath and whispered, "I hate myself sometimes."

"It can't be that terrible, Willa. What'd you do, kill someone?" The slight tease in his voice didn't make headway through the ominous distance that separated them.

"Yes." The word croaked out. She grabbed a pillow and used it to cover herself. A weak sort of protection when the damage done wouldn't be physical.

"Self-defense? Was your ex hurting you?"

Now the literal moment of truth was upon her, she found the story ready to burst from her like an infected wound needing cauterizing.

"Not my ex, my best friend. She died of a drug overdose."

"Did you make her swallow pills or force her to shoot up?"

"Of course not." She buried her face in the pillow and didn't worry about whether he could make out the words. Her confession was as much for herself as him. "But I introduced her to my boyfriend. Derrick sold pot around our high school. He was funny and charming and made me feel . . . important."

The high school social hierarchy seemed so unimportant now. If-onlys went on repeating as usual.

"What happened to your friend?"

"Her name was Cynthia." Her best friend had snorted when she laughed and bit her fingernails to the quick. She'd loved pineapple on her pizza and listened to old-school R.E.M. She wasn't a nameless, faceless, forgotten statistic. "She loved Derrick's parties. Neither one of us had ever been popular in school. It seemed harmless, mostly pot and alcohol."

Willa had felt so grown-up with a beer in one hand and a joint in the other. She'd even considered dropping out, but Cynthia wouldn't hear of it. She had loved school. Her dream had been to go to college and teach elementary school. So Willa had stuck it out, but after graduation, she'd drifted, lost and rudderless, while Cynthia had started classes at the community college.

"After high school, we didn't hang out as often. Maybe I was a little jealous that she seemed to know what she wanted out of life. I don't know." Her feelings back then were like a faded black-and-white picture. "But she never missed one of Derrick's parties, and he and I stayed together for a while. Until I found a stash of heroin in his trunk."

She'd been shocked and terrified, of course. Confronting him had only confused her. He'd told her it was a one-time deal. God, she'd been so naïve.

The bed shifted as she continued to excise the story bit by bit. "Cynthia wanted one hit, she said. Just to say she'd done it. I tried to stop her, but not hard enough. Derrick said it would be fine, even tried to talk me into taking some, but I was scared."

"Did she OD?"

"No. When she came down, she said it wasn't even that good, and I was relieved. After that, Derrick changed, or maybe he stopped pretending with me. He could be mean."

"Did he hurt you?" Anger roughed his voice even more than usual.

Derrick had shattered her in ways she was still understanding, but that's not what Jackson was asking. "He broke up with me. Said I was too immature and needy. It was hard, and I pretty much shut myself off from everyone including my dad and Cynthia. At the time, I thought it was the worst thing that could ever happen to me."

"But it got worse."

"Way worse." She made a sound halfway between a laugh and a sob. "Cynthia still went to Derrick's parties. I was so mad and hurt. I thought they had started dating so I ignored her calls and texts. Turns out she had tried heroin again. And again. She needed my help and I . . . I ignored her. Once I realized, I went looking for her and found her in his basement, high. Her arm was lined with at least a dozen needle tracks. I didn't know what to do or who could help me."

"Why didn't you go to your dad?" He sounded closer, but she didn't take her face out of the pillow.

"He'd remarried by then, and I was being a total bitch to his new wife. Dad and I were barely talking at that point. I was afraid I would get Cynthia in trouble or get in trouble myself."

"You were still his daughter, no matter what had happened."

His words resonated as only the truth from hindsight could. "Cynthia refused to go to a clinic. Said that she could quit whenever she wanted. That it was all for fun. I should have dragged her to the hospital."

Tears crawled up her throat. His hand brushed her arm, but she jerked away, her skin as raw and sensitive as her feelings. "I found her the next night at Derrick's. As soon as I saw her I knew but I tried to revive her. I screamed for help. Prayed. Didn't matter. She was dead."

"Is that why you ran?"

She shook her head. "I got mad. At myself. At Derrick. His parties were nothing more than a means of getting kids hooked and then feeding their addictions. It should have been me, not Cynthia. And if I didn't do something, it would be another girl, another party. I took his stash so he couldn't sell to anyone else. I buried everything in the middle of nowhere." A sob escaped with a trickle of tears. That last image of her best friend was branded on her brain.

"I didn't realize at the time how the supply chain worked and how low Derrick was on it. Some very pissed-off big-time dealers expected their money. Plus he had the police all over him about Cynthia. He threatened to kill me and my dad if I didn't give him the drugs or give him money.

"Dad scared him off, but I knew he'd be back to make good on his threat. Either him or the police. My fingerprints were all over Derrick's apartment. I promised Dad I'd tell him everything in the morning. I left that night, and I've been running ever since."

"What happened to Derrick?"

"He ran too, but the police got him and found more drugs in his car. But there are men that still want their money. I thought I could keep my dad safe if he didn't know where I was. So far it's worked."

"The man who showed up to collect Ford's debt . . . You thought he'd come for you, didn't you?"

She nodded. "Derrick or one of his suppliers will eventually find me."

"You're going to keep running? Until when?"

She hadn't wanted to run in the first place and didn't want to keep running. Especially now. Another sob broke free and another, a wave of grief over past and present.

"Do you hate me?" The words emerged on gasps.

A harsh muttered curse registered a second before his arms came around her. "Of course not. Jesus, you were in a terrible situation."

She didn't drop the pillow but allowed herself the weakness of leaning into his chest a few inches. Regret and guilt dogged her for many reasons, but one had become a recurring nightmare. "I left her, Jackson. Left her lying there, vulnerable and exposed."

"You were in shock." His chest rumbled the matter-of-fact response.

It sounded like a copout. "I should have stayed with her until the police got there."

"Do you remember the day Pop died?"

The sudden veering of topic threw her. She'd been a horrified bystander to their father's collapse. "Of course."

"He died at 2:05 P.M., and I was on the track racing that night. Does that sound normal or rational?"

For a run-of-the-mill man, perhaps not, but he was anything but. "Racing is how you cope with . . . well, everything. Grief, stress, uncertainty."

He stilled against her, not even his chest rising for a breath. "I should have been with my brothers."

She loosened her death clutch on the pillow and turned

fully into his body, her hand landing on his shoulder. "They understood."

"Maybe." He cleared his throat, but his voice was still roughened with emotion. "My point is that I can picture every detail of Pop's death, but afterward, everything is fuzzy. I wasn't making good decisions. It's a wonder I didn't get myself killed."

Was he right? Had she been in shock? The hours and days after she'd found Cynthia were fuzzy. Her headlong drive into the woods to get rid of the drugs. The wait for either Derrick or the police to show up at her house. The shock of Cynthia's death weaving through the town and the inevitable questions from her dad and Cynthia's grief-stricken parents. Willa had borne it all without shedding a tear, ready to accept her fate. It was the threat against her dad that had prompted her into action.

Jackson's absolution didn't magically wash away her guilt, but the burden felt lighter now it was shared. She wasn't aware of time passing, but eventually, he worked the pillow from between them, maneuvered them down, and pulled the covers over them.

The cold nights of fitful sleep in the trailer plus the cathartic summoning of her demons had exhausted her. Wrapped in his arms, feeling truly safe for the first time in years, sleep claimed her fast and hard. Her last thought wasn't narrowed to the sins of the past, but a new hope for the future.

Chapter Twelve

Jackson woke long before the sun rose. Moonlight shaded the darkness. With her face smoothed in sleep, the toll worry and exhaustion had taken the past few weeks was evident. He hated to think he'd been the cause of any of it.

The revelations from the night before rolled around in his head. It was easy to picture a younger, less worldly version of Willa caught up in something beyond her control. He ached for her losses, both real, like Cynthia and her innocence, and self-imposed, like her father.

Whether or not she wanted to admit it, her tendency was to believe the best of people. Life's experiences may have dented her natural optimism, but why else had she stuck around Cottonbloom for so long?

His arms tightened at the stab of worry. She would need to confront her past and make peace with it before any sort of future was possible. He wanted to help her. Protect her. He would move mountains for her if he could. But he had a feeling her past was a mountain she would have to summit alone.

With his thoughts and emotions in turmoil, his body was distracted by something more primal. Covered by a thin white cotton bra, her full breasts were pressed against his bare chest. Her pants rode below her belly button. The curves of her waist and hips should have danger signs posted.

The natural morning inclination of his body was stoked by the sight of her in his bed and the feel of her body close. Their brief exploration had only whetted his appetite for more. For everything.

But the night before had revealed fault lines in her defenses, and he didn't want to take advantage. After all, he wasn't after a one-night stand. Or one-morning stand as the case may be.

Sunlight crept across the room, lighting the corners and dissipating the mystery and intimacy of the night. Her eyes fluttered open and she blinked a few times.

"Good morning." He kept his voice low so as not to spook her.

A blush suffused the exposed curves of her breasts and crept into her cheeks. She touched her hair and tucked a piece behind her ear.

"I should go," she whispered.

"You don't have to."

"Do you want me to stay?"

He was used to bold, brash Willa in the garage. The woman in his bed radiated uncertainty. He ran a hand up her arm, and she shivered. His gaze dropped to see her nipples peak against the thin cotton. He wanted to answer in the basest way possible and take the point in his mouth.

He took a breath to control the urge. "I want you to stay. I might have to handle a thing or two in the garage, but you can hang out and stay warm. Watch TV or read. Relax."

He trailed his fingers down the valley of her spine to the hollow of her lower back, pressing lightly. Like a choreographed dance, she arched her back and twisted her hips closer. Her slight intake of air signaled her awareness of his erection.

"Are you sure?" Her voice was breathless. Their gazes met and held, raw need on display in hers. The combination of bold and unsure was sexy as hell.

"No reason for you to freeze in your trailer. I've got plenty of room."

Except there was hardly any room between them now. He smoothed his hand over her bottom and squeezed. Her moan crumbled his good intentions.

A dog's bark and the scratch of nails on his door fractured the moment. Like she'd been given a shot of adrenaline straight to her heart, she scrambled away, grabbed her shirt off the floor and held it over her breasts. "River needs . . . I should . . ."

She disappeared and the door opened a second later followed by the patter of dog feet racing down the stairs. After she'd been gone for several minutes, it became clear she was using River as an excuse. He flopped onto his back and did his best to ignore his throbbing dick.

Hell, maybe it was for the best. The garage was officially closed until after Christmas, but afterward, they would still need to function as coworkers. How would having sex change their dynamic under a hood?

He dragged himself up and went to the window. The sun was already melting away any snow within its reach. River bounded through the scant patches under trees, but Willa wasn't in sight. Finally, he gave up and headed for a cool shower. By the time he emerged, Willa and River were back. She had put out dog food, poured herself a bowl of cereal, and was talking to the dog.

"What'd you think of the snow?" A pause. "It's going to melt soon, so you'd better enjoy it."

"You always talk to her?" he asked.

She swiveled around to face him. "It's slightly less weird to be talking to a dog than myself, right?"

The joke landed too close to his heart for comfort. She had suffered through her loneliness out of a mistaken sense of penance. A return smile was beyond him. "I need to talk to Mack and Wyatt about Ford. Make yourself at home."

Without a car at her disposal, she was effectively trapped, which made him feel comfortable enough to leave her alone. The pocket of cold air at the top of the stairs was jolting even though the back doors of the barn were closed, leaving the interior dim.

He clomped down the steps, the cold still seeping through the sweatshirt he'd pulled on after his shower. Mack's deep voice and Wyatt's answering laughter drifted to him before his eyes had adjusted.

He followed the sound as if it were a beacon, his brothers coming into focus sharing the beat-up couch in the back.

"A family meeting and I wasn't invited?" Jackson asked.

His brothers' heads turned in synchronicity to greet him.

"Merry Christmas," Wyatt said in a chirpy voice.

"River trotted over and dropped a deuce in my front yard, so I assumed you were busy—or getting busy—this morning." Mack's smile held an uncharacteristic tease. He'd shouldered more of the burden of the garage than any of them and it showed in the strain around his eyes and scarcity of smiles.

Which was one big reason Jackson's knee-jerk refusal to contact their mother in order to find Ford was weighing heavily on him. But it was Willa's story playing itself out over and over in his dreams that had highlighted his self-ishness.

Ford was their brother and he was in trouble. One of

them needed to extend a helping hand. If Ford chose not to take it, then at least his conscience would be appeased.

"You're hiding Willa upstairs?" Wyatt's feigned shock was ruined by the twinkle in his eye.

"Her trailer has a kerosene heater. She would have frozen last night." Jackson grabbed a Coke from the fridge. "And nothing happened." That was almost the truth.

"Well now, that's disappointing," Wyatt said with an eyebrow waggle.

Mack shoved Wyatt's shoulder. "Are you going to tell him your news or what?"

Jackson's gaze shot to Wyatt's, and in a flash of intuition Jackson said, "You're going to make an honest woman out of Sutton Mize, aren't you?"

Mack muttered a curse. "How do you two do that?"

"Guess it's the nine months we spent squished up together." Wyatt grinned. "I asked her to marry me yesterday, and shockingly, she said yes."

"She does know that she can do a sight better than you, right?" Jackson's tease was all bluster. Truth was, Sutton was lucky to have Wyatt's love and devotion.

"Don't tell her until it's official." Wyatt stood up and hugged Jackson.

Jackson dropped his forehead to Wyatt's shoulder for a moment before pulling back. "How was the 'Cuda?"

"Amazing. Perfect. I can't thank you enough for helping Sutton. For being so good to us."

Jackson tapped him once more on the back with his fist and stepped away. "Always, bro."

"You know what this means, right?" Wyatt snapped his fingers. "The curse is broken."

"Careful. You still have to make it legal," Jackson said.

"But when I do, you'll be next." Wyatt's lighthearted prediction didn't feel so light in Jackson's chest.

The three of them chatted a few minutes about the engagement and the reaction of her father, who was a well-off and well-connected judge in Cottonbloom, Mississippi.

"You'll be the most useful relative that's married into that family. Everyone needs a good car mechanic." Mack stood up and clapped Wyatt on the shoulder. "I'm cold and need some coffee. Aunt Hazel is bringing the Crown Vic by in about an hour. I'll take care of it since you have a visitor."

"Let me handle it. I need to talk to Aunt Hazel anyway," Jackson said.

"In that case, unless another emergency comes in, I'll be at the house binge-watching all the *Die Hard* movies."

Jackson held up a hand. "One more thing. I'll do what I can to find Ford, including calling our mother."

A few beats of surprised silence ticked off.

"Why the change of heart?" Mack asked.

"Something Willa told me last night got me thinking. As much as Ford gets under our skin, he's our brother and in trouble."

Wyatt pulled at his chin hair, a smile playing at his lips. "Weren't you the one that suggested stripping him naked and dumping him out in the swamps when he threatened to sell his stake?"

"Yeah, well, not saying he doesn't deserve a hundred mosquito bites where the sun don't shine, but he's got to be scared and panicked about some bookie shaking him down for that much money."

Mack's expression turned darker and inward. Mack's relationship with Ford had been poisonous since Jackson could remember. Less than eighteen months separated them, and a competitive fire burned in them both, stoked unintentionally by their pop. It made for a messy dynamic.

"Let me know what you find out." Mack walked away, his shoulders more tensed than they had been. Jackson muttered a curse. His goal of lightening Mack's worries had backfired.

"You need to talk about anything else?" Wyatt pointed at the ceiling.

"If you mean Willa, then no."

"Are things progressing?"

Jackson considered telling Wyatt to mind his own business. Wyatt would take his brush-off in stride, but the truth was Jackson felt unusually adrift and fearful of the changes looming both personally and for the garage.

"She finally told me more about how she ended up here and what she's running from."

Wyatt gave a low whistle. "Is it bad?"

"Yes and no. She's not a criminal, but it's a sad story." It's all Jackson could say without betraying her trust.

"Are you going to help her?"

Jackson grimaced. "If she'll let me."

"She's a mite independent." They exchanged dry smiles at the understatement.

"She had to learn real quick what it took to survive." At twenty, without a degree and growing up relatively sheltered, Willa must have been terrified setting off on her own. It was a miracle she'd come through the past five years with her humor and heart intact.

"She trusts you now. Just don't screw up."

Jackson rolled a side-eye toward Wyatt. "No shit."

"Go ask Dear Abby if you don't like my advice. You'd better go open up the garage for Aunt Hazel." Wyatt bumped his shoulder and shuffled backward, heading for the door. "If you don't need help, I'm going to head over the river. Don't forget, Sutton's counting on you to come to her New Year's party."

"You know parties aren't my thing." He had zero desire to rub shoulders with the upper crust of Mississippi.

"If you really feel that way, I'll send your regrets."

Wyatt's smile signaled a kind of trouble that had baited Jackson into doing something stupid more times than he could count. "A shame though. I guess you'll miss Willa's big reveal."

"Wait, what?" Jackson halved the distance between them. Close enough to see the puckish twinkle in his twin brother's slate eyes.

"Sutton's designing a dress for Willa to wear. Something super-sexy. She said Willa has a banging body and deserves a nice dress after wearing coveralls all day, every day. But you're probably not interested in seeing Willa out of coveralls, are you? Or maybe you already have?"

Dammit, Wyatt was too good at navigating the rivers of emotion Jackson did his best to avoid. He narrowed his eyes, pointed a finger, and backed away. "I'll be there."

Wyatt's laughter trailed after him and reverberated in Jackson's head long after he'd left. Wyatt's happiness was borderline nauseating, no matter how much Jackson liked Sutton.

Aunt Hazel turned into the parking lot, only the top half of her head visible over the steering wheel, just as he'd cleared out a bay. Every so often, he tried to talk his aunts into buying something smaller and with better gas mileage, but so far, neither had been willing to part with the Crown Victoria.

Even though Hazel was smaller and could barely see over the wheel, she was by far the more responsible driver. His aunt Hyacinth had gotten several speeding tickets over the years and considered them a point of pride. If car racing had been an acceptable pastime for women in Hyacinth's youth, Jackson had no doubt that she would have smoked all comers.

Jackson motioned Hazel forward, and she edged into the bay in a series of starts and stops. He offered a hand out of the car. She looked up at him, a question in her eyes.

The opening was there for him to ask about his mother, yet he bypassed it, knowing blasting through that door would leave painful marks.

"What seems to be the problem this time?" It was difficult to keep his sarcasm at bay when it came to the Crown Vic's frequent trips into the garage. At some point there really would be something wrong, and they were likely to overlook it.

"A funny noise at idle."

Jackson slipped around her to start the engine. Instead of retreating to the waiting room for coffee, Hazel followed him to the front where he found the latch and propped the hood up. Engine noise filled the space, yet an uncomfortable vibe had Jackson glancing over at his aunt.

"I'll replace your air filter and see if that fixes things."

She wasn't looking into the engine compartment but at him. The questions he needed to ask her built like a pressure cooker until they were all he could focus on. He turned the ignition off and half sat on the front seat of the car. She followed him and waited, her eyes almost level with his.

"Wyatt said you know how to get in contact with our mother." He put it out as a statement, but needed confirmation.

"I do."

"Do you talk every Sunday or something?" Resentment seeped through his usually rock-solid defenses like river mud through a sieve.

"Nothing like that." She shifted on her low-heeled sensible black shoes, the lines around her eyes deepening. "She contacted me about ten years ago."

"Ten years?" An agitated energy popped him up and got him pacing beside the car.

He would have been graduating high school. The day he'd donned the cap and gown and walked the stage in front of his best friend-slash-brother, he'd scanned the crowd and wondered if she would show up. Every birthday and seminal event in his life, he'd done the same. It was an instinct or compulsion he'd never admitted to and couldn't seem to stop.

Hazel didn't answer him.

He stopped and faced her, feeling for a moment as if they were enemies instead of allies. "What did you tell her about us? What did she want?"

"She wanted to see you."

"Then why didn't she?"

"Your father, of course. Hobart was a good daddy to you boys, but the man was stubborn as all get out and held on to too much hate where your mama was concerned."

That much was true. He'd gotten rid of any evidence their mother had existed—minus them, of course. Not a single picture remained to stoke even vague memories of her. "What's she after? A cut of the garage? I'm surprised she didn't roll up the day after Pop died with her hands out."

"Have you never made a mistake, Jackson Elkanah Abbott?" Hazel shook her head, the use of his full name a sure sign of her disappointment. And, like when he was six and a Hot Wheels car had found its way into his pocket at the store, he felt it keenly.

Easier to avoid her grenade of a question. "She abandoned us by choice."

"All right then, have you never done something you regretted?"

He glanced toward the barn as if he had X-ray vision and could see Willa. What was she doing? Wrestling with her own regrets?

"Regrets have a way of growing deeper roots every year," Hazel said gently, as if sensing his softening.

"When's the last time you talked with her?"

"Late this summer. I had hoped Wyatt would reach out to her, but he's too wrapped up in Sutton."

He would let Wyatt share the happy news with their aunts. "Does Ford know where she is?"

"I don't know. Why?"

"We're wondering if maybe he's with her."

Hazel made a throaty sound of surprise. "It's possible, I suppose." She opened her pocketbook and removed a folded piece of stationery. When he reached out, she pulled it away. "Are you only contacting her because of Ford?"

With his aunt staring at him with the same eyes that stared back at him from the mirror, he could only be truthful. "Yes."

She gave a sharp nod. "Promise me you'll hear her out and give her a chance."

A chance to what? Reenter their lives and play a happy family after being gone for twenty-plus years? His resentment ebbed as quickly as it flared. Before Willa, he would have never given his mother a second chance. His black-and-white world view had been blurred to gray by Willa.

"I promise," he said gruffly.

She extended the paper, and he took it. With fingers that felt too clumsy to even tighten a bolt, he unfolded the sheet. Belinda. Oak Grove, Louisiana. She hadn't gone far. Oak Grove sat a few hours away, close to the Arkansas border.

Did he have a passel of half brothers or sisters running around? "Did she remarry? Have more kids?"

"Nope. She pined for you boys and Hobart too."

He wasn't sure how to reply, and Hazel's knowing, too-wise eyes weren't helping. He turned to the nearest supply bin. "Let me get a new air filter."

When in doubt, he always changed the filter. The air circulation in the Crown Vic was the cleanest in Cotton-bloom Parish. It took him a scant ten minutes to button everything up and drop the hood. He followed his aunt to the driver's side.

She fired the car up and rolled down her window. "When are you going to call?"

"Soon." After he had a chance to mull over every implication and write his playbook.

"I'll see you at church and for Christmas Day lunch, won't I?"

"Of course." He bussed her cheek, and she rolled up her window, seemingly satisfied.

He waved her out of the garage, locked everything back up, and took the stairs to the loft two at a time, anxious to verify Willa hadn't magically disappeared.

He slowed at the top and eased the door open. She was lying on the couch, her eyes closed and a book tented over her chest. River lifted her head from where she was curled at her feet, but otherwise seemed as loath to disturb Willa as he was.

He sat in the armchair close to her head and watched her sleep. Did she feel safe with him? He hoped so. Even more, he hoped she considered him as more than a protector or friend, although he wanted to be both those things for her too.

But if she woke up to find him staring at her like this, she might decide he was a creepy weirdo. He picked up the top book of the stack she'd brought from the trailer. The fact her most precious possessions included borrowed library books said a lot.

He turned to the first page. It was set in the Wild West. He read a page and then another and another, going slow and running his finger along each line until he was caught up in another time and place.

"Do you like it?"

His gaze shot off the page to meet hers. Her eyes were soft and sleepy and sexy in a way that made him want to take her back to bed. He nodded, unable to knit together letters to form coherent words.

She spun her legs to the floor and stretched her arms above her head. The thin cotton T-shirt emphasized the curves of her body. He swallowed and forced his gaze off her breasts and back to the pages of the book, but the black-and-white text ceased making sense.

"I should go." Her voice lilted on the edge of a statement and question.

"No, you shouldn't." His voice emerged too harsh, and he forced a coaxing tone. "It's not snowing anymore, but it's still bitter cold out. You'd be miserable in your trailer."

"I've survived worse." The rawness of the admission had him closing his hands into fists to keep from grabbing her.

"I know," he whispered. "But this isn't about surviving, okay?"

"It's Christmas Eve."

"So?"

"Aren't you going to spend it with your brothers?"

Christmas Eve had never been a huge holiday for the Abbotts even before his pop had died. It had been up to the boys to get down the artificial tree and decorate it. Eventually, they had outgrown the magic and had stopped celebrating it at all. Except, Hazel and Hyacinth made sure they went to church Christmas morning, followed by a big supper and a present apiece.

Jackson assumed that tonight Wyatt would be with Sutton, and Mack would be asleep before eight. "We'll go over to the aunts' house for Christmas Day supper, but I've got nothing going on tonight. Stay."

When she didn't answer right away or even look at him, he took her hand in his. She turned her hand and skimmed her fingers over his wrist. His heart thumped faster and harder against his ribs. He massaged his thumb down the middle of her palm. His body was asking a question he couldn't verbalize.

He could back away now and pretend the sexual currents sizzling between them didn't exist. Time and inattention would squash whatever struggled to break ground between them. He could go back to his tidy half-life. Or could he?

If she stayed the night, they would be burning bridges and altering their relationship forever. Change was bearing down on him like the sharp corner in a race he was sure to lose yet was determined to see to the finish line.

His hand tightened around hers and the words welled up from his chest. "Please stay."

Chapter Thirteen

Willa was taken aback at the almost begging tone of his voice. He wasn't being polite. Need and want and desire were naked in his eyes. Her lips formed her answer before her brain could process the implications. "Okay, I'll stay."

In the split second after the words left her mouth, her brain caught up. She understood exactly what her answer meant. She was terrified, but the past few weeks had unlocked a part of her that craved his touch and attention and wanted him no matter the consequences.

It reminded her too much of her teenage self, but she wasn't that naïve, stupid girl anymore. Could she have Jackson and protect herself at the same time? As impossible a task as it seemed, she would try.

The first step in self-protection was to break contact before he read the depth of her desire in her eyes. She disentangled their hands and stepped to the window.

She glanced over her shoulder. He sat and watched her like a hunter waiting for his prey to exhibit a sign of weakness. With the silent declarations hanging between them, a constant thrum of arousal vibrated the air.

"Want to watch a movie?" His smile was so slight his

dimples remained hidden, but it was enough to settle her nerves.

"Sure." She forced a casual stroll back toward the couch and plucked the remote from the coffee table. "But I get to pick."

His groan was good-natured and eased the intensity of the mood. She flipped on the TV and found a funny holiday movie she remembered as a kid. The promise of what was to come simmered underneath their laughter, but a budding excitement overtook her earlier trepidation.

This was Jackson. The man she'd worked side by side with for two years. She'd confessed the worst about herself the night before and yet he was here and still wanted her. He was honest to a fault, honorable, and sexy as hell with his perfect stubble and dimples and jacked biceps. The sexual energy heated up a notch.

"You're not watching the movie." His face remained in profile.

She cleared her throat and tried to focus on the grown man in an elf costume on the big screen, but her gaze kept finding its way back to him.

"Have I grown an extra head?" This time a dimple creased his cheek with his smile.

"Yep. You sure have." She smiled back even though he wasn't looking.

She swallowed, gathered her courage, and ran her fingers over his lips. His bottom lip was fuller than his top, but both were masculine to the extreme. A little hard, a little unforgiving, but they'd been unbearably gentle on hers the night before.

Her bones turned to taffy, and her breathing bottomed out, her lungs working faster but pulling in less and less oxygen. His gaze roved her face and he raised a hand. She flinched slightly, and his eyes narrowed, but he didn't speak. He cupped her jaw, his thumb stroking across her cheekbone while his strong fingers massaged the back of her neck.

Had she ever felt anything so amazing? She hadn't until his mouth dropped to hers, and he worked his magic. This time, though, she wasn't planning on running—unless the destination was his bed. He set the pace of the kiss. Slow and devastating to all the defenses she'd spent years perfecting. A languid sensuality filled the space that caution had vacated.

He pulled back and the loss of his lips had her prying her eyes open. He looked at her like she was special and precious and her heart felt like a fragile ornament he could easily break.

"How blind was I?" he asked.

"What do you mean?" Her tingly lips formed words with difficulty.

"To have you by my side all this time and not notice how beautiful you are."

"I'm not."

His smile held a hint of sadness but she wasn't sure why. He tucked a piece of her butchered hair behind one of her ears. "It took you threatening to leave to open my eyes. Promise me you won't run away."

Guarantees and promises were useless. "I'm scared."

"Of me?" He speared his hands into her hair, his fingers working her scalp and sending waves of sensation through her body. He hadn't even touched her below her neck yet her body was impatient for more.

His eyes demanded the truth, and she swore she would give him as much truth as she was able. "Of how you make me feel and what we're getting ready to do. I haven't gotten close, you know, physically, with anyone since I ran away from home."

He blinked and tilted his head as if rolling the fact around in his brain. "Five years?"

"Five years and three months, but who's counting?" A strained laugh escaped.

He didn't show any signs of amusement. Dropping his face to nuzzle his nose next to hers, he whispered, "I won't hurt you, darlin'."

The endearment sparked a fire in her chest. She'd been called darlin' and sweetheart and sugar but never by a lover and never in a rough, honeyed voice. But she wasn't fooled. He might well break her heart.

"Will you make me feel good?"

"I'll make you feel better than good." With his declaration ringing in her ears, he stood and held out his hand, waiting for her to choose.

She chose him. No matter what happened tomorrow or down the road, she would never regret this moment and hoped he wouldn't either. Maybe she was undeserving, but luck didn't bend her way often, and she would grab hold of whatever good the universe offered.

She slipped her hand into his and stood. He smiled and scooped her into a cradle hold. Tucking her face into his neck, she laid kisses on his hot skin as his stubble scraped pleasurably against her lips.

He set her down on the bed. With her legs dangling over the side, she propped herself up on her elbows. What was next? Should she get naked so they could get down to business?

She hooked her thumbs in the waistband of her yoga pants, but froze when he grabbed the back of his T-shirt and pulled it over his head. Her head went swimmy, everything but his chest a blur.

He'd been shirtless the night before, but it had been dark and she'd been trapped in her nightmare. And the morning had been both super awkward and arousing. Enough light filtered through the windows to emphasize every ridge and plane of his hair-covered chest. He grabbed her knees, pulled them apart, and stepped in between, the muscles along his chest and arms popping.

"Dear Lord." The words registered in her ears as her own. "Are you doing that on purpose?"

"Doing what?"

Before she had a chance to answer, her T-shirt was gone. She was in the same cheap white bra as the night before, its shabbiness highlighted. Embarrassment flushed through her. Yet what could she do except own who she was and what she had? If he laughed or teased her, then so be it. Forcing her hands to her sides, she raised her chin and looked him in the eyes.

Except his gaze was lower, his smile appreciative. He traced over the edge of the bra with the rough pad of his finger. Her nipples were visible and peaked against the thin fabric. In a lightning-fast movement, he dropped to nip at the tip of one breast with his teeth. Her hands came to the back of his head without conscious direction, but once there she tightened her hold in his hair.

He moved to her other breast to give that nipple the same attention, and she arched closer. He slipped a hand behind her and fumbled with the clasp. It took three tries before the fabric loosened, and he brushed it aside to cup her breast.

His gentle, sure handling of her was something unexpected and unfamiliar. He rose over her, drew her bra off, and tugged her pants down her legs, leaving her panties in place. She was exposed physically and emotionally, without anything to hide behind.

He unbuckled his belt and made short work of his pants and underwear, not experiencing the same level of shyness she battled. A dark cloud of wariness joined her modesty.

"Wait a second." She scooted back on the bed and pointed. "You didn't warn me about Goliath."

He glanced down and grinned, his dimples creasing his

face. "I'm not one for naming body parts but I could get on board with that one." He crawled toward her, Goliath bobbing.

"You promised not to hurt me." She protested even as foolishness joined the disorienting stew of emotions battering her chest.

He dropped to her side, spread his hand over her rib cage, and pushed her flat, his fingers caressing the underside of her breasts. His erection was pressed against her hip, and her intimidation pivoted to curiosity and arousal muted her wariness. She squirmed and parted her legs a few inches.

He laid a soft kiss on her lips and moved his hand down until his fingertips slipped under the waistband of her panties. "Trust me?"

She did trust him to make her feel good and deepened the kiss, slipping her tongue to touch his in answer. He groaned, his hand drifting down. She tilted her pelvis as if she could shorten the distance. Wetness had dampened the cotton between her legs but any embarrassment was burned to ash by the feel of his hand inching closer.

Finally, after eons, he stroked a finger over her. She clutched at his shoulders, needing something solid and warm and real to cling to.

"Does this feel good, baby?" He rumbled in her ear as he tugged at her earlobe with his teeth and played between her legs.

Her eyeballs may have rolled back in her head. The noises she made had a begging quality but she was too far gone to care. She lifted her hips and tugged one side of her underwear down. He helped her get them off and returned to stroke every bare inch of her. She spread her legs even wider and pulled at his waist, wanting more of his weight over her.

"Not yet." His words were injected with enough gravel to make them almost incoherent.

"Please?"

What might have been a laugh vibrated his chest against her. "I'm a man of my word."

He was as honest and steadfast as she was deceptive and flighty. She might have vacillated over the disparity, but he slipped a finger inside of her, and her worries went up in smoke.

The burst of ecstasy was acute and traveled through her body from the top of her head to her toes in aftershocks of pleasure. She chanted his name and this time when she tugged, he moved over her, his hips between her legs, his erection gliding between her legs on the evidence of her climax.

He tilted his head toward the ceiling and muttered a curse. Shifting away from her, he reached for the nightstand. She wrapped her legs around his thighs to keep him from going far, but it didn't take long for him to return with a foil packet. A condom. Another rush of heat raced over her chest.

This was happening. Not that his finger inside of her hadn't felt very real, but in a few seconds, Goliath would be next.

"I'm surprised they make condoms to fit you." Her laugh petered into a hard swallow.

"Darlin', I'm not sure what you're used to, but I'm not *that* big." He rolled the condom on and positioned himself between her legs.

"Tell that to my vagina."

Another of his rumbly laughs sent vibrations straight to where he was rubbing the head of his erection. "Shall I make introductions?"

He pressed inside of her a few inches and she gasped,

but not from pain. It was closer to the euphoria of fitting the last piece in a thousand-piece puzzle into place. A space filled. A need assuaged.

"Are you okay?" His voice was strained unusually thin. He was still and waiting for her to answer.

If she said no, he would pull out. The certainty echoed in her heart, and tears sprang to her eyes. To cover the rash of vulnerability, she forced a half smile and whispered, "I think my vagina and Goliath are going to be great friends."

His chest convulsed with laughter. He tightened his hands on her hips and pushed all the way in. Buried deep, he didn't move, only raised his eyebrows. With words unnecessary, she nodded, and he took his first stroke. His rhythm increased until he was pounding into her steadily. He dropped closer, fit a hand under one of her buttocks, and tilted her to his pleasure.

And, hers too as it turned out. The new angle did something to her insides and drove her toward another climax. This one more like a wash of pleasure than the wrenching ecstasy of the first. He followed before she was even off the high, pulsing inside of her with a hoarse primal roar.

He collapsed over her, and she welcomed the solid bulk of his weight. As the physical satisfaction waned, her chaotic thoughts tumbled to the forefront.

Sex changed everything. For the worse in her woefully limited experience. She tightened her arms around his back, the skin taut over bunched muscles. She didn't want to let him go. Not yet. Could they find a way to work together without things being awkward? Maybe there was a path forward for her to forge a real future instead of living like a ghost.

Or she could leave Cottonbloom. Keep running. He didn't know her real name, and she was good at disappearing. A stab of guilt dimmed her afterglow.

He rolled off her with a deep sigh and disposed of the condom. Turning back to her, he gathered her in his arms, his body heat banishing any chill. They lay for a long time, neither of them talking, but it wasn't weird. Which was weird.

"That was way better than any dream I had about you." The admission popped out as if sex had broken her internal filter.

He propped his head up on his hand. "You've had sex dreams about me?"

She'd already named his penis Goliath. Dare she feed his ego even more? She peeked up at him, but it wasn't arrogance or a smug sense of ego that reflected in his smile, but wonder. She snaked her hand around his nape and fisted her hand in his hair.

"I never thought you'd—" She bit her lip.

"Make your dreams come true?" He came halfway over her and propped his elbows on either side of her head.

"Want me."

"Willa." He had a way of saying her name that settled a melancholy longing in her heart.

The physical complications she could handle, it was the emotional ones that would require time to pick apart and examine when she was alone and her body wasn't feverish for his. The hair on his chest made her already sensitive nipples harden and send ready-to-fire signals where his thigh pressed between her legs. Obviously, her body was looking to make up for lost time.

"Don't start something you can't finish, Jackson Elkanah Abbott."

"Elkanah, huh? That's like throwing down a gauntlet."

He was hard again, and she was eager. "Consider it thrown. In fact, make it a dozen gauntlets."

"Damn, woman, even Goliath can't handle a dozen in one night." He snagged another condom, but hesitated with it halfway on. "It's been a while. Are you sure you aren't too sore?"

"I might be tomorrow, but right now, I need you."

He entered her, and she tiptoed the line of pleasure-pain. She grabbed both his biceps and dug her fingernails into the hard muscle. The gesture was like applying spurs to a racehorse. He jerked forward and took short stabs, staying on his knees between her legs.

He pushed one of her legs up and out and skimmed his other hand between her thighs, driving her closer to another orgasm. Their joining was fast and dirty and a little rougher than the first, but just as amazing. She closed her eyes and surrendered.

The buzz in her ears drowned out any noise he made, but she could feel every inch of him inside of her. He fell over her and pushed himself even deeper with the whisper of a groan. She crossed her ankles around the back of his thighs to hold him inside of her.

He ran a hand up and down her thigh, the calluses along his palm sending shock waves along her skin. Everything the man did was sexy and arousing. She pictured him with a wrench in his hand and the flex of his biceps as he torqued a bolt. Her inner muscles clenched. Next time she saw him do that she might require resuscitation on the shop floor.

He unhooked her ankles from around him, got rid of the second condom, and tucked her under the covers. The heat and length of his body imprinted deeper than the physical. She had been his since almost the moment they'd met, but for this one moment at least, he was hers. While she was in his arms, the future didn't stretch out bleak and hopeless. Instead, a wavery picture of happiness and joy and laughter in the loft and garage emerged like a mirage.

But her past lingered like rotten garbage to ruin everything. If Derrick found her, he would fulfill his promise to destroy everything she cared about. She'd been the cause of enough pain already, and even imagining Jackson hurt sent her skittering toward panic.

Whatever luck came her way was temporary, and she embedded the memory of Jackson to draw upon when hard times inevitably circled back around to engulf her.

"How do you feel?" His breath was warm and tickled her ear.

"Amazing. You're amazing. I never thought it could be like this." Secrets and lies dominated her life, but she refused to temper her response in bed with him. In this at least, she could be honest.

His laughter vibrated his chest against her back. "You ain't seen nothing yet."

She started and turned around to see his face. His smile was genuine and open, his dimples cutting deep. His smile had always been endangered, but it had become nearly extinct since his father's death the year before.

Because she was finally able to, she ran a finger down his cheek and into the crease of his dimple. "What do you mean?"

"We've only hit the basics."

The basics was all she was acquainted with, but she'd read books—lots of books—and her heart leaped into a quickened rhythm at the possibilities scrolling through her head. How much time would they have together? Not enough. Never enough.

"What if I don't know what to do?" Her embarrassment didn't come close to dampening her curiosity and excitement.

"It's not hard."

Her gaze dipped to where he was pressed against her hip, and his rumble was part humorous and part sexual. His kiss was slow and languorous with a promise of pleasure that made her toes curl. He gathered her close, her face pressed into the warmth of his neck, the smell of him at once comforting in its familiarity and arousing in its newly discovered nuances.

"I got you something for Christmas," he whispered into her hair.

She smiled even though he couldn't see her. "Goliath?"

"That was your stocking stuffer." His laughter was like the slow crank of an old engine. "Hang on."

She sat up and adjusted the sheet under her arms. He came back and laid a folded quilt in her lap. She ran her fingers over the stitched-together triangles of red and blue and green plaids on a background of cream.

Was he a mind reader? A heart reader? How else could he have known she longed for one of the Quilting Bee's specialties? "I love it. It's beautiful." The wobble in her voice migrated to her chin. She would not cry, dangit.

He tilted her face toward his. "You can return it and pick one you like better."

"No. I want this one." She hugged the quilt close. "It's been a long time since anyone got me anything for Christmas. Thank you."

He laid a kiss on her lips, soft and simple. "You're welcome. I thought it could keep you warm if I wasn't there to do it."

She nuzzled his neck to hide the spring of tears. "I didn't get you anything. I'm sorry."

"You're in my bed. Finally. Best present I've ever gotten, hands down." He tucked a piece of hair behind her ear but it sprang back in an awkward in-between stage of growth.

Exactly the way she felt sometimes. Her leap from adolescence into adulthood had left her too experienced in some ways and entirely innocent in others. The last time she'd had to navigate a relationship of any sort, she'd been a teenager and the rules had been less complicated. Jackson was a man—more of a man than most, she would guess despite his teasing—with a man's experience and expectations.

"You've given me more than I ever imagined. More than I deserve." Tears made her sniff. She rolled away and lay on her back, blinking away evidence of her vulnerability.

"Because of your past?"

One tear conquered gravity and snaked out of the corner of her eye and into her hairline. "Of course."

"You shouldn't have to pay for what happened when you were nineteen or twenty the rest of your life."

"That's what murderers do though." The words came out waterlogged.

"You didn't kill your friend, Willa. You're a smart, logical person. Deep inside you know that's true." His thumb glanced over one of her tears.

"I'm not that smart."

"The stack of books on my coffee table would disagree."

Looking to change the subject before she was forced to lie, she asked, "Why don't you have a tree?"

"Wyatt usually puts one up, but he's basically living with Sutton now. Anyway, Christmas isn't my favorite holiday."

"Why not?"

His shoulder moved under her cheek. "Pop never had time for Christmas and it only reminded me we didn't have a mom around."

She had loved Christmas when it had been just her and her dad. Her stepmother had ruined the holiday for her. Not through her actions, but her mere presence.

"What is your favorite holiday, then?" she asked.

"New Year's Eve has a shot at the top spot this year." The flirty tease in his voice brought her head up. He was smiling again. Sex had fostered an ease between them that was a far cry from their professional interactions in the garage.

Sutton's offer scrolled through her head. Did Jackson know about it? "You'll be at Sutton's party?"

"Yep. You too?"

"She's insisted that I come."

"How about we go together?"

She'd learned to recognize and could parry a come-on like an expert swordsman. But this casual invitation sounded more like . . . "You mean, a date?"

"Is that what the kids are calling them these days?"

"What about your brothers?"

"What about them?"

"You're okay with them knowing about us?"

"Wyatt knew I wanted you even before I could admit it to myself." Sarcasm tinged his voice. "Are *you* okay with them knowing?"

"Of course." Her ready agreement was followed by a shadow of doubt, yet her quick answer made his body go lax. "It's going to be weird our first day back at work though, isn't it?"

"Let's worry about that later." His voice drifted into vagueness. He closed his eyes and yawned. "I'm going to close my eyes for a second. You tuckered me out."

He was asleep within minutes, his head tilting to the side, his chest lifting her head in steady intervals. Her body still buzzed like a live wire from her orgasms, sleep an impossibility. Gathering late-afternoon clouds cast long shadows across the bed. In sleep, his face was cast with an innocence she knew was false. He'd seen his share of heartache.

A whine from the other room made her gasp. Poor River was probably ready to burst. Willa slipped out of bed, threw on one of Jackson's sweatshirts, and pulled on her yoga pants. River pawed at the loft door and shot out as soon as Willa cracked it. Slipping on her shoes, Willa followed quickly to let her outside.

River made a beeline to the magnolia tree in front of Mack's house to take care of her business. Willa stamped her feet to keep the chill out. Afternoons like this in her trailer were miserable and boring with the promise of a long, sleepless, cold night stretching out. Books were her salvation during days like that.

She glanced back at the barn. She had her books, but tonight her salvation would be Jackson. She didn't have to be cold or alone and felt both undeserving and grateful.

Mack stepped out onto his porch, his features indistinct, but his bulk identified him. Willa whisper-called for River to come back, but the dog was closer to Mack than her and trotted over to him.

Mack squatted down and gave River an ear rub, her tail wagging at warp speed. Willa's hope at blending in with the side of the garage died at Mack's two-fingered wave. "Merry Christmas, Willa."

She fiddled with the hem of Jackson's sweatshirt and walked over, but not up the steps to his porch. While she respected Mack and trusted him to a point, she didn't want to answer questions about her and Jackson. Not until she had a chance to come up with something to say that didn't give her true feelings away.

"Merry Christmas to you too."

He rose and swayed enough that he had to grab hold of the porch railing. She took the first step, her hand out as if she could catch him if he collapsed. Before she could ask if he was okay, a smile lightened his usually somber expression.

Astonishment kept her on the bottom step. Mack Abbott was drunk, and by the glassy look of his eyes, he was drunker than Cooter Brown.

"Are you okay?" she asked tentatively.

"Let's see . . . second Christmas without Pop. Not only has Ford threatened to sell out, but he's gotten himself in a heap of trouble and if I wasn't so worried about his neck, I might wring it myself." He waved a finger in her direction. "Worried about you too."

"I'm fine." Defensiveness shot the words out.

"Yeah." He drew the word out. "I don't think so."

She stumbled off the step. "Come on, River, time to go in. It's cold."

The dog trotted down the steps, and Willa leaned over to spear her fingers in her fur.

"I like you, Willa, but I know you're hiding something. Don't you dare hurt my brother." A threat she'd only heard him use with Ford sharpened his voice. He would go to battle to protect the people and things he loved. Apparently, she didn't make the cut.

Instead of making a promise she might not be able to keep, she retreated, waffling at the bottom of the steps to the loft. Maybe she should borrow one of the garage's cars and head back to her trailer.

The door opened at the top, light spilling around a bare-chested Jackson. River threw herself up the stairs in a clumsy gallop. The welcome in his face was too much for her better judgment to fight, and she mounted the stairs in an equally graceless run, falling into him. He wrapped his arms tight around her and shifted them enough to close the door against the cold.

"What's wrong?"

"Nothing." Nothing he could help her with anyway. "But you should go check on Mack."

"Why?"

She hesitated, not sure whether Mack wanted anyone to see him drunk. She had a feeling he would regret their conversation, if he even remembered it. "He's drunk."

He muttered a curse and ran a hand through his hair

without letting her go. His worry was palpable and made her think he wasn't surprised Mack was drunk. "Are you good for a bit?"

"Take as long as you need. He's your brother."

He grabbed a T-shirt and disappeared out the door with a grimace in her direction. Once he was gone, the silence closed around her. She had learned to embrace silence, but this one was tinged with a bittersweet loneliness. How much harder would it be to face the countless nights alone now she knew what she was missing?

She crawled into the bed with her clothes on and huddled under her new quilt, not seeking warmth as much as stability. Without Jackson to anchor her to the here and now, her dreams meandered into the past.

Two hours later, Jackson eased back into the loft. The first thing he did was verify Willa's presence. The lump under the covers settled the lump that had risen in his throat. River hopped up from the corner of the couch she'd claimed and stayed on his heels into the kitchen. He gave her some water and kibble and grabbed some OJ for himself.

Mack had been more than drunk; he'd been obliterated. His ramblings had covered their pop's death, his worry over Ford and the garage, and even concern over Willa and her intentions regarding Jackson. He'd mostly listened, suppressing a sad rawness at times and a smile at others. Mack kept everything pent up, his grief, his worry, his anger.

Honestly, it had been good to hear Mack unpack his feelings, no matter how painful they were. Jackson had left him covered up on the couch with a glass of water and two painkillers on the table by his head.

A mewling cry came from his bedroom. He shoved the OJ back in the fridge and ran-walked to his bed. Willa thrashed as if something in her dreams were attacking her, childlike whimpers coming from her throat.

He pulled the quilt back and climbed in beside her, trying to calm her with nonsense words and shushes. Her hair was damp with sweat, and she tugged at the collar of his borrowed sweatshirt as if it were strangling her. He whipped the sweatshirt off, the beauty of her naked torso giving him pause, but he ignored the base desire and instead pulled her close and rubbed her back.

She calmed in his arms although her breathing remained fractured and gaspy.

"I don't want to." The words emerged on a pain-filled moan.

"You don't have to do anything you don't want to do." He wasn't sure if she was talking to him or someone in her dream. "I'll protect you, Willa, I promise."

After what felt like an eternity, the hand curling around his neck signaled her wakefulness.

"Jackson." His name fell from her lips like an endearment.

"I'm here and not going anywhere." If only he could extract the same assurance from her. He wasn't after a grand declaration or commitment, only the knowledge she would be around when the sun rose in the morning.

"I had a bad dream." Her arm tightened around him.

"Want to tell me about it?"

She hesitated before saying, "It was nothing. Nothing at all."

He wanted to believe her, but he didn't. A nightmare like that wasn't nothing. He'd battled enough of them when he was a kid to know. After two years working side by side and the mind-altering sex, she still didn't trust him and it hurt like an ache he couldn't ice away.

Her grief and guilt were living, breathing gremlins that hunted her even in her dreams. Her confessions the night before rang true but incomplete. What else was she not telling him?

"How was Mack?" she asked.

"In a rare talkative mood. He's snoring on the couch. I'll check on him in the morning. Speaking of tomorrow, the aunts host a Christmas Day dinner. Do you want to come?" Although Hazel and Hyacinth would no doubt be bursting with questions, they were too old-school polite to ask during the breaking of bread.

"Marigold invited me to her house ages ago."

"You could send your regrets and come with me."

"I'd like to be with you, but I'm not sure I've got the gumption to face your aunts after today. Anyway, I promised Marigold I'd help with her car."

"Tell her to bring it the shop. Easier to work on here."

He could feel her hesitation. "She can't afford it, Jackson. Dave's medical bills have been piling up. He can't work and their son is a year away from college. It's been a strain."

"I didn't realize . . . We could do it free of charge."

"She's got too much pride for that." She turned and scooched until her back fit to his front, her head pillowed on his arm. Like a contented cat, she sighed and went boneless against him. Darkness had fallen, and with her in his arms, he followed her into sleep.

Chapter Fourteen

Jackson sidled into the Cottonbloom, Louisiana, police station as if he were turning himself in after a crime spree. And in fact, guilt ate away at his stomach like battery acid. Not because he had robbed a bank, but because he was about to do something worse. Betray Willa's trust.

Yet was he really? Because he obviously hadn't earned her trust. Lies and omissions hovered and the longer she stayed silent the heavier and more devastating the potential fallout grew.

His mission was to put his mind at ease. He had her plates and Gloria would run them. Her car could be stolen. If that was the case, he would help her make things right and give her a new car. The problem was his imagination was going wild with possibilities, each one worse than the last.

Afraid she would pull away—or even worse, run away—if he outright asked, he was getting sneaky, and his conscience paid the price. He liked absolutes, but with Willa he found himself toying with murky justifications. The situation was as uncomfortable as it was unusual.

Willa was complicated and skittish and unforthcoming, yet her heart was good and strong and pure. He'd bet his stake in the garage on it. Which is why he was taking drastic measures to get at the truth. Not to confront her or accuse her, but to help her. She wouldn't see it that way though. She had spent too long with only herself to count on. How could he convince her that she could count on him too?

"Jackson Abbott, how are you doing, young man?" Gloria, a deputy, the unofficial office manager, and his former Sunday-school teacher, waggled her fingers at him from her desk before continuing to file her long fingernails.

"Slow day?"

"Same as usual which means, yep." She grinned. "Are you 'bout to liven things up?"

"I need a favor."

"You want me to arrest someone for you?" Humor glinted in her dark eyes, and she tossed her braids over her shoulder.

"Could you run a plate for me?" He held out the card he'd written the numbers and letters on.

"Is that all?" She made a phishing sound and took the card. "Is someone trying to sell you a hot car? I can pick them up and we can question them."

The last thing he needed was for Gloria to get on the scent and question Willa. She'd go to ground faster than a field mouse. "Nothing like that. I need to know who it's registered to. Nothing illegal." At least, he hoped not.

Gloria straightened and focused on her computer screen. The tap of her nails on the keyboard filled the silence.

Her gaze skimmed the screen and Jackson wished he could angle himself to see too. She hummed. "Registration expired years ago. Is someone currently driving with this tag?"

"No." The lie hurt and he was sure Gloria would see straight through him, but she didn't even look up.

"It was last registered to a Mrs. Wilhelmina Buchanan."

Wilhelmina? Could be short for Willa. But Mrs.? His head went swimmy, and he grabbed the edge of the desk. She was married.

Gloria's voice cut through the buzz in his ears. "Deceased."

"I'm sorry, what?"

"The car was last registered to a Mrs. Wilhelmina Buchanan. Deceased."

"Dead?"

"Let's see . . ." Gloria ran her finger over the screen. "She died four years ago, age ninety-two."

"What make and model was the car?"

"A Honda four-door sedan. Model year, '91." Gloria glanced over the top of the montior, her gaze narrowing. "You want to tell me what's so special about a dead woman's crappy Honda?"

"Not really, no."

"Jackson Elkanah Abbott." Gloria's tone was a spot-on mimic of his aunts'.

"You've been hanging around Hazel and Hyacinth too long."

"You're not in any sort of trouble, are you?" Gloria was one of the kindest people on either side of Cottonbloom, but she was still sworn to uphold the law. No matter what, he would protect Willa. Whatever her reasons for taking a dead woman's name and car, they would be good.

"I'm not in trouble. Promise." Jackson grabbed the piece of paper with the plate information on it before Gloria could tuck it away. Not that she couldn't jot it down from the computer, but having evidence in his handwriting seemed a dangerous paper trail. "Thanks for your help. Appreciate it."

He forced his mouth into a smile, but knew it must be anemic when she didn't return one. Before she could launch into more questions, he retreated to his Mustang.

The rumble didn't soothe him like it normally did, and he sat in the parking lot debating his next move.

Getting a library card these days required identification, and Marigold was as close to a friend as Willa had in Cottonbloom.

He headed across the river to the Cottonbloom library. Running his hands down his jeans, he stepped inside and shuffled to the side of the door. The smell—a combination of ink and paper and something intangible like knowledge—cast him back to his school days and set him on edge. He'd not been the best student and books still had the power to intimidate him. He'd been lucky to find his calling under the hood of a car at a young age.

His work boots squeaked on the wood floor and drew an annoyed stare from the white-haired lady behind the desk. At least, it felt like annoyance. He approached and cleared his throat. "I'm looking for Marigold. Is she working today?"

He waited for her to tell him he didn't belong, but she only flipped the open book over on the desk and smiled a smile that only reflected welcome and pointed. "She's shelving books upstairs in the paperback fiction room."

After thanking her, he soft-footed to the stairs. They creaked all the way up. He found Marigold in the second room he popped his head into. Her red hair stood out like a flame against the drab spines. She stood with a book in her hand and looked out the window at the gray skies.

No one else was in view. He cleared his throat and knocked on the doorjamb.

She turned, her slow, tight smile almost banishing the glimmer of tears in her eyes. "Why as I live and breathe, if it isn't Jackson Abbott. Are you lost?"

"Not lost. Looking for you, actually." He stepped farther into the room, the cart of books between them.

Confusion knitted her brow before she nodded with a soft, "Aha. You're here about Willa."

"Has she said anything about me?" He felt like a teenager for even asking. Cars he understood; people were much more difficult. Which was a big part of why he was there.

"She might have mentioned you a time or two." Marigold raised her eyebrows, tucked a book onto the shelf, and picked up another one.

"What did she say?"

"Lots." Marigold slotted two more books on the shelf.

When it was clear she wasn't planning to elaborate, he said, "I care about her."

"Good. She needs someone to care about her."

"I need information, though."

Marigold propped her hands on the handles of the cart and stared him down. "Why are you asking me? Go ask her."

"I've tried, but she's so secretive. I was hoping you might have documents from when she applied for her library card that would clear things up."

"You want me to share personal information?"

The way she said it settled a cloak of shame around his insides and made him a little sick. "I don't think Willa Brown is her real name."

A flash of anger crossed her face, earning her right to her red hair. "If she's keeping secrets, it's for good reason. Have you thought about that?"

"Of course I have." Voices outside the door had him dropping his to lower tones. "I want to help her face up to her past. I'd protect her."

Marigold's face softened. "Maybe she's trying to protect you, did you ever think about that?"

"Protect *me*?" He couldn't keep the incredulousness out of his voice.

Marigold rolled her eyes. "You don't need protecting because you're a big strong man? So was Dave, but cancer has cut him down like a sapling in a strong wind. I wager that girl has seen and dealt with more than you and me combined. Whatever else has happened, she's survived and held on to a sense of humor. Gives me hope."

Marigold was right. If Willa stole a car and took on a dead woman's name, then it was for good reason. If he were patient, once she truly believed she was safe, she would tell him. She was worth waiting for.

"How is Dave? Last time I dropped by he was too tired to visit," Jackson said.

"The days after chemo are the worst. That old saying about the cure being worse than the disease? Well, it's true. But his doctor says he's responding well, and God willing, he'll beat the cancer. He gets bored and would love a visit, I'm sure."

Jackson raised a hand to pat her on the shoulder, but ended up scratching his ear when she turned away to slot in another book. He wasn't good at giving or receiving sympathy. The weeks after his pop had died had been a torture of never-ending, well-meaning platitudes.

"If you ever need help with your cars, we'll fix you up. No charge."

"I appreciate the offer, Jackson." She didn't meet his eyes and he was grateful, not sure he could mask his pity.

When he had a foot out the door, she said, "Willa never applied for a card."

He half turned toward her. "How does she check out books then?"

"She would come on the weekends and spend all day reading at a table, put the book back on the shelf, and repeat until she'd finished it. We started talking, became friends, and I offered to check out books for her under my name."

"You've never asked her?"

"Nope. Even if I had, she wouldn't have told me. Just like she's not telling you. But I trust her to return the books every Saturday morning like clockwork." She returned her focus on the job, her back to him and softly humming. He was dismissed.

He trotted down the stairs, the creaks and squeaks not bothering him now. Picking apart what he'd learned, which wasn't much, he resolved to quit digging, but he would keep his eyes and ears open for any hint of her past, and whether she wanted it or not, he would do his best to help her move on, preferably with him.

Willa stepped under the car on the lift, scanning the work order Mack had left for her. She felt small under the two-thousand-odd pounds of car. It could crush her like the Wicked Witch of the West, leaving nothing but her work boots sticking out from under the bumper. Being put out of her misery sounded pretty good.

Jackson's and Wyatt's heads were close across the garage next to the break room and she couldn't help but wonder if they were discussing her. How much nitty-gritty detail did men share about their conquests? Considering they were twins, they might be discussing things as intimate as whether or not she snored. Did she? She honestly wasn't sure. Or maybe what she called out during sex? Some variation of *oh God* or *more, please* if she remembered correctly.

Anything they said was muffled by the grinder's peculiar music. Mack worked in the corner on a piece of metal, sparks flying from his hands like he was an alchemist. His specialty was molding and melding metal into new, perfect shapes.

As dawn was breaking Christmas morning, she and Jackson had had sex again. This time she'd been on her hands and knees. It had been incredible and animalistic and sexy as all get out. But after their respective showers, she had to face the awkwardness of a parting. He was on the hook to attend church and the weird vibe had sent her retreating to her trailer to prepare for dinner with Marigold.

She hadn't heard from him that night. And he'd arrived late this morning. In the fifteen minutes since he'd walked in, all she'd received was an indecipherable look. The anticipated awkwardness of their first day back to work registered at a hundred—on a scale of one to ten.

Her sixth sense registered his presence before any of her conventional senses. She spun around, her nose three inches from his chin. His invasion into her personal space made her want to surrender and lean into his strength. Instead, she took a step back, her heel landing on the handle of a tool. She teetered, and he caught her elbow, closing the distance between them once more.

"Are you okay?" His rumbly voice cut through the grinder's noise.

"Fine. I should know better than to leave tools on the floor." When she tried to bend down to pick up the socket wrench, he held her fast.

"I mean, us. Are you okay about us?"

"Is there an us?" She honestly didn't intend the question to sound like a snarky ultimatum. She was curious and more than a little desperate.

"I hope so. Did you get cold last night?"

Winter in Louisiana varied wildly, and their pre-Christmas snow flurries had given way to milder temperatures. "River kept me company. And I had my new quilt."

"I expected to find you at my place when I got home."

"Why? You didn't invite me over."

Still holding her arm in a gentle but implacable grip,

he ran his other hand through his hair. "I thought the invitation was a given."

"It wasn't, and I have a place to live."

"But it's . . ." He shook his head as if recalibrating his argument. "I'm inviting you now, okay? Will you stay with me tonight?"

Her heart quit flip-flopping in her chest like a dying fish and instead swooped like a bird in flight. The danger of loving him was thrilling and tingle inducing.

"What are we going to do?" Even before she finished the question, she wanted to stuff it back in her mouth.

His smile exposed his knowing and naughty dimples. She fanned herself with the work order. Spontaneous combustion was a distinct possibility. Except, instead of being embarrassed by her naïveté, she found herself smiling as a reel of possibilities unspooled like a porno.

"Strike that question. I have a vivid imagination," she said.

He skimmed his hand from her upper arm to her hand for a brief caress before stepping back and crossing his arms over his chest. The moment took on a clandestine feel. She glanced around and Wyatt's head swiveled away as if he had indeed been watching them.

"I guess your brothers know I spent the night."

"Hard to hide things when we all live and work on top of each other."

"Are they okay with us?" She assumed his invitation established the existence of an us.

"I didn't ask since it's none of their business. But if you're curious, Mack told me I better not eff things up since you're the best mechanic this side of the Mississippi. That's high praise coming from him, by the way."

High praise, indeed. Mack's standards were impossibly high. She switched gears, injecting some tease. "Did you oversleep this morning?"

"No. I had some business to take care of." He didn't even crack a smile.

A commotion at the door saved her from having to navigate the sudden uncomfortableness of the moment. Sutton Mize leaned over to give Wyatt a kiss but slapped his dirty hands away when he would have pulled her in for a hug too. Still laughing, she weaved her way around a toolbox and the car in the first bay and stopped in front of Willa and Jackson.

"It's time." Sutton propped her hands on her hips and called out. "Mack, I need to borrow Willa for a couple of hours."

He tipped up his mask. "Go for it. It's going to be a slow week."

Jackson slipped the work order from Willa's slack fingers. "I'll handle the Jeep. You go."

Willa wasn't sure she wanted to leave with Sutton. She honestly hadn't thought the other woman was going to follow through on her offer. Polite overtures were common; action was not.

Wyatt joined them. "Sutton's been looking forward to this all week. You don't want to disappoint her, now do you, Willa?"

With the announcement of Sutton and Wyatt's engagement, she was practically an Abbott, which held some weight. Willa adjusted her cap and smoothed a hand down her coveralls, feeling overwhelmed. "I guess not."

"Good." Sutton slipped an arm through hers and guided her toward the door with a stride that seemed impossible in her heels. "We have lots to do."

How long could it possibly take to try on a dress? A half hour tops including travel time. She'd be back before Jackson could even finish the Jeep's exhaust-system check and would make up the time by skipping her lunch break. Feeling better, she trailed Sutton to the parking lot.

"I'll drive," Sutton said, sliding behind the wheel and cranking the engine.

Sutton's car wasn't anything special, but it was a luxury vehicle compared to Willa's piece of crap on wheels. Still, she hesitated. Getting into Sutton's car meant giving up a getaway. A rope of anxiety tightened around her chest and left her feeling trapped.

Sutton rolled down the passenger window, leaning down to catch her eye with a genuine smile. "I'm not a crazy driver. Promise."

If Wyatt trusted her, then Willa could too. At least for a half hour. She opened the door and plopped down. The interior was still warm from the drive over. Willa unzipped her coveralls halfway, revealing a ratty black T-shirt at least two sizes too big and intended for a man, and promptly zipped it back up.

Sutton pulled around to a narrow alley at the back of Abigail's Boutique. Willa followed her through a heavy, serviceable door and into a utilitarian storage area. It reminded her a little of the shop floor and her trepidation receded. This would be over in no time.

The clack of Sutton's heels echoed off the expanse of concrete. She bypassed the office and pushed through a set of floor-to-ceiling swinging doors.

A couple of women browsed through racks at the front of the shop. Another woman wearing glasses and with her brown hair pulled back in a low ponytail sat behind the counter reading a book.

Sutton pointed. "My sister, Maggie. Maggie, this is Willa."

The woman's smile was friendly enough but distant. While Willa noted a superficial resemblance to Sutton in a shared build, Maggie's expression was more serious and reserved. She lacked the dazzle and welcome Sutton wore so naturally.

"Nice to meet you. Can't wait to see you in the dress Sutton designed." One of the shoppers waved from the front of the store, and Maggie set her book down. "I'll handle them while you two work some magic."

Sutton gestured her toward the nearest changing room. "Your dress awaits. Be careful because there are still pins in the hem."

Willa took one step toward the room and stopped. "Look, I can't pay you. Or not much anyway."

"Was I not clear? Consider this a gift. Or a favor, if you'd rather. Next time I have car trouble, I'll bring it to you instead of Aaron's Garage." Sutton winked, and Willa couldn't help but smile back. As if Wyatt would trust anyone else but him to work on her car.

Willa took a deep breath, steeling herself for what she'd find inside the changing room. The concoction of fabric on the hanger looked too delicate to wear. Instead of the expected blue, it was a mossy green. She might have gasped.

Sutton shut the door, but not before Willa caught a glimpse of her satisfied smile in the mirror. Willa ran her fingertips over the gauzy layers of skirt which looked like it would hit her above the knee. In contrast to the demure bottom, the top was strapless, the bodice stiff. It was gorgeous and no way would she be able to do it justice.

She pulled off her cap and ruffled her hair. Even when she didn't have hat-head, it was a mass of split ends and uneven edges. And what about shoes? Her choices were scuffed work boots or flip-flops.

She would try it on, thank Sutton for the time, and tell her to put it on sale in the boutique. Someone would buy it before the end of the day.

She laid her coveralls and T-shirt over the chair and stood there in her clean but worn-out underwear. Unclipping the dress from the hanger felt like a travesty. Something so beautiful wasn't meant for someone like her.

She unzipped the side, stepped into the dress, and wiggled it up. At first she thought it was too small, but the zipper closed easily, her curves on display. The top of her white bra edged over the green gauze of the bodice.

She stared at her reflection. Even barefoot and with her hair a mess, she looked like a different person. A woman. Maybe it was the culmination of excising her past to Jackson and the sex and the last two years of relative safety that enabled her to realize how much she'd changed. Why did it take a pretty dress and a floor-length mirror to reveal it?

The terrified girl who'd run away was now a woman strong enough to make a stand. What form that would take didn't come in a rush of particulars, but she would make a plan to face her past. Finally.

Something inside of her cracked open with the decision, and a tangled rush of emotions closed her throat to a pinhole and sent stinging tears to her eyes.

A soft knock sounded on the door. "Everything okay in there?" Sutton asked.

There was no escape from the tiny dressing room, or the boutique for that matter. She would have to suck it up and get through this before she could decide what road to navigate from here.

Without bothering to answer, she turned and opened the door.

Sutton gasped this time and clapped her fingertips together. "The green is magnificent. I'm glad I changed my mind." An uncharacteristically uncertain look passed over her face. "What do you think?"

Willa chuffed. "It's amazing and you know it. I've never felt . . . sexy before, you know?"

Sutton arched her eyebrows. "Not even when you spent the night with Jackson?"

An emergency flare went off in her chest and spread heat through her entire body. Splotches broke over her chest resembling a virulent rash. She sputtered something that wasn't exactly a denial.

"Don't be embarrassed. I have a feeling all those Abbott brothers are good with their hands. I know Wyatt sure is. Comes from working on cars, I'd guess." Sutton made a sound like she'd tasted something delicious.

The isolationist part of Willa wanted to stick her fingers in her ears and hum "The Star Spangled Banner," while the part of her that was starved for friendship and connections wanted someone to talk to. "You don't understand. Things are complicated. Not straightforward like they are between you and Wyatt."

Sutton's laughter pealed. "Straightforward? Remember how we got together?"

"You've got a point there." Willa turned to the bank of mirrors.

The bra was an unsightly slash of cheap cotton against the rich green. She shimmied out of it and dropped it at her feet. The neckline was low but the bodice was stiff and molded her breasts. The skirt flared over her hips. Even her legs looked longer.

"Jackson is going to lose it when he sees you. God, your body. I'm so freaking jealous. Once we get your hair done, you'll—"

"My hair?" Willa smoothed her hair back and caught Sutton's gaze in the mirror.

"You don't want a fairy godmother, but as your friend, I cannot possibly let you pair that hair with my dress." She paused before adding, "No offense."

"I can't let you—"

"Do you love your hair? If so, I'll back off."

She *had* loved her hair. And so had Derrick. Cutting it had been her sacrifice to appease her guilt. Plus, practically speaking, her long hair had been her most identifiable feature. Easier to go incognito without it.

"I don't like it. It's horrible." She fingered the uneven ends at her nape.

"Then we're in agreement. The appointment's been on the books since before Christmas." She glanced at a slim silver watch on her wrist. "In fact, we'd better hustle. Brenda gets in a snit when you're late. Let me repin the hem. It needs to be a tad shorter."

Sutton dropped to her knees and fiddled with the hem. Willa couldn't take her eyes off the new her in the mirror. Not new exactly, but newly discovered. She wanted Jackson to see her like this and not in a ball cap and coveralls, but owing Sutton didn't settle well. Debts had a way of being collected one way or another.

"Why don't you run a tab of expenses and I can pay you back over the next couple of months," Willa said.

Sutton looked up from her position on the floor and took a pin from between her lips. "If that's what you want."

"It's what I need."

"Fine." She stuck the pin into the cloth and shook her head.

Willa had probably set TNT under whatever bridge to friendship they were building. She opened her mouth to apologize, make an excuse, joke—anything to break the sudden tension—but Sutton rose and dusted off her knees, her gaze skimming Willa's body critically.

"I don't think I need to make any other alterations. You look gorgeous." She gave Willa a little push toward the dressing room. "You can leave your coveralls here. We'll walk over to Brenda's."

Willa removed the dress as if it were breakable and hung it back up. Seeing herself back in the ratty shirt and ripped-up jeans was a shock. She turned her back on the mirror. "Could you pass over my bra? I dropped it in front of the mirror."

"Sure. Hang on." Sutton's voice sounded like she was moving away and not toward her.

Just when Willa was ready to step out and retrieve the bra herself, a hand holding pristine white appeared over the top of the door. Sutton dropped a bra over, but not the one Willa had put on that morning. She lifted it up by the straps and examined the satin and lace as if making a scientific discovery.

"This isn't mine."

"Oops. I burned your bra. Consider yourself liberated." A tease lightened Sutton's voice. "Don't worry, I'll put it on your tab."

Unless she wanted to walk out braless, she didn't have much choice but to slip it on. She stepped out of the changing room with her hat on expecting a comment, but Sutton only smiled and said, "Let's go."

Maggie waved them off and ensconced herself behind the counter with her book once more.

Without her coveralls as protection against the cool wind, goose bumps stood up over her arms. Sutton kept up a brisk pace down the street away from the river.

"Brenda can be a little off-putting, but she's the best. She stays booked months in advance in spite of her personality," Sutton said.

They passed the pizza place and Regan Fournette's interior-design shop and the ice-cream parlor until they reached the end of the street where A Cut Above was tucked into the corner and marked by a simple dark-stained wooden placard. No neon sign or striped barber pole. The more discreet the sign, the more exclusive the establishment.

Sutton pushed the door open. The poof of air drew her inside with the scent of expensive hair products undercut by a slight chemical tang. The woman who greeted Sutton with two air kisses was heavily made up with hair too big for her petite frame. She wielded a vicious-looking pair of scissors like they were part of her hand. Willa guessed she was in her early fifties, but she could have been off a decade in either direction.

"Is this our project?" The lady reached for Willa's ball cap, but Willa pulled back.

Sutton looped their arms and leaned close. "I haven't failed you yet, have I? What's the worst that could happen?"

Willa widened her eyes and tilted her head slightly toward the woman that greeted them. Brenda looked like a splinter got lodged under her finger, her mouth pinched, the fine lines along her top lip hinting at a nicotine habit.

Sutton smiled, her suppressed laughter sneaking into her voice. "Brenda. This is Willa, and as we discussed, she needs a cut and color."

Brenda waved a pair of scissors around Willa's face. "Can I see what I'm dealing with, young lady?"

When Willa balked, Sutton pulled her hat off.

Brenda's exclamation was not at all ladylike. "Well, I can't say you didn't warn me, Sutton. Follow me." Her tone was militant, and Willa followed automatically even as she shot Sutton a dirty look.

Sutton smiled and waggled her fingers good-bye.

Willa was whisked to a secluded cubicle in the back of the shop and pushed into a cushioned chair, a satiny cape snapped around her neck. Brenda paced behind the chair, the metal slice of the scissors opening and closing accompanying the older woman's rhetorical musings. At least, Willa assumed they were rhetorical.

"Harder to style short hair. The color is dull, but not one-dimensional. I can work with that." She took Willa's chin and tilted her face back and forth. "Extensions?"

Before Willa could reply in the negative, Brenda muttered, "No. Better to emphasize your unusual face shape. And a dry cut for precision."

The woman operated the scissors with a comfort and confidence Willa could appreciate. It was the same way she felt about her tools. Without ever directing a question toward her, Brenda spun her chair around so she faced away from the mirror.

A comb appeared in the hand not wielding the scissors, and Brenda went to work. Willa didn't enjoy relinquishing control, but it was just hair, and the only way it could get any worse was if Brenda shaved her head. Actually, even that might be an improvement.

"All done." Brenda slipped her scissors into the pocket of her smock. The haircut had been quicker than an oil change.

Willa twisted to check out her new cut, but Brenda stopped her with a clawlike grip on her upper arm. "No peeking until the color is in. Come with me."

Brenda led her to another chair, this one without a mirror but with a rinse sink. Willa tensed, expecting Brenda's hands to be rough, but the massage of cool paste over her head was soothing and she closed her eyes. As long as she didn't end up as a fake blond, she didn't care.

Two more rounds of similar cool, sweet-smelling rubdowns followed, each one washed out with warm water. Finally, Brenda towel-dried her hair and said, "Back to my chair."

Brenda shuffled through Willa's hair while a blow-dryer provided white noise and warmth. Willa wasn't sure how much time had passed when Brenda put everything aside and whipped off the cape.

"Are you ready?" Brenda had a smile on her face for the first time.

"You can't have made it worse, so why not."

Brenda spun her around. Willa blinked at herself in the mirror. She wasn't unrecognizable. In fact, it was more like she'd been cast back in time. Her brown hair was a rich chestnut with hints of auburn. It was trimmed and evened out and tumbled in waves around her face that looked deliberate instead of messy.

She tucked one side behind her ear, the strands silky and bouncy. "It's great."

Brenda's smile was closer to a smirk. "What did you expect?"

Willa turned her head this way and that. The woman was an artist with her scissors. "Not this. Thank you."

Brenda patted her shoulder kindly, but her voice was brisk. "You're welcome. Now, if you don't mind, I have another client."

Willa smothered a laugh, hopped up, and weaved her way back to the front. Sutton was slouched in a chair, one high heel dangling from her crossed foot, reading a gossip magazine. She glanced over the top when Willa cleared her throat.

Her eyes flared wider and she stood up, the magazine falling to the floor. "Perfect. Do you like it?"

"How could I not?" Willa ruffled the back, which was slightly shorter than the top now. "You were right about Brenda."

"Now do you trust me?"

Sutton was teasing, but the question held deeper meaning for Willa. She guarded herself fiercely, but she was finally ready to trust Jackson with all her secrets, wasn't she?

She gave Sutton a tight-lipped smile and held out a hand. "My hat?"

Sutton started to hand it over but jerked it out of Willa's reach. "Are you going to put it back on?"

"I'm going back to work, so yes."

"But you'll squish your hair."

"Yes, but I'll also look like a mechanic. And fit in with the boys."

"They're aware you're female."

Willa snatched the hat, mashed it down on her new and improved hair, and walked out. Sutton was at her side. They didn't speak until they were halfway back to the boutique.

Finally, Willa said, "You grew up in Cottonbloom and lived a charmed life." She ignored Sutton's snort. "You've never gone to bed hungry or cold or worried about what your boss might say or do to you the next day. I had to watch my back. And front. I quit good jobs because of bad men. I had to protect myself. You get that?"

"I didn't realize." The wind had reddened Sutton's cheekbones, but the rest of her face was pale. Defensiveness pitched her voice higher. "Wyatt and Jackson and Mack aren't like that. You *like* Jackson."

The Abbotts reminded her of the men who'd hung around her father's garage when she was growing up. Respectful and decent. Her first mistake on leaving home had been thinking all men were like that. She'd learned hard and fast they weren't, but she'd learned her lesson so well that she'd forgotten decent, honorable men still existed. She was lucky to have stumbled into an entire family of them. Even Ford, through all the family drama with his brothers, had been nothing but polite if a little dismissive.

"I do like Jackson." Admitting it aloud stripped away another layer of hard-fought protections.

"Then why don't you see where things go with him?"

"I might," Willa said vaguely. While she wanted to trust Sutton, she wasn't quite ready to yet. Not until she confided in Jackson and gauged his reaction. "Can you take me back now?"

Sutton sighed but opened the door of the boutique for Willa. "Grab your stuff. We can go out the back."

After Willa pulled on her coveralls, she glanced in the mirror. She was dressed the same as she was when she arrived, but she wasn't the same. What had fundamentally changed was still unclear.

Sutton didn't attempt small talk on the ride back to the garage. Willa fiddled with the thick, rough canvas of her coveralls. So different from the fragile fabric of the dress Sutton had made for her. As soon as Sutton pulled to a stop, Willa had one foot out the door. Sutton grabbed her sleeve.

"Come to my house early on New Year's, and we'll get ready together." Warmth and excitement sparked in Sutton's eyes as if the branch of friendship she had extended was intact and even thriving.

Willa hesitated but nodded. She understood now why Wyatt had moped around like a lovesick cow over the fall. Sutton was hard to resist.

Willa adjusted her ball cap and coveralls before she opened the door that led into the bays. The sound of work getting done echoed off the concrete. River was the first to trot over and greet her as if she'd been gone for days. She crouched for a moment to let the dog get her snuffles and wags out. Mack was in his office on the phone, and they exchanged a little wave. Wyatt had his Christmas present from Sutton up on a lift.

The Jeep she'd been assigned that morning was already done, and Jackson was cleaning up the bay. She shuffled over, her hands stuck in her pockets, and he glanced up.

"How'd it go?"

"Sutton is talented. And a little bossy." She smiled, but Jackson didn't return it.

"Yeah, she's nice." He continued to sort the tools into the proper drawers without making eye contact.

She had studied and classified his every mood over the past two years, yet instead of strengthening her intuition, their intimacy had muddied the water. Was he upset with her? Or had being back at work together made him realize he'd made a mistake?

"What's wrong?" The question squeaked out of her tightened throat.

"I've got something personal to take care of. You want to come? Have to keep it on the down low from the boys though."

His question unfroze her lungs, and she gulped in a breath. "Are we scouting a car?"

"We're going north to Oak Grove."

A shot of adrenaline propelled her heart into a sprint. Her hometown was a hop and skip from Oak Grove. "What for?"

"My mother is there. Ford too maybe."

Relief slowed her heart rate and returned rational thought. She needed to remember not everything was about her. Jackson grappled with his own messy past. She was an expert at messy pasts and would do anything to help.

She raised her hand but pulled back and stuck it in her pocket once more. She wanted to touch him, but wasn't sure where the line between lovers and coworkers was drawn.

She compromised by taking a step closer to him. "Have you talked to her?"

He rubbed his hand over his forehead, leaving a dark streak. "Not exactly."

"What does that mean?"

"I hung up when she answered. At least, I assume it was

her. I don't know." His unusual lack of confidence left her nonplussed.

"I'm sure she would have welcomed your call. Why'd you hang up?"

Chapter Fifteen

"If Ford is there, I don't want to scare him off before I can talk to him." It was a reasonable answer if not exactly the truth. Jackson had hung up because the lilting feminine voice had incited a panic like he was eight again and making crank calls around town with Wyatt. His stomach flickered with remnants of nerves.

"Are you sure you don't want to take Wyatt or Mack with you?" She had stepped close enough for him to see her big brown eyes under the brim of her cap.

He should take one of his brothers, but he didn't want one of them. He wanted Willa next to him, holding his hand and telling him without words she would back him up. Willa was stronger than any of them.

He fought the urge to toss her hat aside and kiss her. The knowledge his bed was only steps away was difficult to resist, but eight to five, Monday through Friday, they had to stay coworkers. Except he was asking her to go with him, not as a coworker, but as someone who'd become an integral part of his life.

"No, I want you." He forced himself to meet her eyes.

Her tight mouth and crinkled eyes gave the impression of wariness. "I need to clean up and change."

"You left some things in the loft if you want to clean up here."

"You sure it will be okay? I missed almost two hours this morning." She glanced around.

"It's slow between the holidays. Anyway, you'll be with me." He crossed his arms over his chest. "I'll go by myself if—"

She touched his wrist and slipped her fingers under his sleeve. The caress settled his prickly nerves. "I'll come, but I don't want your brothers to think I'm taking advantage of the situation because you and I . . . you know."

Considering he'd beat himself to a pulp worrying about the fact he was taking advantage of her because he was sort of her boss, her admission made him smile. "It'll be fine. Go change. I'll clear it with Mack."

She quickstepped to the back of the shop and disappeared through the door that led to the barn. He knocked on the doorjamb of the office. Mack's face was drawn tight. Stress did not look good on him, and he'd been wearing it too often of late.

"What's wrong?" Jackson asked.

Mack threw a pen down. "The usual. What's up?"

"We don't have another job, so I'm going scouting this afternoon and taking Willa with me." He posed it as a done deal, not a request.

"Is this work or a date?"

"Work." The twinge of his conscience was almost painful. He hated lying, especially to Mack, but taking Wyatt or Mack with him would look too much like they were ganging up on Ford. If he was even there. But if Jackson could talk Ford into coming home and negotiating, then maybe some of the strain Mack carried would ease.

Mack glanced away. "You know I like Willa, right?"

"Sure."

"I hope I didn't say anything while I was blitzed that was insensitive."

"You're worried about her *feelings*?" Jackson couldn't help but laugh a little. "Getting soft in your old age, bro."

Mack cursed and threw his pen in Jackson's direction, but the smile on his face was welcome.

"You mind keeping an eye on River?" Jackson nodded toward the dog who'd staked a claim on a spot in the corner. One of Mack's old blankets was folded as a makeshift bed.

"Not a bit. Aside from pooping in my yard, she's a well-behaved mutt."

Movement from the corner of his eye drew his gaze toward Willa. She slipped in the back door in jeans, an oversized army-style coat probably from the thrift store, and her ball cap pulled low.

Something uncomfortable squatted on his chest. He trailed his gaze from her hat to her boots, carnally aware of the curves that she hid under the bulky clothing.

"What?" Her eyes narrowed as if she could read his mind.

"Nothing. You ready?" His voice was too brusque, but he couldn't admit the strength of his feelings to her. Not until everything was out in the open between them. His head and heart were at war.

"What about—"

"Mack's going to watch River." He herded Willa outside.

It was chilly but not cold. The sky was a slate gray, and encroaching clouds promised rain. Willa picked up her pace and overtook him on the way to the Mustang, rounding the front to the passenger seat. The sight of her sliding into the car next to him eased his mounting tension. A temporary reprieve.

The car's heater kicked in as they crossed the river into Mississippi. Willa shimmied out of her coat and tossed it on the narrow backseat. With a lack of her usual grace, she pulled her ball cap off and ran her fingers through her hair, keeping her face averted.

He looked from her to the road and then took a long second glance that sent him over the center line before he corrected. Her hair was a mass of waves on top and trimmed shorter in the back. The color was different too, but not in a way he could put his finger on. He only knew it looked richer and softer than before. His hands squeaked on the leather wheel, and he wasn't sure how to attribute the rapid beat of his heart.

"Your hair." The words came out between a statement and a question.

"Sutton insisted. Said my hack job didn't go with the nonhack-job dress she made me." Her voice lilted uncertainly. She was a combination of bold sass and shy naïveté, and she could pivot between the two in a matter of seconds.

"It looks good."

"Yeah?" She fiddled with the wavy strands behind her ear.

"Better than good." He grabbed her hand in his and pulled it away. Her hand was small and soft in his, and he wanted to keep hold of it, but he didn't. Instead, before he could question himself, he added, "But then I've always thought you were pretty."

The sidelong look she shot him was both thankful and mocking. "I call bullshit. Until a few weeks ago, you never saw me as more than a wrench with a brain and legs."

"Yeah, well, I never claimed to be more than a blind idiot with a brain and legs."

"What changed?"

"You were acting like you wanted to leave the garage. Cottonbloom. I couldn't let it happen."

"Because I'm an invaluable mechanic?" A teasing bite was in the question.

He chanced a glance over. In contrast to her tone, her face was serious, her eyes wide and searching. He tightened his grip on the steering wheel and stared off in the distance where the stretch of road curved out of sight. "Because you're invaluable to *me*."

The longer the silence went on the drier his mouth got. Had he said too much, too soon? The last thing he wanted was to scare her off before he could convince her to trust him with all her secrets.

"Jackson." His name came on a choked-up whisper. She touched his forearm and his hand loosened around the wheel. She knitted their fingers together. Handholding wasn't his thing, and it felt a little awkward at first, but as their thumbs danced in a more erotic version of thumb wars, he relaxed.

After several minutes of no conversation, they eased into small talk about seemingly inconsequential things, starting with football. She was a Cowboys fan because that had been her father's favorite team, but she liked the Saints okay too. Her favorite food was lasagna, and she loved root beer. He relished every tidbit, no matter how minor, that she shared with him.

His Mustang ate up the miles. He drove north into Mississippi sticking mostly to back roads, crossing a two-lane bridge over the Mississippi and back into north Louisiana as dusk was falling. Christmas wreaths and lights still decorated most houses they passed.

His concentration slipped the closer they got to Oak Grove. The drive into town was mostly scrub and pine trees, but as they approached downtown, huge live oaks highlighted a white-columned county courthouse. The downtown mimicked many Southern small towns—its charm past its prime and tarnished, but still visible.

He took a turn off the main street, having committed the directions to his mother's house to memory. He slowed to a crawl and counted down the numbers on the mailboxes until he reached a small single-story brick house of nineteen seventies heritage. He cruised past going suspiciously slow if anyone was watching them out their front windows.

Willa twisted around in her seat. "Wasn't that it back there?"

"Yeah, it was." He fought the urge to keep driving them out of town and back over the Mississippi River. He reminded himself this wasn't about his mother, but about Ford and the garage and their future. He did a wide U-turn in the deserted street. "Do you see Ford's car?"

"No, but the garage door is closed."

He parked on the street, but blocked the driveway, in case Ford decided to make a run for it. He didn't make a move to open his door.

The yard was well kept, and although rosebushes along the path were dormant and stark, he could imagine them fragrant and blooming. A long-forgotten memory surfaced of full red blooms in a vase on their kitchen table while he ate pancakes. The memory was so vivid, he could almost smell them. What he couldn't do was picture his mother or remember her voice.

"I'll be right there with you." She touched his arm, her voice strong with a confidence he could borrow from.

He nodded, unable and unwilling to put into words what her support meant. He got the door open on the second try. She was already out and waiting for him on the cobblestone path to the slab porch.

His boots felt like clown shoes as he trudged up the

walk. Willa pressed the doorbell, the tones slightly disso-
nant. A shuffle could be heard on the other side, and he
ran his hands down the front of his pants. The door opened.

The woman on the other side was a stranger, yet his
gaze catalogued familiarities faster than his brain could
note them. Wyatt had her eyes, clear gray with a constant
twinkle, and hair, almost black but shot through with an
attractive silver. And, like with his twin, an instant connection tugged him forward.

"Hi . . ." What did he call her? Not Mom. "Hi. I'm—"

"Jackson." Her eyes brimmed with tears, and she raised
a hand as if she were going to touch him, but didn't.
"My son."

He stood there like a mute, his mouth working, but
nothing making it out of the tight squeeze of his throat.

"I'm Willa." She saved him by sticking out her hand and
taking his mother's still raised one in a shake. "We're here
because . . ." She paused as if leaving him an opening, but
he was stuck and unable to take it. Finally, she asked, "Is
Ford here?"

"Not at the moment, but he'll be back shortly." His
mother stepped back and gestured. "Please come in."

Like a robot, he moved forward. His mother ushered
them into a den with brown carpet and brown wood paneling all around, even the ceiling. It was dim and cave-
like. "Can I get you something to drink? Coffee or hot
chocolate, maybe?"

Another buried memory surfaced—a woman making
hot chocolate for him after a nightmare. He'd inserted Aunt
Hyacinth into the memory, but the woman had been his
mother. She fidgeted and stared at him. Was she trying to
locate the little boy he'd been in the man before her?

"Hot chocolate would be welcome." His voice came out
rougher than usual. "It's a mite chilly out."

"Make yourselves at home." She flashed a smile, a set

of dimples creasing her cheeks for an instant. He took a step back, seeing a piece of himself in her for the first time.

"You okay?" Willa whispered.

"I don't know." He was too restless to sit and pretend this was a normal visit. A line of photos on the mantel drew him farther into the room.

With a jolt, he recognized old school pictures of all of them. Aunt Hazel and Hyacinth's work, no doubt. They had always asked for extras for their wallets. He picked up the picture at the end. He and Wyatt were in their caps and gowns at high school graduation, their arms across each other's shoulders. Wyatt's smile was open while he was barely smiling at all.

Willa was by his side, stroking his arm lightly. A throat cleared, and he turned with the picture in his hand. His mother held two steaming mugs.

"You hate me." It was a statement. "I get it. I hate myself for leaving the way I did."

She set the mugs down on the coffee table and took a seat in an old wooden rocking chair with a plaid ruffled seat cushion tied to the back rails. It too held a vague familiarity.

Hate was too simple and easy a feeling. He sank down on the couch and stared at the bobbing, dissolving marshmallows on the surface of the hot chocolate. "Why did you leave?"

The squeak of the rocking chair brought his attention back to her. Her head was tilted toward the ceiling, but her eyes were closed as if she were looking inward or backward for the answer. "I was young and overwhelmed with the four of you. No, more than overwhelmed. I was depressed, and it got worse with each one of you. I thought something was wrong with me. Your father was obsessed with the garage and—"

"Don't blame Pop."

She opened her eyes and met his anger head-on. "He didn't know how to help me. The more I cried, the more he retreated to the garage. The day I almost hurt you is the day I left."

"Hurt me?"

"You'd had an accident in your bed. Shouldn't have been a big deal, but I almost hit you. You were barely four. I packed a bag, told Ford to look after all of you until Hobart was done working, and left."

He racked his memory, but came up with nothing. He didn't remember the day she'd left, just a gradual fading of before into after. "I don't remember any of that."

"I regret leaving, but I would have regretted hurting any of you boys even more. I missed you all terribly, but I thought I was doing the right thing by staying away. It took therapy and going on medication before I got myself together. By then, your father wanted nothing to do with me."

"You contacted him?"

She nodded. "Many times over the years, but he stonewalled me. Finally, I went to your aunts."

"When did Ford find you? Or did you find him?"

"He called me a few months ago." Her gaze skated off to the side, but a hint of strain pulled lines out of her forehead. For the first time her youthful face betrayed her age.

"He wanted money?" His gut knew the answer to the question.

She gave a brusque nod and didn't look over at him.

"Did you give what he asked for?"

"I gave him everything I could afford."

The kid in him that had heard his pop rail against her selfishness countless times decided she deserved it. The grown-up part of him recognized she didn't. Like Willa, she was trying to atone for her mistakes.

"Ford's taking advantage of you," he finally said.

She swept her gaze to his. Her sadness sped through him. "I know, but I would do anything to make up the past to you. To all of you."

"Did he tell you what the money was for?"

"He said the garage was in financial trouble."

Jackson rubbed a hand over his jaw to stem a curse. "The garage is fine. Ford's dug a hole with a bookie down in Baton Rouge."

"Gambling." His mother laid a hand over her chest, shock flittering over her face before her expression steeled itself. "I would have still given him the money."

"Don't give him any more. I'll cover his debts." His offer pulled a soft gasp from Willa.

The sound of the front door rattling sent all three of them to their feet. "That's him," his mother whispered.

Jackson waited. Ford would have recognized the Mustang, of course.

"If it isn't my little brother." Ford propped himself in the doorway, his cheeks reddened, his eyes bloodshot. The smell of bar smoke and whiskey soured the room. He looked like shit.

"We need to talk," Jackson said softly.

"Catching up on the past twenty-five years with our mother?" He weaved his way to the couch, his eyes fixed on Willa, whistling softly. "If I had known what you were hiding under those coveralls, I might have made a move."

Jackson took a step forward to lay into Ford but stopped short. If he hadn't been watching Ford so closely, he might have missed the flash of self-disgust. Was Ford trying piss Jackson off on purpose?

"She's off the market." Jackson forced his voice calm.

"I'm not a car, boys," Willa muttered.

A shot of humor cooled Jackson's burn of anger, and he sat. Willa sank down on the edge of the cushion to his left, and Ford sprawled across a love seat on the other side of the coffee table. Their mother was a gray-faced statue in the rocking chair. Anxiety zinged around the room like a pinball machine.

Jackson picked up his hot chocolate and took a sip. "Your bookie came by the shop."

"Which one?"

Abandoning his mock casualness, Jackson set his mug down with a thump, his stomach souring. "What the fuck do you mean, 'which one'? How many people do you owe money to? And how much?"

"None of your business." Ford's gaze flicked to their mother.

Ford was not their mother's problem. As much as the brothers cursed and railed against him, Ford was their problem. He could pay their mother back with the money Jackson planned to offer to get him out of trouble.

"How much did she give you?" Jackson nudged his chin toward their mother, but didn't take his eyes off Ford.

Ford took a check out of his shirt pocket and held it out long enough for Jackson to see their mother's name scrawled at the bottom. Belinda Abbott. The fact she hadn't shed their name was like a bloodletting.

"Didn't cash it." Ford ripped the check into tiny pieces. "It would have only been a Band-Aid. I need a chunk of big money fast, so I'm selling my stake. The deal is in progress."

A numb acceptance came over him. It was the outcome he'd been dreading, yet he wasn't surprised. "Why didn't you come to us? We would have paid off your debts without you having to sell out."

"And then what? Mack would have rubbed it in at every turn. Anyway, I don't want to work at the shop. Never did." A sadness cloaked Ford's bravado, making him appear smaller and less sure of himself. "I couldn't be the man

Pop wanted. It was always Mack even if Pop couldn't see it."

"Any chance you could cancel the deal?"

"Too late." Ford rubbed his hands together, his gaze down. "I'll pay my debt and have enough left over to make a life somewhere else. I'm headed to Memphis."

"What's going to happen if you gamble your way into debt again?"

Ford's half-shouldered shrug wasn't reassuring. "I won't. I'm going to make something of myself without being compared to Mack every hour of every day."

More than the garage had trapped Ford. Jackson worried his brother's feelings of inadequacy would be an even stronger cage, but what could he do at this point except damage control?

"Who'd you sell to?"

"Can't say until the papers are signed. Mack would try to stop it." Ford's voice was devoid of emotion. "But some fresh blood might do the shop some good."

Fury rolled through Jackson like a thunderstorm. The garage should only be owned by Abbotts. It was their pop's legacy. He squeezed his hand into a tight fist, ready to let loose. His focus narrowed on Ford, the accumulations of past and present suffocating. A soft touch dissipated the storm. Time and space widened, and he forced his hand to open if not exactly relax. Willa's touch restored a sense of order in the chaos.

"I can't do this." Jackson stood and skirted around the coffee table. With his hand clamped around Willa's, she was forced to follow him.

He stopped in the doorway of the den and looked back at his brother. Ford was leaning over, elbows on knees, his head in his hands. Ford had taught him how to swim in the river and where the best places were to catch a fish. He wasn't a bad man, just a lost one.

"Ford." Jackson barked his name and waited until Ford shifted to meet his gaze. "You're my brother and I love you, dammit. If you need help, you call and I'll answer."

He was sure he wasn't imagining the tears in Ford's eyes when he nodded. Jackson held his stare a moment longer before hitting the front door. His mother followed them out onto the porch.

"Please don't go." Her voice was pinched in a squeak of emotion. "I can make dinner."

Night fell like a blanket over them, clouds blocking the rising moon. Jackson faced his mother. It was bizarre that the momentous occasion of reconnecting with his long-lost mother had been overshadowed by Ford. "I can't stay."

"Can I see you again? Or can we talk? Your brothers . . . ?" She held her throat as if the question hurt. Or maybe it was the answer she dreaded.

Wyatt would see her. He was the one who had been feeling the family out after discovering Aunt Hazel had been in contact with her. He wasn't so sure about Mack. He had been older and wrestled with memories of her that he and Wyatt had been too young to form.

"They don't know I came up here today. Let me talk to Wyatt first. Pretty sure he'd like to see you." She looked so starved for information, he added, "He got engaged over Christmas."

"Did he? To a nice girl?" Her smile was tremulous and her eyes watery.

"Very nice. From the Mississippi side of Cottonbloom."

"I'm glad." She looked away and swallowed, but when she spoke again, her voice was teary. "I wasn't a mother to you boys, but I'm begging for a chance to be forgiven. I'll be in your lives as much or little as you'll allow."

Sincerity was all he sensed. The most he could offer at the moment was a nod and a warning. "Don't let Ford take advantage of your guilt, because he will. He already has."

"He's my son, and he needs me." The simplicity shattered Jackson's false sense of calm.

His heart bled a little more for what they'd lost as children, and he tightened his hand on Willa's. Instead of doing something foolish like giving his mom a hug, he dug out one of his cards and handed it to her.

"Call me if you need help with him. Or to talk or whatever."

She ran a finger over the embossed logo and numbers, her eyes downcast. "Hobart did real good with you boys. He'd be proud. I was so terribly sad to hear of his passing last year. I loved him."

Loss was a strange thing. Some days the pain of not having his pop around was like a room he could close off and ignore. But, in this moment, even though it had been more than a year, his pop's death crashed through the walls that had formed around his emotions like a wrecking ball. The pain felt as fresh and eviscerating as if his pop had died yesterday.

His pop's feelings about his former wife hadn't mellowed over the years, and Jackson had a pretty good guess as to what he would have said about this meeting and the tentative connections forming. But his pop hadn't been infallible. He'd been blind to Ford's unhappiness and Mack's potential.

"I'll call you tomorrow, okay?" He reached out and covered her hands with his own and gave a brief squeeze. Hers were cool but smooth. What had she done all these years? All of a sudden, he wanted to stay and find out.

Instead, he turned and walked away, not looking back. Willa was at his side, saying nothing, but the worry in her face didn't go unnoticed. Only when they were back in the Mustang and out of town did he speak. "Did I break your hand?"

"Only a momentary cutoff in my circulation."

"Thanks for . . . well, everything."

"All I did was stand—or sit—next to you."

"Exactly." At his side was where she belonged.

"This is bad, isn't it?" Her hands were tucked between her legs and her shoulders were hunched forward.

"It's not good." He eased his foot off the accelerator when it crept up to eighty. Getting pulled over would be the crap topping on an already shitty day. "Any guesses who he might have sold to?"

"Best-case scenario, he sold to another mechanic looking to expand or play a silent-investor role. Worst-case, he sold to someone who has it in for the garage, but it's not like you boys have any enemies, right?"

"True." Superficially, her answer seemed correct, but as he ruminated on it, names popped into his head. "Ah, hell."

"What?"

"Don could probably afford to buy Ford's shares."

"Who's that?"

"The driver who was at the track."

"The one you punched?"

He grimaced. A wreck on the track was one thing, humiliation in the pits was another altogether. For the most part, racing was still a man's sport at the local dirt tracks which meant testosterone rose to obnoxious levels more often than not.

"And Sutton's ex would love to stick it to Wyatt." Jackson banged his skull against the headrest hard enough to add to his headache. Andrew Tarwater not only had the money but a strong motive. Granted, Tarwater had been caught cheating with Sutton's best friend, but the man hated Wyatt for taking advantage of his stupidity.

"And what about Mack? Any disgruntled customers with means?" she asked.

"Anything is possible. He's been keeping things to

himself the last few months." Jackson muttered a curse. "Tarwater is the most likely buyer."

She turned toward him. "Three-quarters of the business is still under your control. What can he really do?"

"Make our lives a living hell? Blackmail the bank into calling our loan?"

She fell silent. The Mustang ate up the miles, his anxiety growing the closer they got to Cottonbloom. Not only would he have to break the news about Ford finding a buyer, but he had to handle the delicate task of discussing their mother.

He glanced over at Willa. Without her calming presence, he might not have been able to keep from jumping Ford. Truth be told, he might have turned the Mustang around before he'd made it over the Mississippi.

"Thanks for coming with me," he said.

"Anytime you need a wingman—er, girl—I'll be there." Her smile was a little sad, a little knowing, and a lot beautiful.

He took her hand and pressed his lips against the pulse point of her wrist. Was it his imagination or did it jump?

He pulled into the garage's parking lot and stared out the windshield, the silence eerie after the hours spent with the engine growling. The moon was haloed by clouds, giving it a yellow cast.

"You guys have lots to discuss. I'll head home."

"No." The word came out harsh. "I want you to stay."

"Why?"

Because you're as good as family, he wanted to say but didn't. He wasn't sure she would appreciate the sentiment. "The business of the garage affects you as much as it does us."

Her eyes narrowed on him. "I don't own a stake."

"You're our only employee. That must count for something." When she didn't respond, he tried to keep the begging out of his voice. "Please, Willa."

"If you need me, I'll stay." She pushed the car door open.

No lights shone from Mack's house, but his truck and Wyatt's car were out front. He led Willa around the side of the garage to the barn. His twin's laugh traveled through the space, and his step stuttered. Willa gave him a nudge in the small of his back.

Mack saw him first. "Did you two find anything worth the effort?" He headed to the fridge without waiting for an answer and held out two cold cans of beer. Willa waved him off, but Jackson popped the top and took a swig, hoping it would give him courage.

"I lied." His soft words launched like a grenade. Everyone stilled for the explosion.

Wyatt shifted forward on the couch. "I had a feeling something was up. Did you find Ford?"

Jackson wasn't surprised Wyatt cut to the heart. "I found him."

"Good or bad?" Mack asked.

Jackson hesitated, not sure how to frame the complications of the day. Mack popped the top of the beer Willa had rejected and drank half in one go.

"You'd better tell us everything," Mack said when he came up for air.

Willa gave Jackson a nod and tight smile. It was enough.

"I tracked Ford down at our mother's house in Oak Grove."

Mack opened his mouth then clamped it shut and looked off to the side. Wyatt's eyes sparked and energy released through his tapping heel. "What was she like?"

"Nice. Normal. Still pretty and young-looking. You look a lot like her, Wyatt."

"Nice? She abandoned us. Have you forgotten that?" Mack crumpled the beer can against his leg and tossed it toward the bin. The discordant clang upped the tension.

"I'm not saying we have to invite her over for the holidays, but she seemed sorry and sincere and wants to mend things."

"There's no mending what she did." The bitterness in Mack's voice poisoned the air.

Jackson exchanged a telling look with his twin. "We can discuss our mother later. It's Ford that's the more immediate problem." He took a deep breath. "He's in the process of selling his stake."

Mack closed his eyes, his head falling back and his lips mouthing something—a prayer, a curse, either would be understandable. "To who?" he finally asked aloud.

"He wouldn't tell me; afraid if he did, you'd try to kill the deal, but the obvious person would be Tarwater." Jackson kept any blame out of his voice. Even though it wasn't Wyatt's fault, he would beat himself up anyway.

Wyatt groaned and ran both hands through his hair, linking them at his nape. "What a d-bag."

Jackson wasn't sure if he was referring to their brother or Tarwater. "Ford's taking the money to pay off his *bookies.* The hole was way deep. He plans to make a clean start in Memphis."

"Any of us really think Ford can give up gambling?" Mack paced.

Their collective silence could fill an old-school encyclopedia.

"If it means anything, Ford seemed . . . broken. Trying to live up to Pop's expectations when it was never what he wanted got to him. Said you should have been Pop's favorite, not him." Jackson punched Mack lightly on the arm.

"Is Tarwater going to be at the New Year's party at Sutton's?" Willa asked.

Mack stopped and stared as if he'd forgotten she was there.

"Hell, no," Wyatt said. "Her parents blacklisted him."

"Get him invited. If he's sworn Ford to secrecy, then he wants the upper hand. You should confront him and put him on the defensive." Willa picked at her fingernails but she was looking at them from under her lashes. "He's a butt kisser, right? He'll be on his best behavior with Sutton's daddy around. In fact, can her daddy apply pressure to get him to sell it back?"

Mack's focus bounced to Wyatt. "You think the judge could work a deal?"

"He and Pop were friends, and I'm engaged to his daughter. I don't see why he wouldn't help. Tarwater's made no secret about the fact he wants to run for Mize's judgeship as soon as he retires. Or before. Let me grease some wheels." Wyatt rose, pulled out his phone, and retreated to the back of the barn.

"Good idea, Willa," Mack said.

Jackson smiled at her. He expected her to be preening from Mack's rare compliment, but instead her face was serious, reflecting troubles he couldn't identify.

"Listen, you guys have lots to discuss. I'm going to head back to my place." She tucked her hands into her back pockets and shuffled toward the door. Something in her face stopped Jackson's protest even though he didn't want her to go. The squeak of the back door on her exit expanded the fissure in his chest.

Wyatt returned with a grim smile. "The judge will personally invite Tarwater tomorrow morning."

"Good. Let's sleep on it and brainstorm options over coffee." Mack's voice was steely as he walked to the door.

A few beats of silence fell. Wyatt's arm was draped over the back of the couch in a pose of relaxation, but his bouncing foot gave him away. "What was she really like?"

"She had our high school graduation picture on her mantel. And other school pictures of us around."

"I'll be damned," Wyatt muttered. "Has she lived in Oak Grove all this time? What does she do for a living? Does she want to see me?" The eagerness in Wyatt's voice recalled something childlike.

"Of course she wants to see you and Mack. But listen, I don't know anything about her. Not really. She never remarried and is still using Abbott as her last name. But for all I know she could up and move again." Even as he issued the warning, he didn't believe it.

"You have her number?"

Jackson fished the piece of paper with her info out of his pocket and handed it over. "She wrote Ford a check that he ended up not needing because of the sale, but I'm worried."

"Worried Ford will bleed her dry?"

"Something like that."

Wyatt glanced over his shoulder to the door. "You think Mack will come around?"

"Let's you and me pave the way. Feel her out before we drag him down that road."

Wyatt stood up and stretched. "Good idea."

"Where's Sutton?"

"Working on final details of the party with her mom."

"You want to crash here? It'd be like old times." Jackson, who usually craved solitude, suddenly dreaded heading to the empty, quiet loft.

"Nah. Thanks for the offer, but I'll wait for her at home." Wyatt slipped on his jacket and sent Jackson a not-so-subtle side-eye. "Why did Willa head out?"

"I don't know." Jackson kicked at a buckling board.

He'd get his tools out and fix it. Or maybe he'd go a couple of rounds with the punching bag. It wasn't that late.

"Things are progressing between you two though, right?"

"I guess." He wanted to talk to Wyatt about the information he'd obtained about her car registration, but it would only compound his sense of betrayal.

"Okeydokey." Sarcasm was rife in Wyatt's voice, although it vanished when he clapped Jackson on the back on his way out the door. "Hang in there. Time has a way of unraveling complications and getting to the heart of the matter."

His heart didn't feel like it even belonged to him anymore. The silence reverberated in his ears. Oh hell, it didn't.

His heart belonged to Willa.

Chapter Sixteen

New Year's Eve dawned with a clear blue sky so deep, Willa had to squint against its brilliance. Looking out at the sun and sky, one would think it was summer, but a crack of the door revealed nature's joke. The wind whistled with a chill that made her stomp her feet.

The garage was closed. So was the library. She'd left River at the garage knowing she'd be gone all afternoon and would spend the night with Jackson. It was strange and too lonely to contemplate being in the trailer without her. Willa settled herself on the couch and opened a new book.

The words failed to work their magic. She used to spend days reading in her trailer, escaping to other worlds and places. But lately something had shifted. She didn't want to escape her life anymore. Not if that meant escaping Jackson.

She wished she was curled up on his couch, or better yet, in his bed, talking or maybe not talking but doing. She smiled, but it faded fast.

Their trip to find Ford and meet his mother had complicated things further. She'd physically ached for Jackson, both from the implications of Ford's betrayal and the impact of meeting his mother. He'd hit a brick wall of emotions and it had knocked him backward. Not much she could do except help hold him up until he got his bearings in the new world.

She'd wanted to plant herself and be his rock. Forever.

Which is why she'd retreated. If she'd stayed, there was no way she would be able to hold back the way she felt about him. It was frankly terrifying.

The morning and afternoon passed in bursts of reading and thinking and killing time before heading to Sutton's house to get ready for the New Year's Eve party and wait for Wyatt and Jackson to pick them up.

She packed a small satchel with the little makeup she owned—a mascara that was old enough to talk if it had been a child and a cracked blush she had found on the sale rack.

Sutton's house was a surprise. It wasn't trendy and new, but older with character. The bushes out front were a patchwork of green leaves and bare limbs. She parked on the street, tucked her bag under her arm, and trod softly to the porch.

Before she even rang the bell, the door opened and Sutton ushered her inside with an infectious energy.

"I've been watching for you. I half expected you to cancel on me."

"I can't say I didn't think about it." What stopped her was Jackson. Like in her work on cars, she didn't want to let him down. He was counting on her.

"We're going to have fun." She glided into the kitchen. It was airy and remodeled. Modern black-and-white tile and gray granite countertops were offset by homey gingham curtains and dark-stained swivel chairs at the bar.

"Coffee?" Sutton waved toward the pot. "It's going to be a late night."

Willa fixed a mug and took a sip. Its rich flavor set it

apart from the basic black she was used to from the shop.
"It's good."

She peeked out of the window above the sink. The
backyard was eighty percent taken over by roses, the stems
deadheaded and bare at this time of year. "I'll bet your
backyard is pretty in the summer."

Sutton sidled closer until they were shoulder to shoulder. "Sure is. The roses are what sold me on the place.
The woman who lived here never married. Her health
wasn't good, and she had to move to Cottonbloom Comfort Home, but the Realtor said that she wanted someone
to buy the house who'd take care of her roses. I promised
I would."

"How did she know you'd keep your promise?"

"She didn't. Sometimes you've got to have faith." Although Sutton said it lightly, to Willa the words felt heavy
with portent of the future. Could she put her faith in Jackson? Sutton broke the silence. "But she didn't have to wonder. I brought her bouquets at the Comfort Home until
she passed."

Sutton was a good person. The Abbotts were good
people. Did her past mistakes exclude her from ever be-
longing? For the first time, she could see herself earning
a place with them.

"I can see why you and Wyatt got together."

"Why is that?" Sutton's brows drew in, but a smile still
turned her lips.

"Because you're both ridiculously nice."

Sutton's bark of laughter was unexpected. "Wyatt is
nice. I'm not. I basically blackmailed him into going out
with me. Neither one of us thought it would turn into
more." She twisted the engagement ring on her finger,
chuckling. "I mean, he was a little jerk to me as kids."

Sutton nudged her head in the universal signal for *follow me* and swept out of the room. She stopped at a door

halfway down a short hall. "I know you've seen the dress, but it's finished and freaking beautiful."

Sutton pushed the door open, and Willa tightened her grip on her mug. Sutton wasn't bragging. The dress wasn't beautiful; it was a work of art. Willa was afraid to touch it, much less wear it.

As the artist, Sutton didn't have any such qualms. She ran her hands over the bodice.

"The headless mannequin wears it better than I will." Willa was only half joking.

Sutton made a scoffing sound, examined a seam, and picked at a loose string, everything about her serious. "Ridiculous. You have *way* better boobs than my mannequin."

"Uh, thanks?" Willa couldn't stop a small laugh from spurting out.

"How about a shower first?" Sutton backed out into the hallway and pointed to a room down the hall. "I left a robe on the back of the door. Everything else should be out. Just holler if you need me." Sutton walked away with a little wave over her head.

Willa took her time. The endless hot water and the choice of bath washes and shampoos would make going back to her bargain-brand shampoo and the bar of soap she used in her five-minutes-or-less showers depressing.

She toweled off, thankful the steam fuzzed out her reflection. The robe was a thin cotton, and she clutched the lapels together as she opened the door to peek out. The puff of chilly air made her shiver. She picked up her mug, but the coffee had cooled during her epic shower.

Sidling down the hall toward the kitchen, she stopped when it was clear Sutton wasn't there. Alone in silence was a comfortable place for her and the tension across her shoulders loosened. She put her coffee mug down and moved to the shelves of books in the den. Regret and desperation were familiar companions, but the spike of jealousy was an unwelcome guest.

The books represented something more than pleasure and escape, but an alternative life she'd burned to the ground. If things had been different, where would she be? In a nice place like this with a college degree framed on the wall? Would she have a full bookcase?

Maybe, maybe not. School had never been her priority, and she hadn't appreciated books until she had nothing else. And that alternate life wouldn't have Jackson in it. Any jealousy vanished, leaving a pang that felt suspiciously like thankfulness.

She turned away from the books and packed her regret away. She would always carry it with her—Cynthia's death was something she would never forget—but maybe she could forgive herself and claim a piece of happiness with Jackson. Was that too much to ask of fate?

"Are you out? Come on back." Sutton's voice drifted from the room at the end of the hall.

Even though a dark part of her popped up with a warning of self-preservation, Willa wanted—or maybe closer to needed—hope to cling to and shoved the feelings down like a game of whack-a-mole.

Willa pushed at the half-open door with her foot. Sutton sat on a wooden kitchen chair in front of a mirrored bureau, flipping through a fashion magazine. As soon as she spotted Willa, she stood, tossed the magazine on the bed, and gestured to the chair.

"Have a seat. I'm going to attempt to re-create Brenda's magic with your hair, then I'll do your makeup. Unless you want to do it yourself." Sutton's voice veered high as if she were afraid she'd offended Willa with the offer.

The role reversal helped de-rust Willa's friendship skills. She laughed and gave a half-shouldered shrug.

"Makeup wouldn't last five minutes at the garage so I never bother."

She didn't add that makeup wasn't a consideration when keeping her car running and food was a priority. People like Sutton had never experienced that type of gnawing hunger.

"Good, because I've been looking forward to this all week." Sutton's excitement was genuine.

Willa slipped onto the chair and met Sutton's eyes in the mirror. "Obviously, Wyatt is falling short if this is the highlight of your week."

For a split second, Willa worried she'd overstepped, but Sutton's pealing laugh set them on new footing. "That man has rocked my world in every way. Besides the obvious"—she waggled her eyebrows—"he's given me the confidence to show off my designs. I used to make things and shove them into a closet. Seeing women wear them is a dream come true. And you are the perfect model."

Willa made a scoffing sound. "Shockingly, Victoria's Secret has not come calling."

"Those aren't real women. They're robots, haven't you heard?"

They shared snickers. "Rich robots, though," Willa added.

"Yep. But there's more to life than money." Sutton squirted hair product in her palms and shuttled her fingers through Willa's hair, ruffling it.

"Spoken like someone who's never had to worry about it." Willa kept her voice from veering dark. The last thing she wanted was to topple the fragile camaraderie they were building like a Jenga tower.

Sutton's hands stilled for a moment, her eyes downcast, before resuming to work her hair. "You had a rough childhood, huh?"

If she had then it would be easier to shuffle blame to someone or something else, but her hardships were all of her own making. "Actually, I had a pretty great childhood. I mean, my mom died right after I was born, but my dad was really great."

She raised her hand to touch the fraying emblem on her hat before she remembered she didn't have it on. Fisting her hands, she forced them to her thighs.

"Did he inspire your love of cars?"

"Yeah. He owns a shop. I would hang out there all summer and after school. Once I was done with homework, he would let me help him. Soon enough, I was working there. Mr. Abbott reminded me so much of my dad." The sting of tears surprised her, but she wasn't sure which man they were for. Both of them were lost to her in different ways.

"Mr. Abbott and my dad were both into cars and friends of a sort, I suppose. I barely knew him though. I hated being dragged to the garage when I was a kid." The regret in Sutton's voice was something Willa recognized. "I thought it was dirty and smelly and Wyatt was *so* annoying."

"Boys can be pretty dumb, huh?" Willa attempted to inject some humor into the moment.

Sutton's laugh was more sardonic than amused. "Girls too. Lord knows, I've made my share of mistakes."

Was she referring to her disastrous engagement to Andrew Tarwater? "It's not your fault."

Sutton stilled. There was no need to explain what she'd meant. "But it is," she whispered. "What if Andrew—"

"Stop it." When Sutton wouldn't meet her eyes in the mirror, Willa twisted around in the chair. "Trust me on this: what-ifs are useless. All you can do is move forward and try to mitigate the damage."

The advice echoed in Willa's chest as if she were the one hearing it instead of the one giving it. Had she moved forward or had she run away? And why did it feel like she was circling right back around to where it all started?

Sutton nodded, but she didn't look convinced. The noise of the hair dryer covered the need to speak. Willa studied the room in reverse through the mirror. Touches of Wyatt were everywhere. A shirt tossed over the pillow, a pair of boots sticking out from under the bed, a brush and male deodorant on the bureau in front of her. Wyatt had basically moved in with Sutton and would be living there full-time after their wedding.

By the time Sutton was finished, the mash of worries and emotions had been put away. The artful tousle of her hair was something Willa wasn't sure she'd ever learn how to replicate. But she liked it. Liked how it made her feel feminine and pretty for the first time in forever.

Willa stared into the mirror; the woman staring back was familiar yet somehow irrevocably changed over the last weeks. "It's great. Thanks."

Sutton patted her shoulders. "You ain't seen nothing yet. Makeup is next."

Willa opened and closed her eyes on command and didn't complain. She trusted Sutton not to turn her into Bimbo the Clown. In fact, she trusted Sutton more than she had another woman since Cynthia so many years ago.

"How about some lip gloss instead of stick? It'll look more natural." Sutton's gaze was narrow and assessing.

"Whatever you think."

A corner of Sutton's mouth quirked in a flash of amusement. "Says the woman I nearly had to blackmail into getting a new dress and haircut."

"Considering I've cut my own hair the last five years and shop at the secondhand store while you honest-to-God could be a model somewhere, I'm learning to trust your judgment." Willa's voice was teasing, but any humor drained out of Sutton.

"I'll talk to Wyatt about getting you a raise. That's ridiculous."

Willa shifted and grabbed Sutton's wrist. "No. Jackson gave me a big raise. It's not how much I make. It's that I don't—" *Deserve nice things and people.* Willa let go of Sutton's wrist, turned around, and stared into her own wide eyes.

With a worried look creasing her brow, Sutton unscrewed the tube and leaned in to dot the gloss on Willa's lips. "I'm here if you ever need to talk."

"I appreciate that." And she truly did.

She rubbed her lips together, the slick feel of the gloss different from the balm she used to protect her lips from the cold of her trailer.

"Dress and shoes, and then I'd better get ready."

Willa followed her into the sewing room. Sutton handed her a pair of black lace underwear. They were delicate and probably expensive.

"I brought—"

"You're not wearing a pair of cotton granny panties under my dress. Put them on."

Willa shimmied them on under the robe while Sutton worked the dress off the form.

"Drop the robe and step in." Sutton's voice was clinical.

In a fit of modesty, Willa tucked an arm over her breasts, but the dress was up and covering her in seconds. Once zipped, the bodice was tight in a way that made her feel more confident than uncomfortable.

"Check yourself out."

Willa sidled over to a floor-length mirror. She looked . . . pretty. Really pretty. The green brought out the new reddish highlights in her hair. She spun. After wearing jeans and coveralls for so long, the airy skirt against her legs felt decadent and revived memories of high school dances.

"Shoes." Sutton held up two different styles. A pair of high heels in metallic gold and matte gold ballet flats. "I wasn't sure how comfortable you'd be in heels."

"The flats would be smarter." Yet, when she reached out, she took the heels like a raccoon unable to pass over a shiny object. "I'll try on the heels for fun."

"Sure. You decide while I get ready. The boys will be here in a half hour."

Willa waited until she was alone to slip her feet into the high heels. She held on to the dress form's shoulder for balance. Her legs were transformed. They were long and lean and sexy. Imagining the look on Jackson's face was enough to tip the scales. Yes, they'd had sex, but they'd never been out together, and maybe it was silly, but she wanted their first date to be special. The night felt like the start of something important.

She let go and took a few steps, her ankles wobbling a little. If Cinderella could cram her foot into an unbendable glass slipper, then surely Willa could manage an evening in a pair of heels.

She practiced walking up and down the hallway and through the den until she was confident she wouldn't do a face-plant. Sutton emerged from her bedroom in a form-fitting dark blue dress with subtle sparkles in the fabric. The neckline was high, but when she turned, her back was exposed nearly to her waist. With her hair pinned in a twist, she was subtly sophisticated in a way that had to do with more than just a dress. But for tonight at least, Willa was her equal.

The sound of a car engine drew Sutton to the front window where she barked a laugh. Willa joined her. They had driven separately, Wyatt in an old Dodge two-door Dart that looked cheap next to Jackson's cherished Mustang. Of course, as soon as Wyatt finished restoring his dream car, he would drive the Plymouth Hemicuda forever. The Abbott brothers were nothing if not committed and faithful to their cars.

They parked along the edge of the driveway and emerged simultaneously, meeting between their cars and walking up the drive shoulder to shoulder. While they were fraternal twins and had different coloring, their build was identical as was the way they moved, graceful and almost feline. There was no denying which brother was the most compelling though.

She couldn't take her eyes off Jackson. He had shed his customary coveralls and jeans in favor of a dark suit. His white shirt emphasized his tanned skin, and his tie was a plain black. It was simple, yet fit him like it was custom made. He'd bought it for his father's funeral. At the time, she'd tried—and failed—not to notice how handsome he'd looked that day. Now, she didn't have to battle the inappropriateness of her feelings.

Wyatt had similar dark slacks on, but no jacket, a white shirt, and a green tartan tie that was off-kilter. Not bothering with the doorbell, Wyatt stepped inside. His grin froze and took on shades of shock when he met her gaze. Jackson stepped in behind him, his expression serious and unchanging upon seeing her.

A pang of uncertainty had her ankles and knees wobbling. Was it too late to change into flats?

Sutton looped her arm through Wyatt's. "Doesn't Willa look amazing?"

"Jesus! I mean, yes. I'm just . . . you're just . . ." An easiness returned to his smile. "You look really pretty, Willa. Weird seeing you without your hat though. You sure you don't have it stashed somewhere?"

His teasing made things seem not so foreign. "Yeah, in my underwear. I'll whip it out later."

"Are you seriously planning to wear that tie?" Sutton tugged on the length of tartan, her voice disbelieving.

"Apparently not. You got something better?" He flipped the ends of the tie and grinned even wider.

"Come on back." She swept out and he followed, leaving an expanding discomfort between her and Jackson.

Willa wasn't sure what she'd expected, but a smile or even a compliment would go a long way toward soothing her nerves. She decided to throw him a bone. "You look nice."

He smoothed one lapel of his jacket. "It's from Pop's funeral." His voice was rougher than normal.

"I know."

"It's the only suit I own."

"I figured. You still look nice."

Even a tepid *so do you* would have been welcome, but he didn't respond.

His reaction, or lack of, squashed her burgeoning excitement, and all she wanted to do was run like Cinderella before she even got a chance to go to the ball. Actually, to the hell with running, Prince Charming was going to get a piece of her mind. "Was this a mistake? If you don't want to be seen with me then—"

Chapter Seventeen

"Stop." The simple word was all he could manage at the moment. Shock had zapped his heart into a rhythm that left him feeling like he'd crested a hill too fast in his Mustang. Scary and exhilarating.

She didn't look like his Willa. Not the girl who worked by his side and made him laugh and was his constant. Not even the Willa he'd discovered in his bed. She was a woman with an intimidating sophistication. He'd always felt more experienced and in control of whatever they were doing. For the first time, he wondered what a woman like her was doing with a grease monkey like him.

His gaze didn't know where to land. On sexily tousled hair that begged for his hands while he kissed all the gloss off her pink lips. On vulnerable eyes that had been outlined and mascaraed to emphasize the brown and gold. On the narrowness of her shoulders or her delicate-looking collarbones or her breasts . . .

Lord help him but the strapless dress did something amazing to her curves. A primal need fired inside of him. He wanted to skip the stupid party and take her somewhere private. He wanted to run his hands under the skirt, peel the top down, and feast. He'd keep her in bed all night, all week—hell, all year. It was his New Year's resolution.

His legendary control was close to breaking. What was it about her? Or was it everything about her? Engines with all their moving parts and complications were easier to figure out.

She propped her hands on her hips and the corner of her mouth pulled back in a look he recognized as the precursor for one of her barbs.

"What is your problem, Jackson Abbott? It's not like this was a blind date. In fact, you've seen more of me than . . . anyone, actually. If you don't like it, then you can kiss my you-know-what at midnight."

He almost smiled. Her makeup and hair might be more stylish and her body rocking in the bombshell dress, but inside she was most definitely still his Willa.

He stepped closer. She was almost as tall as he was. His gaze finally made it past her hips to skim her long legs and down to a pair of ridiculously high heels. His imagination went wild with possibilities. "My problem is that I'm a jackass."

She blinked, her mouth opening then snapping shut. When she spoke, her voice had softened into a whisper. "Not usually."

"An idiot?"

"Maybe a little." She glanced down and back up at him through her lashes. The gentle, flirtatious look hit him like a punch. This time his heart kicked like he might require someone to call 911. "Do I clean up good?"

He knew what she wanted to hear and later, in the dark solitude of his bed, he'd tell her and, even better, show her. But, for now, he tempered his response, hoping to get a rise out of her. "Not bad."

She stepped forward and punched his arm. It might

have stung if she hadn't tipped to the side as her fist made contact. Her eyes popped wide and a little huff escaped. With reaction times honed on the racetrack, he wrapped his arm around her waist, bringing her flush with his body.

"You sure you know how to operate those shoes?" This time he couldn't keep the smile off his face.

"They don't require a license. And I was doing fine until you showed up."

Her admission made him feel slightly better. He wasn't the only one who was off balance. Her body notched into his perfectly with the added inches the heels lent her. His focus dropped from her sparking eyes to her mouth. Maybe he'd kiss the gloss off them right now. His lips hovered an inch from hers. So close he could feel the ramp-up of her breathing. Or was that his breathing spinning out of control?

"You two ready? Oh, sorry." Wyatt strolled into the den, his hands shoved inside his pockets, his tartan suit tie replaced by a blue and gray striped bow tie. He didn't look sorry at all. In fact, he looked like he was ready to burst into laughter.

Jackson supposed this was payback for the time he'd nearly walked in on him and Sutton. He'd snuck out and let them get on with it though. Didn't look like Wyatt was going to be as polite.

"You look like an effing waiter," Jackson said as he stepped away from Willa. Except he didn't completely release her, only slipped his hand around hers and squeezed.

"I know, but Sutton thinks I look hot, right, darlin'?"

Sutton joined them, a wrap around her shoulders and a clutch tucked under her arm. Wyatt pulled at his collar and slipped his arm around her.

"You know it, babe." Even though her smile was directed toward Wyatt, Jackson could feel the radiating happiness.

"That's all that matters." Wyatt kissed her nose. "Ready to roll?"

Jackson opened the car door, and Willa slipped in with a smile that struck him as very un-Willa-like. It held different sorts of secrets. Sexy ones. The silence between them held a new quality. It wasn't the comfortable silence they enjoyed in the shop. Working together under the hood of a vehicle didn't require them to speak with words. They could read one another's minds.

He had no clue what she was thinking right now. Ever since they'd had sex . . . No, even before. Ever since he'd let himself see her as more than a mechanic, he'd wandered in blind confusion where she was concerned.

Her face was turned toward the passenger window, and her hands were knitted together on her lap, the set of her bare shoulders tense. She acted more like she was waiting for a dentist appointment than headed to a party.

"If it's not fun, we can leave," he said.

"I've never been to a New Year's Eve party." She huffed a laugh. "I've never been to anything fancier than a kegger right out of high school. Sutton's friends are doctors and lawyers and professors. It doesn't matter what I wear, they'll know I don't belong."

He laughed, and she shot around to face him, the slightly pissed-off expression much more familiar.

"Are you laughing at me?"

"No. Yes." He shook his head and glanced at her out of the corner of his eye. "You've probably read more books than everyone at this party put together. We don't call you Encyclopedia Brown at the shop ironically. You know something about everything. I'm the one who should be worried."

"How do you mean?"

"I can talk cars and racing all night long. How far is that going to get me with this crowd?"

"It got you pretty far with me." A flirty promise was in her voice, and he whipped his head around.

"Yeah, well, you're special." He tightened his hands on the wheel and stared at the tail end of Wyatt's car.

"Am I?" she whispered. She brushed the sleeve of his jacket, and although it was impossible, the touch of her fingertips seemed to burn through the layers of fabric to leave his skin tingly.

The moment tipped into a potent intimacy. He wanted to pull over and show her how special she was to him, but he didn't let himself. A dark part of him laughed at his attempt to control his feelings. The truth was deeper and more damaging. There was no "letting" himself do anything, it had happened. He had already fallen for her.

He was saved by their arrival at the Mize mansion. Every window blazed with light and the columns in front were wrapped in twinkly white lights. Cars lined the drive and street leading up to the house. Wyatt gestured out his car window in a follow-me gesture, and they bypassed the parked cars to twin spots near the front.

"It's so pretty," Willa said with her face pressed close to her window.

He turned the Mustang off and reached for her wrist before she could open her door and climb out. "You realize that Sutton's your friend now too."

Her smile held a hint of sadness. "I'm not sure what to do with a friend."

"You could try trusting them." His voice came out harsher than he intended.

Her eyes narrowed on him before she turned away and slid out. By the time he joined her, her face was bland and he couldn't tell if the flash was anger, suspicion, or a figment of his imagination.

After obtaining the information about her car registration from Gloria, he had made a resolution to keep it to himself, but he wasn't sure how long he'd be able to stay silent. The urge to confront her and excise the poison was growing every minute.

He pressed his lips together and offered her his arm. She looped hers through his. He had to steady her twice on their walk over the uneven cobbled driveway to the front door. Sutton opened the door and a swell of soft music and the buzz of conversation enveloped them.

Sutton's parents greeted people in the large foyer. A wide oak staircase rose to a second-floor landing, dominating the entry. A chandelier threw crystal-fractured light into the nooks and crannies. A dining room off to the left had a table covered in food and a buffet stocked with drinks and manned by a tuxedoed bartender. To the right was a great room with furniture pushed against the walls and people milling around.

Wyatt shook hands with Sutton's father. A quick whispered exchange passed between them and Wyatt's smile dropped.

Sutton hugged her parents and waved him and Willa closer. "This is Willa, and you probably remember Jackson, don't you, Daddy?"

While Jackson shook Judge Mize's hand, Sutton's mother gave Willa's cheek an air kiss then took her hands and held them up, examining her head to toe. "Lawsy, you certainly are doing Sutton's dress justice. Very pretty."

Her blush was obvious even through the makeup. "Thank you, ma'am. Sutton is amazing, but I'm sure you already know that." The sincerity and charm in the compliment turned Sutton's mother into Willa's champion right in front of him.

Sutton and Wyatt drifted to the side to talk to someone Jackson didn't know, their arms locked around one another. Jackson turned back to Judge Mize. "Thank you for inviting us, sir."

"Considering we're soon to be family, I hope we'll be seeing lots more of you. Is Mack coming?" He glanced over Jackson's shoulder.

"Later. For the meeting. Is Tarwater here?"

"Not yet." Troubles shadowed the judge's eyes. "I certainly understand the motivation to confront him. Lord knows, I've wanted to take Andrew behind the shed a time or two for how he treated Sutton, but have a care how you approach him. He's slippery."

That was a nice way to put it. "We'll try."

It was all he could promise. The combination of Mack, Wyatt, and Tarwater with the added specter of Ford's betrayal had the makings of a Molotov cocktail.

The judge nodded absently at Willa, but his focus was on the next arrivals, and Jackson drew Willa into the great room, scanning for Wyatt, but he was nowhere to be found. In fact, Jackson didn't recognize anyone. Crossing the river was like entering another world.

"What are you thinking about?" Obvious nerves had her fidgeting.

"I'm thinking how weird it is that I grew up a stone's throw from most of these people but I don't know them and they don't know me."

"Not even from the garage? I see Ms. Vera across the way." She smiled and gave a wave to a white-haired lady who looked vaguely familiar. He squinted in the woman's direction, and Willa laughed. "The Olds 442?"

"Ah, now I remember."

She turned until she was leaning against the wall between a couch and a painting of dogs on the hunt. "Do you see little car heads instead of people's faces? And instead of names, do you label people as a make and model? Like, there's Ford Taurus. I wonder how his mama, Toyota Corolla, is doing?"

He smiled and propped a shoulder on the wall, his back

to most of the room. The position put them close and lent a sense of solitude, however false. "Cars aren't inherited like hair color or eye color or build or something. They're an extension of a person's personality."

She rolled her eyes. "What does my POS say about my personality?"

He hesitated at grasping the opening she'd provided. What did it say that she'd taken a dead woman's name and car? "It says that you're desperate and scared and want help."

She straightened and turned to face him. The hardness in her eyes aged her years in a millisecond. "I'm doing fine, thank you very much."

God, she could turn as prickly as a blackberry patch, but the sweetness she protected was worth it. He reached for her cheek, but she jerked her head back. It didn't deter him. He slipped a hand around her nape and held fast, her hair tickling his wrist. "I didn't say you *need* help. You want it. I wish you'd let me help you do more than just survive."

Her neck relaxed and her head fell back, her lips parted slightly. This time he didn't resist and dropped his mouth to hers for a kiss, brief but sweet. He knew better than to take her yielding as a surrender, but maybe he'd won another skirmish.

Their eyes were still locked when Wyatt's voice cut between them. ". . . here he is, but I doubt he'll play."

Judge Mize probably wouldn't take kindly to Jackson punching his future son-in-law for being a pest. He turned his head and ground the single word out. "What?"

"You really don't want this ray of sunshine on your team anyway, do you, boys?"

Cade and Sawyer Fournette flanked Wyatt, and Jackson forced his jaw to relax even if a smile was beyond his ability at the moment.

"Do you two ever stop recruiting for your team?" He raised his eyebrows at Sawyer. "I thought your wife had strong-armed you into playing for Mississippi anyway."

"She did. But I put my foot down and told her I was playing for Cade this season."

"Don't lie. You begged her. Promised her all sort of favors to *let* you play for me." Cade's smile was sly.

Sawyer's arm came up behind Wyatt and he knuckle-punched Cade in the upper arm. Cade made an exaggerated *ow* sound and rubbed his biceps, while tossing a wink in Willa's direction.

"I'm Cade Fournette and this is my brother Sawyer. You a 'Sip or a swamp rat?"

"Swamp rat, I guess, but I've only lived here a couple of years."

"Willa is a mechanic in the shop," Wyatt said.

Sawyer whistled low. "I'll have to bring my truck in sometime. You're a sight prettier than these two."

"I'm a sight better mechanic too." Willa's voice held a familiar bite that skated between teasing and tart.

Sawyer tapped Cade's shoulder and caught his brother's eye behind Wyatt's back. "This is who you need." He returned his attention to Willa. "Do you play ball? We need some kickass women on the team. Monroe's heart isn't in it anymore."

"My heart's not in what?" Monroe Fournette slipped next to Cade and wrapped her arm around his waist. He pulled her into his side and nuzzled a kiss into her temple.

"Playing in the baseball league since Rachel was born," Cade said. "We're trying to talk Willa here into taking your place since I can't seem to convince these sorry Abbott boys to play."

"Don't let them bully you into playing," Monroe said to Willa. "You'd think they didn't have a business to run. Mother said Rachel is fine, by the way."

Cade's lips twitched, but his voice was all warm comfort. "Just like she was fine the last three times you called." He turned his attention to Willa and Jackson. "First time we're leaving the baby."

"That must be hard, but if she's with your mother, I'm sure she's fine," Willa said.

Monroe gave a small huff. "You don't know my mother, do you? Your dress is stunning, by the way." She effectively cut Willa out of the herd of Abbott and Fournette men.

"Heard a rumor from Regan," Sawyer said. "Is it true Ford sold his share of the garage?"

"Unfortunately, true." Jackson hated their family troubles were the talk of Cottonbloom, but it wasn't unexpected.

"To who?" Cade crossed his arms, an intimidating expression on his face.

Jackson and Wyatt had run in the same crowd in high school with Sawyer, the all-American good-old-boy. The three of them had shared many an illicit beer at parties out in the boonies. Cade had been older and forced to drop out of high school to work after their parents were killed by a drunk driver. Looking back, it must have been a hard time for all the Fournettes, but Sawyer wore his past lighter than his brother.

"We suspect to Tarwater," Jackson said softly after taking an inventory of ears around them.

Sawyer asked, "What's wrong with Ford?"

"He's looking to move north to Memphis." People may already be aware of Ford's gambling problem, but he was still an Abbott and Jackson's instinct was to protect him.

"Easy solution: buy Tarwater out." Cade spoke like a man used to wielding money and a lot of it if rumors were true.

"Doubt we could raise that much ready cash. We invested in substantial upgrades to the shop the past couple of years. Anyway, not sure Tarwater's motivation is all money." Jackson looked anywhere but at Wyatt, but by the way the Fournettes shifted, they'd heard all about Wyatt and Sutton.

Wyatt's jaw was set as if he were itching to go a round with the punching bag in the barn. "I can't say I'm sorry or regret how things turned out. I have Sutton and she's worth whatever grief Tarwater can cause us."

"Mack and I have your back." Jackson caught Wyatt's gaze, and his twin's shoulders lowered a couple of inches as the tension ebbed.

"If you need anything—advice on negotiations, a loan—you come on by Fournette Designs anytime." Cade held out a hand and Jackson shook it.

"Appreciate it." And Jackson did, but that didn't mean he'd ever take Cade up on the offer.

The Abbotts would ride out this storm like they had their mother's desertion, their pop's death, and all the trouble in between—together. Well, minus Ford this time.

The Fournettes ambled away and were pulled into other conversations. Monroe left after giving a Willa a small hug. Willa stayed motionless through the gesture.

"I'm going to find Sutton and keep a lookout for Tarwater and Mack. I'll text you." Wyatt weaved through the crowd until he disappeared out a door in the back.

"Monroe seemed nice." Willa's tone was distinctly suspicious.

"From the little I've been around her, she is nice. She and Regan, Sawyer's wife, were friends in high school and came to the occasional party. I didn't have much to do with them though."

"Them in particular, or girls in general?" She cocked her head.

"Most girls thought I was boring."

"Boring?" Her shock transmitted through the barked-out word.

He reached out to play with a piece of hair that had fallen over her forehead. "My life is cars. Most women find that boring. Didn't you accuse me of wanting to marry my Mustang?"

"Your life is more than cars. It's your brothers and your aunts." She glanced away, but unspoken words hung between them.

He took a risk. "And you."

Her throat muscles worked and she peeked at him from under her lashes. What he really wanted was to stare into her eyes and beyond to whatever she was hiding from him. He didn't like the gray between.

"Jackson, there's something—"

His phone dinged. He ignored it. "What?"

"Shouldn't you . . . ?" She pointed at his chest.

It dinged again. He slipped his phone out of the inner pocket of his jacket. Two texts from Wyatt.

Tarwater.

Mack too. Let's roll.

"It's time." The acceleration of adrenaline was eerily similar to how he felt at the starting line of a race.

"I'll be waiting." She squeezed his arm.

He gave her a nod and worked his way out of the great room and into a short hallway. They were meeting in the judge's office. He knocked once and opened the only door in the hall.

Tarwater half sat on the desk, a snake-oil-salesman smile on his face, texting. Wyatt took up the middle of the small room in a predatory loose-limbed stance, giving the impression that blood would be spilled.

Mack was planted next to the door, his feet set wide and his arms crossed over his chest. He hadn't bothered to dress for the party, his jeans and black ABBOTT GARAGE T-shirt in stark contrast to the rest of them. In fact, with his beard and frown, he looked more like a bouncer than a guest.

"Is that everyone, then? Ford's not gracing us with his presence?" Tarwater straightened and placed his phone on the desk at his hip.

Whether or not Tarwater knew Ford had hightailed out of Cottonbloom was a mystery, but Jackson had to assume his question was meant to bait them.

"Ford's not important. Not anymore," Jackson said.

Tarwater's smile grew in size and brightness. "I wondered when he was going to drop the glad tidings. I thought he might have told you at Christmas. That would have been quite the present."

Mack stepped forward. Jackson put his arm up like a guard rail. Mack stopped, but his voice carried a real threat. "I'm surprised you didn't sashay into the garage and tell us yourself. Seems to me that would have made your Christmas really special. But then again, you would've had to congratulate Wyatt and Sutton. They're engaged, you know."

"Congrats." Tarwater's smile was wiped clean, the word disingenuous. His phone vibrated, and he glanced down before flipping the phone to conceal the screen. He shrugged a smile back on his face, but it was smaller. "It's not my place to tell you boys anything."

"What do you mean?" Wyatt moved to Jackson's other side, putting the three brothers shoulder to shoulder and facing down Tarwater.

Tarwater's gaze darted to the door as if measuring the distance. The man shouldn't have put himself in such a vulnerable position, but then again, maybe he was counting on them to remain civil in Judge Mize's home. Considering Wyatt tackled Ford in the middle of a swanky fund-raiser at the country club earlier that fall, he really should know better.

"I was asked to keep quiet until my client decided to reveal themselves."

It took several beats for the meaning to change the course of Jackson's assumption. "You're not the buyer?"

Tarwater leaned farther back, his gaze sweeping from Wyatt to Jackson to Mack and back again. His laughter bordered on mocking. "What in tarnation would I do with a stake in a car garage? I pay men like you to fix things so I won't be bothered with it. Jesus."

"Then who the hell is it?" Mack growled out.

"The buyer is on the way. A new start for the new year?" Tarwater's barely veiled glee darkened the silence that gathered. Things had gone from bad to unpredictable, which in Jackson's opinion was almost worse.

More than anything, he wished Willa were with them to skewer Tarwater with her sarcasm. But she wasn't.

A soft knock at the door had them turning to face a new, unknown enemy. The handle turned and the door opened on a long squeak.

A woman was silhouetted in the doorway. She was tall, close to six feet in her heels. The light from the foyer chandelier made her fitted dress shimmer. Her dark hair brushed the thin shoulder straps of her red dress. Something about her struck Jackson as timeless, like one of the old-school stars in the movies their pop liked to watch on Sunday afternoons.

Wyatt stepped forward and pointed. "I remember you. From the gala. You and Ford and Tarwater were huddled up right before I—" He cleared his throat.

She stepped inside the room and closed the door. Her perfume stirred on the air, sweet but with a citrusy bite. "I was afraid you and Ford were going to kill each other. I'm glad neither of you drowned." Her smile was unexpectedly open and warm. "And I hear congratulations are in order."

Jackson and Wyatt exchanged a glance. Now that the buyer was revealed as a woman whose intentions were unknown, they might as well burn their game plan.

Wyatt shrugged and looked like Jackson felt, at a loss for what came next. "Thanks. I guess."

Mack took a step toward her, and she matched him with a step back, her hand playing with a silver locket on a delicate chain. "You've run into Wyatt and presumably know Ford rather well, but we've not met. Who are you?"

"Ella Boudreaux." She held out a hand. While her accent reflected a Southern birth, it wasn't as Cajun flavored as her name implied.

A long pause followed where Mack didn't do anything except look at her offering. Her hand took on a noticeable tremble, but she didn't drop it and try to gloss over the awkwardness. Jackson held his breath.

Finally, Mack engulfed her hand with his. "I won't lie and say it's nice to meet you, Mrs. Boudreaux."

"Ms. actually. I'm divorced."

"And may I ask why you decided to buy Ford's quarter of Abbott Brothers Garage and Restoration?" In contrast to the almost polite question, his voice was harsh.

"Because I can." Underneath the breeziness of her answer was the steel foundation of a challenge. "Could I have my hand back before you squeeze it off?"

Mack looked down like he was surprised their hands were still joined. He let go, flexing and fisting his hand at his side. She ran her hand down the curve of her hip as if wiping away his touch.

What did Ms. Ella Boudreaux want with a small-potatoes car garage? Imagining her on the shop floor with its noise and grease was laughable. While she didn't appear to be in need of money, her expensive-looking dress and heels and perfectly manicured nails could be a front. The smart thing would be to retreat and gather information.

Unfortunately, Mack's temper burned on the edge of control and chaos. He took another step forward and this time she held her ground. They were uncomfortably close. "Lady, my pop founded Abbott Garage. Built it up from nothing. It's my livelihood and my passion and we're going to have big problems if you plan to drag it down."

"Why would I spend good money on something I plan to drag down?"

"Because you can?" Mack threw her words back.

A flash of strong emotion—fear, anger?—was quickly replaced by serenity along with a small smile, but it seemed fake, like a pageant contestant in front of the judges. "I can assure you—all of you"—she made eye contact with Jackson and then Wyatt—"that I have no intention of doing you harm. In fact, you might find I possess rather helpful skills."

"I expect you to be a silent investor until I can gather the funds to buy you out."

"Do I seem like the silent type to you?" The humor leaned more good-natured than biting, but Mack's expression remained stony.

"Then we should expect you Monday morning?" A mocking smile twisted Mack's lips. "Are you good with a wrench?"

"Depends on what you mean?" Her voice was full of innocence even as she propped a hand on her hip, the vibe sultry. Mack's smile disappeared faster than a deer spotting a hunter.

"Selling it back to us would be in everyone's best interests," Mack said softly, but with an obvious threat still pulsing from him.

"Do you have the funds now?"

Mack's silence was answer enough.

"Maybe you'll end up thanking me one day."

"Never." Mack ground the word out between his teeth. He inched even closer, and Ella leaned backward although she didn't retreat. Mack sidestepped her, threw the door open, and stalked out. It bounced closed again.

Ella turned her attention to Jackson and Wyatt. "So I shouldn't expect a welcome sign my first day at the garage, huh?"

She was holding all the cards. Whether she was bluffing or not remained to be seen. "You're not actually planning to work at the garage, are you?" Jackson asked.

"I've found myself with an extraordinary amount of free time since my divorce."

Tarwater remained silent, but observed them like a Roman emperor in the Coliseum. How fast would this news travel? Faster than the river's current through Cottonbloom, no doubt.

"This isn't a game, lady. This is our livelihood." Wyatt took a step toward her and Tarwater made a move to keep them apart, his fist pressed into Wyatt's chest.

"Step off," Tarwater said.

"Why don't you fuck off?" Wyatt knocked Tarwater's hand off him.

"I never understood your low-class appeal." Tarwater shoved Wyatt's shoulder in a weak move. If his aim was to start a fight with a chance of survival, he should have punched Wyatt and run.

Wyatt inhaled sharply, a signal he was ready to pour gasoline on the Dumpster fire Mack had started with the confrontation.

"Andrew, no," Ella said sharply, with none of the tease and charm Jackson had assumed was natural.

When the situation didn't defuse, Jackson elbowed Wyatt and gave a little shake of his head while keeping his eyes on Ella. She was turning out to be as difficult to get a read on as Willa. And that was saying something.

"Let's go. Not the time or place, bro." Jackson grabbed Wyatt's forearm and maneuvered him to the door. They left Tarwater and Ella Boudreaux behind to probably exchange celebratory high fives.

Sutton and Willa waited at the foot of the stairs. His gaze locked on Willa.

The ramifications of what had transpired hit him in a rush. Everything was changing. Nothing would be the same. Their pop's death had caused a fissure that grew longer and wider by the day. Jackson's security in knowing who he was and where he fit into the world was on shaky ground.

He pushed Wyatt toward Sutton, absolving himself of taking care of his twin, and grabbed Willa up in a fierce hug. He wanted to sink into her and use her as his touchstone even as the sane part of him protested the foolishness. She wasn't secure. She wasn't even his. Not yet anyway.

"You wanna get out of here?" No way could he stay and make small talk and smile.

"Sure."

He let out a long breath before loosening his hold and taking her hand. The cold air brought with it a clearing of his head. He slipped off his jacket and draped it over her bare shoulders.

"I'm being selfish. You got all dressed up to go to a party and have fun and here I am dragging you out. We should go back and ring in the new year."

She put her arm around his neck. Her weight anchored him. "I didn't get all dressed up for a party; I got all dressed up for you."

The puffs of white between them ceased as if both of them had forgotten how to breathe. He shuddered in a lungful of air, the cold painful in his chest. Or maybe it was something else that hurt.

Afraid he'd mangle anything that came out of his mouth, he knitted his fingers between hers and led her toward the Mustang, taking care not to let his eagerness quicken his step too much. She wobbled in the heels on the uneven ground.

Once they were inside the car, the noise of the heater preempted any need for conversation, but an unspoken tension ratcheted up with every turn and curve. Changes were afoot between the two of them. Would she stick or run?

Chapter Eighteen

The intensity building in the car was like an unexploded bomb. Jackson made her feel invincible and vulnerable. It was enough to give her whiplash. She wiggled in the seat and pulled at the lapels of his jacket.

The road they traveled led to sex. They'd done it already. Multiple times in fact. But tonight felt different in a way she couldn't pinpoint. They were at a turning point, but she couldn't make out the signposts. The garage came into view through his headlights. He parked around the side, close to the barn.

Home.

The word came unbidden. She wasn't sure whether it was a response to the garage, the barn, or the man at her side. It had been so long since she'd truly belonged anywhere or with anyone.

She pushed the door open. Between the low-slung seat and her lack of experience walking in heels, working her way out was a challenge. He stood by the door, and she looked up. Her lungs squeezed at the sight of his tall, broad frame. His dimples carved furrows in his cheeks, and his husky laugh sped through her like a shot of liquor.

Sliding her hands into his, he pulled her out. Before she

could take a step toward the barn, he swept her into his arms. Her yelp was cut off by his lips. They were cold and soft and still curved into a smile.

Jackson Abbott was special. He'd been her crush since the first day she'd walked into Abbott Garage. She idealized him until she watched him struggle with his father's death. The pain he did his best to hide under a stoic mask had turned her crush into something muddled and complicated. But now everything was clear. She had fallen for him. Hard. Like Wile E. Coyote, she'd fallen off a cliff and left a Willa-shaped hole in the ground.

Had her fate been set before she'd even met him though? Had her past choices destroyed any chance she had with him? A bittersweetness had her burying her face in his neck, afraid he would guess the truth.

She loved him.

Somehow, he opened the barn door with her still in his arms, and River shot out to do her business. He left the door cracked for her return and weaved past the punching bag and the tarp-covered cars to the loft steps in the back.

On the cusp of a new year, the night teetered on a beginning or an ending.

Once inside, he put her down and his suit jacket fell from her shoulders to the floor. With callused fingertips, he traced the side of her neck and across her shoulder. Shivers passed through her, tightening her nipples and growing the ache in her belly that wasn't merely sexual. It was longing.

"You're beautiful."

Her first instinct was to deny, but in his eyes, she felt beautiful for the first time in a long time. Maybe forever.

"Thank you." She took hold of his tie and ran it through her fingers. "You're awfully handsome too."

"I know it's not a typical dude line, but I want to slip into something more comfortable. Apparently, I've put on some weight since Pop's funeral." He loosened the tie, pulled it over his head, and unbuttoned the top buttons of the dress shirt.

Now he mentioned it, she couldn't help but notice how tight the shirt was along his shoulders. Her gaze trailed lower. And how his butt and thighs were outlined in the pants. What he'd put on was all muscle.

"It's all the punching you do because of Ford." She ran her hand over his biceps, feeling it twitch under her touch.

"I haven't punched Ford one time. Not even when we were kids. I left that to Wyatt."

"Not the actual Ford, but the bag in the barn. It was every day for three months after your pop died. And then again the last month and a half." How long would it take to get him out of his shirt?

"You noticed?" The edge of wonder in his voice brought her gaze up to meet his. His eyes reminded her of his father's. More depth and more complicated than they first appeared. But mostly, they were kind eyes.

Beginnings . . . endings . . . Either way, why not finally be honest? "Of course, I noticed. I notice everything about you, always have. From the day I started, I had a huge crush on you, but it seemed safe."

He put his hands on her waist and walked her backward. She didn't fight him or ask him where they were going. She wanted him with an urgency that scared her.

"I'm a fool for not noticing you sooner."

The back of her knees hit his mattress. "I did my best to make sure you didn't. It's too . . . complicated."

"You make it sound like a bad thing." He wrapped a hand around her nape and massaged. She tilted her head back into his touch. Everything he did to her felt amazing, and it was about to get even better. Case in point, while his hand turned her neck to taffy, he traced the neckline of her bodice. "This dress needs a warning label."

"Something like 'may cause spontaneous combustion in men's underwear'?"

His laugh charged all the tiny nerve endings in her body.

She touched the place where his dimples had flashed. "I used to try to get you to smile, even for a second, so I could see these."

"You were obviously desperate." His voice was self-deprecating in a way that made him even sexier in her eyes.

"I was obsessed. Day and night. Even in my dreams."

"As much as I want to rip this dress off you, Sutton would kill me." He pulled her closer and worked the zipper. The fabric sagged. "Tell me about these dreams."

"Some were very, very naughty."

"But some weren't?" How did he cut straight to the heart?

She didn't want her nightmares to intrude on the moment. The ones where he discovered the truth and hated her. Or she had to leave him behind. Or Derrick appeared and hurt him.

"Some weren't." She stared into his eyes, and he seemed to understand her fears. Or maybe that was what she wanted to see. Forgiveness.

He pushed the dress over her hips to puddle at their feet. She forced her hands to stay down. Standing there in only a pair of heels and a lace thong, her heart ripped from its protective cage, she was exposed in every way.

"I've dreamed about you too." He worked his shirt buttons open, his gaze on her breasts. His heat and desire would have been apparent even without the display in his pants.

She didn't second-guess herself and laid her hand against the length of him. His hips bucked. He was even bigger and harder than last time.

"What did you dream about?" she asked.

"That you were going down on me in the middle of the garage. When I saw you the next morning, I was sure you'd know, but everything was normal. Except, I kept having dreams."

She was glad not to be alone in her nightly torment. And if it was in her power to make his dreams come true, shouldn't she try? She sat on the edge of the mattress, grabbed his hips, and pulled him close. Going purely on instinct and what she'd read, she ran her mouth over his cloth-covered erection.

"What are you doing?" Even as he asked, he speared his hands into her hair and held her fast.

"Making your dreams come true. Or one dream, at least." Her voice was muffled against his pants. He undid them, and she helped push them down. His underwear followed to sag low on his thighs. His shirt hung open, exposing a muscled line of his chest, dark hair in contrast to the pristine white.

There was something decadent about coming together half clothed. It wasn't neat and tidy, and she appreciated messy. Even more, she was turned on by it. Rolling her hips on the bed didn't appease her need. Only one thing would. She took hold of him at the base and licked across the tip. Not sure what to expect, she savored the taste of him and explored the shape of him with her tongue.

"Quit teasing me, woman."

The growl in his voice gave her the confidence to take him in her mouth and hollow her cheeks. A sound of pain-pleasure rumbled from his chest, but his hands in her hair held her fast. While still working him in and out of her mouth, she glanced up and stilled. He watched her with an intensity that veered the moment from playful to serious.

"Are you okay?" she asked.

He replied by pushing her to lie back on the bed with

his torso. She scooched farther up on the bed and welcomed his weight between her legs. He ran a hand down her calf and slipped the shoe off, massaging the arch of her foot. He did the same with her other foot. His touch was both a relief and a pleasure. She squirmed like River getting a scratch behind the ears, wanting more.

His chest hair sent tingles spiraling through her, gathering between her legs. All that stood between them was a thin layer of lace. If she pulled the fabric aside, he could be inside of her in a heartbeat.

Her need veered frantic. She was empty in so many ways, but he could fill her. She slipped a hand between them and shifted the fabric. The hard length of him slipped along her folds, but didn't press for entrance. She raised her hips, trying to beg without words.

He pressed his lips against her temple. "What are you doing?"

Frustration was adding fuel to her need. "What do you think I'm doing, Captain Oblivious?"

His rocky laugh was sheer beauty and her focus shifted. Tilting her face, she could see half his smile and one dimple. She kissed his cheek. Being the cause of his laughter and happiness meant more than she could even express.

He pushed off to stand at the side of the bed. The loss of him felt more than physical. Even this small distance between them made her heart ache.

He finished undressing and knelt between her legs. "I don't want it to be over so soon."

She tensed, her heart picking up speed, the pounding like white noise in her ears. She didn't want it to be over *ever*.

Before she could put the wealth of feelings into words, he continued. "And if I'm inside you, I won't last."

Sex. He was talking about sex.

"Scooch back on the pillows."

She didn't argue or question him. Her nerves were too raw. Sure he could see everything she couldn't put into words on her face, she lay back on the pillows and felt as vulnerable as a car that had been stripped to its chassis.

But he didn't call her out. Instead he came back over her and kissed her. A carnal kiss full of promises of pleasure but nothing more. Still, it worked a languorous magic, sugaring her limbs and making her forget her worries about tomorrow. She would live in the moment with him.

The kiss went on and on, their tongues playing, their teeth nipping, their lips tugging. She was breathless by the time he moved south to perform a similar alchemy on her nipples. While his mouth worked one, his fingers rolled and pinched the other, until one need smothered any other thought.

She pushed his shoulders down, ignoring his soft laugh. Instead of ripping her panties off, he ran a finger down the center of the lace, but she was in no mood to be teased or to go slow. She was ready to detonate.

She hooked a finger around the cloth, pulled it aside, and lifted her hips. "Please, Jackson."

Later, no doubt, she'd be mortified by her begging, but he didn't seem bothered. In fact, just the opposite. He scooped his hands under her bare bottom and squeezed, raising her another inch and tilting her. His earlier humor was gone and he looked . . . hungry.

"I've been wanting to do this for a long time, baby."

At the first swipe of his tongue, her eyes closed. Pleasure streaked all the way to her toes, and fingertips, and scalp, but mostly it was centered between her legs.

She wanted it to last forever, but she'd been on the edge for too long already and a slight nip of his teeth sent her careening into an orgasm so intense her world narrowed to the two of them and nothing else. She bit her bottom lip and turned her face into the pillow to keep from saying something she'd regret.

Before she'd recovered, he got rid of her panties and pushed inside of her. The stretch of her already sensitive body sent a shock wave rolling through her. Wrapping his hands around her thighs and opening her, he muttered a curse and pumped, long and hard, on his knees.

She pushed against the headboard to keep from moving up the bed with every strong thrust. With a roar, he held himself deep and pulsed inside of her. She tightened her muscles around him, wanting to give him everything she could.

His grip on her thighs loosened, and too soon, he pulled out of her. He disposed of a condom she hadn't even realized he'd put on and hadn't thought to ask for. At least one of them had been able to maintain rational thought.

He gathered her close and pulled the cover over them. "Happy New Year."

She smiled and kissed him on the mouth. "You too."

He played in her hair as she traced the ridge of his back muscles under his smooth skin. Troubles were waiting outside the door, but for now, they were safe.

"Are you making a resolution?" He ran his hand from her hair down her spine to cup her bottom.

Her breathing quickened. Was that all it took to get her motor running again?

Distracted, she said, "Haven't thought about it. Are you?"

"I'm going to tell the truth no matter what."

The tension flipped as fast as a coin toss from sexual to defensive. She pulled back, but his hand kept them pressed together at the hips. "Have you been lying?"

"Not lying. But omitting some truths."

What was happening? She couldn't think with him so

close. She pushed at his chest, sat up, and pulled the cover around her.

"What truths?"

He propped himself up, the sheet riding low on his hips. "Truth number one: I love you."

It took a long second for the words to penetrate. He loved her? Everything inside of her took flight. She opened her mouth, then closed it. His brows rose at her silence as if daring her to argue. His defiance took the sentimentality out of the confession.

He demanded the truth.

"I love you too," she whispered.

The smile he gave her was the one she had only seen at the end of a well-executed project. It didn't matter that he loved her if lies still lived between them like poisonous mushrooms in marshy ground. He moved closer, but she drew away. His smile darkened.

"There's something else I need to tell you. About my past." She pulled the cover tighter around her, feeling more exposed than she had been naked with his mouth on her.

"Is it worse than what you've already told me?"

"I don't know. Maybe. The other stuff was sort of out of my control."

"I'm glad you can admit that much at least. It wasn't your fault either."

"Yeah, well, I wouldn't go that far, but anyway . . . Willa Brown isn't my real name."

"What is it?" His voice was calm and when she forced herself to meet his gaze, no surprise or shock masked his face.

"It's Willa Buchanan. Wilhelmina, to be exact. My dad's 'Buck' Buchanan. My POS car was my grandmother's. She had told me she was going to give me the car, but got sick with dementia and went into a home. When I needed to get out of town fast, I stole it."

"Wilhelmina Buchanan." He huffed a laugh. "You were named after your grandmother."

"Yeah." She fell back into the pillows, feeling like she could float away. Everything. He knew everything. "Do you still love me?"

"Of course. I knew you had to have had your reasons for taking the car." He leaned in and kissed her.

Instead of getting lost in the sensation, her mind sifted through their conversation trying to pinpoint what was bothering her.

She turned her head to break the kiss off. "Hang on. How did you know I was named after my grandmother?"

"I didn't. Not until tonight."

"Yeah, but still, how did you put that together?"

"Lucky guess?" He tried to reinitiate their kiss.

"What about your resolution to tell the truth?" she asked against his lips.

He pulled back a few inches and sighed, his mouth thinning. "I asked Gloria down at the station to run your plates."

"When?" Her lips felt shot with Novocain.

"Does it matter?"

"Was it before or after we slept together?"

The fact he fought himself on the answer was enough. "After," he finally said.

"Why didn't you say something?"

"Because I decided it didn't matter. Who you were back then doesn't matter."

The lie and betrayal cut deep even though she'd lived lies and told lies for so long, she had no right to outrage. But Jackson was supposed to be better. Better than her.

She scrambled out of bed, turned her back to him, and

shimmied the dress back on, ripping a layer of delicate fabric in her rough handling. Another beautiful thing destroyed. Not bothering with her underwear, she picked up her heels but didn't slip them on. They would only slow her down.

Jackson was up and dressing too, but he was slower, lacking her urgency. She was almost to the door when she realized what he already knew. She had no way to escape.

Her car was at Sutton's, but the Mustang's keys were lying on the table. Taking his precious car would be the final rending of their relationship. He would never forgive her. She might as well go out like a true renegade.

She grabbed the keys and skipped down the loft stairs. River was curled up on the couch and stretched herself up when Willa approached. She couldn't take a dog with her. Her future was too shaky. No matter what, though, the Abbotts would take care of River.

She heard the door at the top of the steps open. She kissed the top of River's head, tears blurring her vision, and ran.

The grass was cold and damp, and mist hung around her ankles. It was like one of her gothic romances, but she was no Jane Erye. She had more in common with the dastardly Rochester. She was shivering by the time she reached his Mustang. She slipped behind the wheel. It took two tries to get the keys in the ignition. The engine cranked with a roar. Jackson was outlined by the red brake lights, ghostly in the swirling mist.

Tears blurred her vision, but she blinked them away as much as she could. Later. She could cry later. Now, she needed to get gone.

She hit the parish road with a squeal of tires. Jackson would hate her for that alone. She didn't have much time. He would grab a spare car from the garage and follow her.

She pressed the pedal to the floorboard. More cars than she'd expected were out because of New Year's, and she got caught behind a slow car on the parish road.

Checking the rearview mirror, she imagined the distant headlights meant Jackson was bearing down on her like an avenging angel. She punched the accelerator and the Mustang leaped like the horse it was named after, passing the car with little effort.

She turned onto Sutton's street. The houses slumbered. Wyatt's car was still gone. They were either still partying or spending the night at her parents'. She parked the Mustang and stashed the keys on the visor. Her shoes were in the passenger seat. She didn't need them where she was headed.

Barefoot, she was halfway to her car when she had second thoughts, not about the shoes, but the keys. Not only would the visor be the most obvious place for them, but someone else could steal the car. Not likely maybe, but it would break Jackson's heart.

Would her leaving Cottonbloom break his heart? She hesitated with her hand on the Mustang's door. Did he really love her? She scrubbed a hand over her face. Later, maybe later, it would all make sense.

She moved his keys from the visor to under the seat, hoping it would slow him down. She cranked her car and prayed it would start and get her where she needed to go. She pulled out of Sutton's driveway with a grinding of gears and squeak of brakes. Her car in comparison with Jackson's really said it all.

One of them had their life together and one of them didn't really have a life at all.

She made it to Country Aire in record time. Booming bass music came from one trailer, and people spilled outside to huddle around a fire pit, still celebrating. The smoky air rocketed her back to days of hot dogs on sticks and s'mores. Time had a way of softening the rough edges of her memories like a river smoothing a stone.

But her life hadn't been idyllic back then. A mother lost forever. A father who was often at work. A stepmother whom she viewed as competition for her father's attention and love. She shook her childhood away while she changed into jeans and a T-shirt. None of that was important.

Pack. She needed to pack up and move on. If she'd done this weeks ago, she could have avoided the pain. But through the cracks of her heart, other memories seeped out. Jackson's eyes, sad but offering absolution, as she'd poured out her shame. His gentleness with her in bed and out. Taking care of her and River when she'd been too proud to ask for help.

He wasn't perfect. He was stubborn as a donkey and as serious as an undertaker. His black-and-white attitude sometimes made him intractable, but he was willing to forgive his mother and give her a second chance. Not only that but he'd waded through all Willa's grayness and still loved her.

He *loved* her, and she loved him. The acceptance swept from her heart and through her body like a gentle wave, uncovering the truth that had been etched there for a long time and only now was truly believed. Whether she saw herself as deserving or not didn't change the facts.

And here she was running away from the best thing to ever happen to her because it had gotten complicated and difficult like the rest of life. But that was just . . . life. Hard as hell and tragic and horrible, interspersed with joy and laughter and love. Maybe the trick was making sure the joy outweighed the tragic.

She wouldn't be surprised to see a lightbulb hovering over her head. Or Oprah giving her an ironic handclap for her aha moment.

She'd told Sutton no one could help her, but that wasn't

true. She could help herself. She was tired of hiding and even more so of running. Maybe things with Jackson were destroyed beyond repair; maybe they weren't. But the only way they stood a chance of moving forward together was if she stopped, turned around, and faced her past.

The decision felt inevitable, as if the road had led to this moment since she'd landed in Cottonbloom and Abbott Garage. She looked around the trailer, but not with the resignation she'd battled earlier.

She swung the straps of the duffel over her shoulder, but left everything else and locked the door behind her. She didn't want anyone stealing her library books. She would be back, one way or another, to settle things.

Chapter Nineteen

Jackson ran to the middle of the road and watched the tail-lights of his Mustang fade. River was on his heels, her bark interspersed with sad-sounding whines. He yelled the one curse word that would have gotten his mouth washed out with soap as a kid. It echoed in the still night. Willa had disappeared. Maybe forever.

"What's going on?" Mack's voice was sleepy. "Was that your precious car spitting rocks down the road?"

The cold seeped into Jackson's feet along with the pain of sharp gravel. He stuck his hands into the pockets of his jeans and jogged to Mack's front door.

"Willa took off in my Mustang."

Mack jerked his head toward the door, and Jackson followed. "Gone for good?"

"Hell if I know." His usually even temper was rocky and volatile. He wanted to hit someone. Too bad Ford wasn't available. A dark humor welled out of his anger and hurt. Willa would have thought that was funny.

"We could call the sheriff."

"I'm not going to have her arrested, for goodness sake. I love her."

"I know, but I wasn't sure if you loved your car more."

Mack's lips twitched. Even if it wasn't a real smile, Jackson was glad to see the evening's events hadn't sent Mack spiraling into a funk. "You have any ideas where she went?"

"A guess? Back to her trailer to pack up. After that, I don't know. Somewhere she can disappear."

"If she's packing up her life, then we should be able to catch her. I'll put on some pants." Mack retreated to his bedroom. His voice drifted out. "You want to go back to the loft for shoes or borrow a pair of mine?"

Jackson leaned in the bedroom doorway. Mack was pulling on a sweatshirt. The room had been their pop's before Mack had taken over. He'd put his stamp on the room and the house, just as he had the garage, but much remained of their childhood. One bedroom still housed the bunk beds Jackson and Wyatt had shared.

A framed picture of all the brothers plus their pop was hanging on the wall. They were younger back then, their current troubles not reflected on their faces, but they were there, growing like a cancer under the surface of their smiles.

Mack tossed him boots and a pair of socks. "Don't want your foot fungus."

"Har-har." Urgency squatted on his chest and he slipped them on while stumbling his way to the door. River was waiting on the porch and jumped into Mack's truck before Jackson could stop her. "You mind?"

"Nah. She can ride along." Mack ruffled the dog's head.

Jackson had a feeling Willa kept a bag packed and leaving would be a matter of minutes, not hours. His impatience must have bled into the cab, because Mack drove fast.

"What do you think Pop would've said about Ford selling his share to an outsider if he was alive?" Mack asked.

Jackson was grateful to transfer his worries, however temporary. "I don't think Ford would have sold if Pop had lived. Even though he didn't want the life Pop built, Ford loved him and wanted to make him proud."

The radio was off, but the heater and the tires on the road filled the gaps.

"What does Ella Boudreaux want?" Mack asked softly.

"My girlfriend stole my car and ran off in the middle of the night. You think I understand women?"

Mack's laugh settled like a security blanket, and Jackson couldn't help but join him. Maybe they'd be all right after all. After their laughter dwindled, Jackson said, "Look, Ella Boudreaux can't be worse than Tarwater, can she? She might even be a sight better than Ford. Once she gets the lay of the land, hopefully, she'll stay out of our hair until we raise the money to buy her out."

"We can hope." Mack turned into Country Aire Trailer Park, and Jackson braced a hand on the dash and one on the door handle, ready to jump out. But her trailer was dark, and there was no sign of his car. He didn't need to bang on the door to know she wasn't there. A feeling of abandonment was stamped on the place.

He made himself get out and check anyway. River followed him and scratched at the front door. Jackson tried the knob but it was locked. He cupped his hands and looked through the window, but it was too shadowy to make anything out.

"Here." Mack tapped him on the shoulder.

Jackson glanced over to see the shaft of a flashlight. He clicked it on and shined it through the window. The inside was in disarray, but everything wasn't gone. He saw clothes on the small couch and pots in the kitchen area. He moved to a back window and scanned the circle of light around her tiny bedroom, passing over a stack of books.

He highlighted the books again and squinted. Library books. His rush of relief weakened his knees, and he turned to lean against the dingy white plastic siding.

"What is it?" Mack asked. "What'd you see?"

"She's not gone for good. She's coming back."

"How do you know?"

"She would never leave without returning her library books."

"It is so weird that you know that." Mack gave a little shake of his head. "Then where is she?"

Where would she go? She wouldn't want to add to Marigold's troubles. Sutton? He couldn't think of anyone else.

He pulled out his phone and hit Wyatt's number. He answered on the third ring. "Is it Mack?"

He glanced at their older brother. Apparently, Jackson hadn't been the only one worried about Mack's state of mind after the revelations of the evening. "Mack's fine and with me, actually. It's Willa. She's run off. I thought she might have called Sutton."

"Hang on. Sutton's down the hall." Fabric rustled for several seconds before low voices sounded, too faint to understand. Wyatt came back on the line. "No word from her. You got a plan?"

"I think she'll be back. Eventually. I could wait for her or . . ."

"Or what?"

"The only other place I can imagine she went was home."

"The loft?" His confusion was understandable.

"No. Home to see her father."

"Did she finally come clean?"

"Sort of." No need to call out his own stupidity on the phone. He already wanted to kick his own butt for not giving her the time she needed to tell him the truth. "The car she drives belonged to her grandmother. Registered in Claiborne Parish. Her real name is Wilhelmina Buchanan. Her dad runs a garage. Shouldn't be hard to track down."

"Swing by and pick me up at the Mizes' place." He disconnected.

Mack had heard his half of the conversation. "We're headed to Claiborne Parish?"

Jackson whistled for River. She came trotting out of the darkness of the field behind the trailers. "You don't have to come."

The look Mack sent him was of the are-you-effing-kidding-me variety. "Are we getting Wyatt on our way?"

"Yep. The Mize place."

River jumped into the cab and hopped into the backseat to curl up behind Jackson. The town was silent and so were they. Wyatt waited at the edge of the driveway, stamping his feet and still in slacks and his dress shirt, although it was untucked and he'd lost the bow tie.

He climbed in the back with River, shoving her over so he could sit in the middle, his arms draped over the two front seats. "I should've called shotgun on the phone."

His grin was infectious, and lessened the weight on Jackson's chest. "I can't believe the Judge put you in separate rooms."

A twist of sourness crossed his face. "Right? When I tried to sneak in her room earlier, she kicked me out. Can you believe it?"

"I would not want to be caught with my pants literally down in Sutton's bed by her daddy. Talk about awkward," Mack said.

They settled in for the long ride, their conversation drying up as they took turns driving and resting. Finally, Jackson ended up behind the wheel. He was too wound up to take his turn and pretend to close his eyes. His brothers slept, Mack's soft snores keeping time. River whined and laid her head on the center console.

Jackson scratched behind her ears and whispered, "We'll find her and bring her home. Promise, girl." If only he felt as confident inside as he sounded. The more miles the truck ate up, the more he was convinced he'd dragged his brothers on a snipe hunt.

Dawn splashed color across the sky. Dark pink and orange chased away the purple. In the days after their pop had died, he'd been up to watch the sun rise more mornings than not. Sleep had become that elusive. He wasn't sure when he'd started sleeping well again, but it had been months since he'd been awake at dawn. Time marched on and scars formed over old wounds.

He shook Mack awake when they hit the parish limits sign. After a yawn and stretch, Mack grabbed his phone and typed. "Buchanan, right?"

"Right."

"Buck's Garage sounds promising. Owner is . . ." A pause. "Mike Buchanan."

"Directions?"

Mack guided him through a typical downtown and across double railroad tracks. The bump woke Wyatt who rubbed his face and sat up between the seats.

The garage was within walking distance of downtown. Jackson pulled into the parking lot. It was deserted.

"Holiday. Everyone is off." Wyatt's voice was rough from sleep.

"Let me see if his home address is listed." Mack typed on his phone.

Jackson's doubts flourished with the wait. "She's not even here. I dragged you guys up here for no good reason."

Wyatt squeezed his shoulder. "Even the possibility of tracking her down is good enough reason for me. We all care about Willa, you doofus."

"Got it," Mack said.

Jackson followed the twists and turns into a solidly middle-class neighborhood that was straight out of an old fifties sitcom. Play sets were in backyards and yards were landscaped.

He parked across the street from the house in question. Nothing moved, but a truck with BUCK'S GARAGE stenciled on the tailgate and doors was parked in front of a closed garage door. No sign of his Mustang or Willa.

He checked the clock. Not even eight in the morning. After discussing options, they headed back toward town for a to-go breakfast of ham biscuits and coffee from a fast food restaurant and settled back across the street to stake out the house.

Just as the voice in his head calling him an idiot was getting too loud to ignore, a figure came into view in the rearview mirror. Jackson turned to get a better look. Jeans, sweatshirt, ball cap. Even though she was too far away to positively identify, he knew. It was Willa.

The relief rushing through him was immense but followed quickly by nerves. What should he say? What if she told him to go to hell or that she never wanted to see him again?

"She's coming up the sidewalk," he said.

Mack and Wyatt both shifted to see her. "You got a plan?" Wyatt asked.

Excuses and arguments to win her back scrolled in his mind. No, there was only one option. The truth.

"Let me talk to her alone for a minute." He slid out and observed her from the far side of the truck.

The LSU hoodie sweatshirt she wore was a size too big and made her look small and vulnerable, which was proof appearances could be deceiving. She was the strongest woman—person—he'd ever met. Could he have left home and survived with his hope and humor intact?

He stepped around the tailgate of the truck when she was even with him. She stopped short and faced him.

"Jackson?" Her voice was a combination of wonder and suspicion.

He ran his hands down the front of his jeans and crossed the street to join her on the sidewalk. Words clawed up his throat, too many to choose from.

She took a step backward. "Did you call the police? Because I don't have your stupid car. I left it safe and sound at Sutton's."

His initial worry wasn't about his Mustang, but the fact she'd driven this far in her piece-of-crap Honda. She'd obviously made it though, and insulting her car would only put her further on the defensive. "We didn't come all this way because of a car. I can replace a car. You, on the other hand, are one of kind."

The tightness around her eyes softened, and she closed the distance between them by a few feet. He didn't move lest he spook her. "We?"

"Mack and Wyatt pretty much insisted on coming too. You're like a little sister to them."

"That was sweet." She sent a half smile toward the truck.

He swallowed past the unexpected emotions welling out of him. Laying himself bare by choice was an uncomfortable feeling. He'd taken care to keep his emotions contained since he was a kid. It was how he'd survived.

He took a deep breath and forced the words out before he lost his courage. "I'm sorry I went behind your back. I was desperate. And scared too, I guess. I had fallen hard and knew you weren't telling me everything. I betrayed your trust, but it won't happen again. I can't lose you, Willa."

She stuffed her hands into her pockets, her gaze skittering toward her childhood home. He steeled himself for her rejection.

"I was going to settle things with my father—my past—

before coming back home to apologize to you. I didn't trust you when I should have. I would have done the same thing you did, believe me. Can you forgive me?"

He tried to logically assimilate the message, but the words that went on repeat were *coming back home* and *forgive me*. Cottonbloom was home. The garage was home. Was he her home?

He threw his usual caution aside and grabbed her up in a tight hug. "Nothing to forgive," he croaked against her hair. His lips went in search of hers. They collided in a kiss as sweet as it was fierce.

Her lips glided over his jaw to his neck. "I was always coming back."

"I kind of figured you'd be back when I saw the library books in your trailer."

Her laughter was the best kind, carefree and light. "Then why did you come all this way?"

"Because I didn't know if you were coming back for the books or to me. I couldn't risk it." The jokiness in his voice fell flat.

She pulled back enough to cup his cheeks and gaze straight into his eyes. The brown of hers were free of defenses and wet with tears. "I was coming back to you. But before we can be together, I need to face up to what I did and who I hurt, starting with my dad."

He tightened his hold around her waist and gave her a little shake. "Don't you get it? I've got your back whether you need it or not. Hell, whether you *want* it or not. You don't have to do this alone."

She looked down, her lashes fluttering, and a tear skittered down her cheek. He caught it on his thumb, his heart aching for her. "I'll go sit in the truck if you want me to but I'd rather stand by your side."

She caught his hand and pressed a kiss in his palm, the heat of her lips branding him in ways unseen. "I want you with me. It's just . . . I haven't had anyone to count on for a long time. It might take some getting used to."

"We have plenty of time to practice, don't we?" He wasn't sure if he intended the question to be rhetorical or not. Luckily, he didn't need to wonder long.

"Forever, if you want." Her lips trembled into a tentative smile.

"I want." He wrapped her in his arms once more, and she clutched him close. "Are you ready?"

Chapter Twenty

Willa's answer to that question would have been a resounding *no* not ten minutes earlier. She'd been sitting in her car around the corner for the last two hours, dozing and wondering whether she had enough courage left to walk up to her old front door.

She'd forced herself out of the car with the intention of walking past the house and scoping out the situation. The last thing she'd expected was for Jackson to appear. For a heartbeat, she'd wondered if he was a figment of her imagination brought on by sleeplessness. Didn't what you most desire appear in times of duress?

Except, he'd proven himself to be warm flesh and strong arms with a declaration she couldn't ignore. The truth was, she didn't want to face up to her past alone. In fact, if he hadn't shown up, she might have turned around and walked back to her car. She glanced over at the man who held her hand and matched her step for step.

"You can do it," he said in the raspy voice that was like the sweetest music to her ears.

He hadn't given her courage so much as helped her locate it. She would tell him later what he meant to her.

Or maybe she'd show him. She squeezed his hand tighter and leaned into his arm.

They walked up the path to the front door. She ran the toe of her shoe along a crack that she'd used to mark the start of her hopscotch game as a kid. The front door was green instead of the red of her childhood. Stands for potted plants flanked the door although they were empty in deference to the cold.

She pulled her father's ball cap off, tucked it into her back pocket, and smoothed a hand through her hair. Her deep breath did little to calm the frantic whirling of her insides, and her finger trembled as she pressed the doorbell. Familiar tones sounded. A part of her hoped for a reprieve. Footsteps sounded, and time slowed like a watch not wound.

The door swung open and there was her father. Grayer, with more lines around his eyes and less hair, but his shoulders were still bull-like and the hand curled around the door was still wide and roped with tendons. She imagined it would feel the same as it had when she was six and it held hers when they crossed the street together.

"Daddy." The childish tenor to the word was only a little embarrassing. Mostly she was just happy to see him. Problem was, she couldn't get a read on him.

"Willa?"

"Yeah. I'm here." It was a stupidly obvious thing to say, but snappy comebacks were out of reach. Her throat was dry, and she tried to swallow, but her voice was scratchy. "I've missed you."

Her father stepped onto the porch and grabbed her up in a bear hug. Jackson dropped her hand, and she wrapped her arms around her dad, fisted her hands in his thick plaid flannel shirt, and buried her nose in his collar. He smelled like soap and grease with a hint of bacon.

The years peeled away. She was young again and his

brown-eyed girl waking up to pancakes and bacon on a Sunday morning before church.

He shook against her, and she turned her head to see a tear trickling into a groove in his cheek. "I was afraid you were dead."

She'd never seen him cry, and her stomach and heart spun in a sickening dance. "Didn't you get my cards?" She'd sent him a birthday card every year without fail, driving to a different city to cover her tracks.

He pulled away, but kept his hands on her shoulders. "Why didn't you come home before now?"

"It's complicated. *Was* complicated. I don't know anymore. Can we come in and talk?"

For the first time, he glanced away from her to look at Jackson. "Of course. Of course. Come on in."

She followed her father inside, reaching blindly behind her. Jackson took her hand. The wood paneling of her youth had been replaced by light gray-painted walls. The furniture was an upgrade from their well-worn overstuffed couches too. House plants decorated much of the small foyer and the corners of the den.

She sat on the edge of a black leather couch. Jackson stayed at her side. His leg pressing against hers offered some comfort. Her father chose a matching armchair across the coffee table. A *Better Homes and Gardens* and a *Classic Car* magazine were on top.

After the initial shock wore off, the awkwardness of too much time passed and too many questions hung between them like dirty laundry, and she didn't know what to wash first. "Is Carol around?"

"Still asleep. Long night."

She could sympathize. Now that the adrenaline high she'd maintained since running from Jackson's bed was fading, her brain waded through sorghum.

He raised his eyebrows. "You going to introduce us?"

"Geez, of course. Jackson Abbott, my dad, Buck. Jackson and his brothers own a garage down in Cottonbloom, Louisiana. Jackson's my boyfriend." She shot him a look, unsure if she'd overstepped, but he smiled and put his hand on her knee. Her shoulders dropped a good three inches, and she leaned even farther into his arm.

"Nice to meet you, sir."

Her father nodded, but his attention was squarely on Willa. It was a look that had inspired babbling and quivery knees when she was a teenager trying to sneak in after curfew. "Your hair's different."

She touched her hair at the nape. "I've kept it short for a long time now."

"That my old hat in your pocket?"

"Yeah. I guess, technically, I stole it, but it's kept me close to you in a weird way." She pulled it out and turned the hat in her hands, tracing the fraying threads of the emblem.

Emotion flashed over his face, but they'd been apart for too long for her to interpret it. "Is he why you're here?" He pointed toward Jackson, but didn't look at him.

"No. Well, yes, in a roundabout way." She heaved in a breath, too tired to censor herself. "I love Jackson, and until I face up to my past, I can't move on with him."

He sniffed, his gaze dropping to their feet. "You don't know how many nights I've dreamed of you showing up like this. Alive and well."

"I sent cards."

His mouth thinned. "You think a scrawled 'don't worry about me' on a birthday card made me not worry?"

"I had no choice but to leave. Cynthia's death was my fault."

He blinked, confusion writ large on his face. "It was ruled an accidental overdose."

"I know." The report hadn't lessened her guilt. "But she met Derrick through me, and he was a drug dealer."

"Went to jail for it too. You didn't do anything wrong." He sat forward and propped his forearms on his knees, his hands fisted. "Did you?"

"Nothing illegal. Except take Nana's car."

"Then why did you up and leave in the middle of the night?"

"Because the night Cynthia died, I took Derrick's stash of drugs and buried it on the edge of the forest. I wanted to square things with the universe to make up for her death. Hurt Derrick. Except, I didn't realize he owed some very bad people big money. He threatened to hurt you or burn down the shop if I didn't get him the drugs back."

"Why didn't you tell me? We could have gone to the police."

Echoes of the day Cynthia died resonated. The pain and terror had tattooed themselves onto her memories, bleeding through everything that followed. Strange how life could pivot on a moment.

"I panicked and . . . I wasn't sure you'd forgive me. Things weren't the same between us after you married Carol." She held up her hands when he tried to argue. "I'm not blaming anyone, just stating the truth and you know it."

"Do you understand the hell you put us—*me*—through all these years?" His face reddened as if he were holding back even more.

Had she understood? Abstractly maybe, but she'd been consumed with her own problems as only a teenager could. And later, the distance had dulled her ability to see a path back home.

"I'm sorry." Years of regrets weighted the apology. It didn't seem like enough, but it was all she had to offer.

"Running was the only sure way I thought I could keep you safe. Plus, I wondered if maybe you'd be better off without me."

Her father sat back and rubbed his face with both hands. "I'm sorry if I made you feel that way. I assumed you were going through a phase or something, that everything would be okay."

"Maybe it would have been if Cynthia hadn't died." She tensed, her leg bouncing. "Do you know what happened to Derrick? He might still be a danger to you."

Her father shook his head. "Was locked up for a couple of years. I saw him around town after he got out, but he never settled into a decent job. Heard he violated his probation."

"So he's back in jail?" Relief unspooled her dread like a reprieve from being hanged.

"I have no idea. But, sweetheart, don't worry about me. I can handle a small-town punk drug dealer." The confidence of a father who could protect his daughter from all comers was in his attitude.

When she was young, still innocent of the underbelly of life and people, it might have absolved her of responsibility. She turned to Jackson. "We'll need to track him down."

"I'll get Gloria on it."

Before anything else could be said on the matter, Carol walked into the room and stopped short, a smile frozen on her face. Her father rose. "Willa's come home."

"I can see that. We've been worried about you, dear." Undertones in Carol's voice struck her as discordant.

Carol didn't look ready to break out the confetti at her return. No doubt, her life had been exponentially easier without Willa in it. She tamped down her resentment and gave her stepmother a half hug.

Introductions were made and the talk was of small

things and not big questions. "Should I get some coffee? Or breakfast?" Carol backpedaled toward the kitchen. "Buck's already fried the bacon. I can make pancakes."

Jackson thumbed over his shoulder. "Actually, my brothers are outside in a truck. I should—"

"Go get them. We've got plenty. If you and my daughter are as close as you seem to be, I should see what kind of stock you come from."

Jackson looked to her for guidance. She nodded. "Bring them in."

"River's with us."

A lump grew in her throat. They'd all come for her. "Her too."

River's buoyant personality and Wyatt's ability to charm put everyone at ease almost immediately. Mack and her father bonded over running garages and loving cars. Carol bustled around pouring coffee and offering up pancakes like a short-order cook.

Conversation dried up as the last of the pancakes and coffee were consumed. It was time to go. This meeting had reestablished their bonds and settled a portion of her fears about Derrick, but it reaffirmed something she'd buried under her guilt.

Her father was a good man, but he wasn't perfect. His authoritarian ways had been part of the reason she'd rebelled. He'd taken her stepmother's side in any disagreements to project a united parental front, but it had left her feeling unloved and neglected by the one constant in her life. The split she'd made five years ago had been brutal and not ideal but ultimately necessary.

Her father's mouth tightened. A tension she couldn't explain stretched between them. Perhaps it stemmed from the fact she was still a child in his eyes.

She stood up and smiled at her father. "We should go."

"We?"

"I'm leaving with Jackson, Dad."

He stood too. "No."

Carol's fork hit the plate, the clang unnaturally loud in the echo of her father's booming command.

"This is your home. You've been gone for too long. You'll stay." His voice was quieter but no less forceful.

All three Abbotts stood. Wyatt and Mack slipped toward the front door with River, silent, but both touching her shoulder in unspoken support.

Jackson lingered. "I'll wait outside." *For as long as it takes.* The promise was in his eyes. If she decided to stay, he would understand. She wanted to tell him she loved him or throw herself in his arms but settled for a nod.

His absence felt like a load-bearing wall inside of her was gone. Her future happiness depended on him, and her heart was in his hands to protect or destroy. The thought would have sent her into a panic a few months ago. Assessing her internals like an engine, she didn't detect anything but an even calmness. She trusted him.

Turning back to her father, she touched his arm to soften her message. "You'll always be my dad, but this isn't my home anymore."

"All these years . . . I want to make up for them." His natural stoicism broke and his chin wobbled.

She didn't hesitate, throwing herself in his arms like she'd done countless times as a kid. But she wasn't a kid anymore. She was a woman with a life and place of her own. "For better or worse, I'm not the same girl who ran off."

"Have you been happy?"

A wave of awareness passed through her. He had been wrestling with his own guilt and self-blame all these years.

"I'm happy now. So happy." She tightened her hold on him. "I'm not disappearing again, Dad, but I can't move back here."

"You're going to leave? Right now?"

She pulled back. Their father-daughter relationship couldn't be repaired or re-created. It had to be built from the ground up, and that wouldn't happen in a day or a weekend. They needed time to get to know each other again.

"You know where I am. We can talk every day. I want you to come to Cottonbloom and see where I work and live, and I'll visit you. I won't disappear again."

The surety in her voice must have made an impression, because her father stepped away from her. She stopped at the door and kissed her father on the cheek, hesitating a moment to breathe him in like so many lost memories, good and bad.

"Love you." She walked out the door. Jackson was leaning against the truck, his arms crossed over his chest, but she knew they'd open to receive her as she got closer.

She turned around halfway down the path. Her father stood on the porch with his hands stuffed in his pockets. She shuffled back to him, fished out her keys, took the trailer's key off the ring, and handed the rest over.

He held them up. Cold sunlight glinted off the metal. Wonder bloomed in his smile. "You're still driving Nana's car?"

An easiness had returned. Cars had always been their bridge to one another. "Can you believe I kept it running? I left it parked around the corner. Consider it returned. I don't think Nana would have minded me taking it, do you?"

"It was going to be yours anyway. Don't you need it?"

"Nah. Jackson's got me covered, but thanks." She hesitated. "I'm going to keep your hat though. You mind?"

"As long as when you wear it, you'll remember to call me."

"Deal."

With that final promise, she walked straight into Jackson's arms.

"You okay?" he whispered.

"I'm good. Can we go home?"

He opened the truck door, and River greeted her with a sloppy lick on the face.

Beyond words, Willa buried her face in the dog's fur and sent thanks to the universe for bringing River and the Abbotts into her life. She and Jackson and River climbed into the backseat and settled in for the drive home.

Nestled against Jackson, his heartbeat pacing her own, she let exhaustion claim her, wandering in and out of dreams. One thing became clear as they drew closer to Cottonbloom. Home was a moving target and had more to do with people than places. Jackson was her home now.

Epilogue

March in Louisiana was fickle. The summery warmth of morning could be replaced by clouds and a cold northerly wind by afternoon. Willa and River were outside next to the garage enjoying the sun before it disappeared again.

Jackson and Wyatt were putting the final touches on the Plymouth Hemicuda. Wyatt was like a father awaiting the birth of his first child, all nervous excitement. Mack was sitting in his office staring at the wall and squeezing a stress ball into dust.

Ella Boudreaux was getting under his skin. After the bombshell announcement at the Mizes' New Year's Eve party, she had stayed away from the garage, and a flickering hope that she would stay out of their business flourished. Mack had reworked their financial plans in order to raise the capital to buy her out, but it would take at least a year.

Mack had spiraled into quiet reflection that periodically exploded into anxiety-driven anger. If Ella Boudreaux did choose to insert herself in the business, Willa worried Mack would detonate as if someone had clipped the wrong-color wire on a live bomb. Honestly, she felt sorry for the woman, but she was smart enough to keep her opinion to herself.

The past three months with Jackson had more than made up for her years alone and lonely. It was still a challenge to accept his help, but instead of getting mad, he'd roll his eyes and call her on her craptastic baggage.

They spent their nights making love then staring up through the skylights of the loft at the endless sky. Wondering at the vagaries of fate kept her awake long after he fell asleep. What-ifs made her hold on to him that much tighter. Her bad luck had splatted against a Jackson-shaped wall. Now, all she could think was how lucky she was to be in his arms and the recipient of his love.

Like stitching together a torn quilt square by square, she and her father were mending their relationship. He'd visited the garage and had been suitably impressed. Jackson's car knowledge had raised him more than a few notches in her father's esteem. She'd shared some of where she'd been and what had happened to her with him, but he didn't need to know everything.

She threw the stick for River and laughed when the dog tripped over the end on her run back. An old Ford truck puttered down the road and turned into the parking lot and out of sight. One of the boys could handle the new customer. She wanted to play hooky in the sun a few more minutes.

"Willa?" The voice had haunted her nightmares.

She whirled. Derrick stood at the corner of the building. He was an older, harder version of the boy she'd known. Multiple stints in prison would do that to a person, she supposed. Gloria's search on him hadn't turned up his present whereabouts.

River, as intuitive and protective as ever, growled deep in her chest and put herself between Willa and Derrick, her back hair standing up like a Mohawk.

"How did you know where to find me?" she said after locating her tongue.

"News is all over the parish. Your mom can't keep her effing mouth shut."

"Stepmom." Her correction was knee-jerk.

"Whatever." He took a step forward. River's growl crescendoed. "You going to call off your mutt?"

"Not until you tell me why you're here. If you're after money or drugs—"

He barked a laugh. "You think I'm still after my stash?"

"You threatened to burn down my dad's shop or break his leg for it."

"Yeah, years ago. Those boys I owed money to are either in lockup or dead. Life expectancy in that line of work ain't great."

"Then what do you want?"

He shifted and looked over his shoulder; a tattoo of a dagger ran from under his ear into the collar of his denim jacket. He probably wasn't after a character reference for an office job then. A roiling fear under dark humor almost made her laugh. She bit the inside of her mouth, the pain grounding her.

"I'm on step nine," he said. At the blank shake of her head, he added, "AA. Twelve steps. I'm on number nine; making amends."

"Oh." It was all she could think to say.

"So, I'm here. Making amends."

"Okay. Consider them made. You can go now and don't come back."

The troubles he wore like a cloak reminded her of Clayton, down at Rufus's, but while Clayton's goodness dulled his dangerous edge, Derrick was downright threatening. None of the good-time charm she remembered remained. It was hard to reconcile the boy she'd thought she'd loved with this man.

"Doesn't work like that. I need to tell you I'm sorry." Aggression beat at his voice.

"You don't sound sorry." She delivered a load of sarcasm with her snark.

He blew out a breath and rolled his shoulders. "This shit is hard. Give me a break."

"Do you think about her?" Anger was superseding her initial fear. "I found her with needle tracks up and down her arms, her mouth hanging open, her eyes bulged out."

He winced like her words were a physical pain. His voice dropped to a near whisper. "I see her like that every time I close my eyes."

A shared regret was a more powerful bond than she imagined. "It was my fault for bringing her around. If I hadn't—"

"I asked you out because I thought you were one of them."

"One of who?"

"Needy girls with easy middle-class money. My bread and butter. But you weren't so easy. I used you to lure in friends instead. Cynthia was ripe to get hooked. If it hadn't been smack and me, it would have been alcohol or pot or pills later."

"You don't know that." She felt obligated to defend her friend, but there was truth between them. Finally. Her guilt lost some of its weight.

The side door opened and Jackson strolled out. "The car's ready to fire up. Thought you might— Who's this?"

His voice was almost as growly as River, his demeanor even more protective. He came up next to her and put a hand on her arm, strong and ready to put her behind him if needed.

"It's Derrick. He's here as part of his twelve-step program. He's . . . well, sort of apologizing."

"This your man?"

"That's right. If you've said your piece, you'd better get gone and never come back." Jackson took a step forward, and Derrick took a step back. Jackson was bigger, stronger, and more intimidating.

Even though she could handle herself, his automatic protection of her only made her love him more. Before things could escalate, she laid a hand on his hard-as-stone biceps and murmured, "Back off, John Wayne, I got this."

He shot her a look that said she'd pay for her dig later, but did as she asked. He planted himself behind her. So close she could feel his heat. The trust he put in her earned him extra points.

Derrick held up his hands in mock surrender. "Look, I'm getting my life straightened out. Got a job up in Little Rock. Apartment. Working on getting a welding certificate. I'm sorry about everything that went down back then. You were a nice kid and didn't deserve someone like me taking advantage of you."

She shrugged, not knowing how else to handle the anticlimactic meeting. In all the scenarios that had kept her up at night, never had she imagined a relatively harmless Derrick seeking her forgiveness.

When she didn't offer him a response, he turned around and trudged toward the parking lot with his head down.

"Wait!" She jogged to catch up with him. Jackson and River were close behind.

Wyatt and Mack were rolling the 'Cuda out of the garage bay, but they stopped as soon as they all rounded the corner.

"You're really sorry?" She stared into his eyes and imagined remorse reflecting back. Was it real? Did it matter? He was giving her the opportunity to close the door on her past. A screen door anyway. Her mistakes would always shade her decisions, but hopefully to help her make better ones.

"I screwed your life up too. Look, you don't have to forgive me, but I had to try. For my own sake," he said.

He'd half turned away, the dagger on his neck facing her, when she said, "I forgive you."

"You do?" He jerked back around to face her.

"Yeah," she said slowly. She might have even meant it, but what she knew for sure was that she had finally forgiven herself. Her trip to see her dad and now this were steps on her own program of forgiveness. She retreated to notch herself under Jackson's arm. "My life's not screwed up anymore."

Derrick nodded and smiled slightly. Whatever load he'd been carrying had lightened. "I'll leave you to get on with life then."

"You too, Derrick. Make it a good one."

He waved over his head and climbed into his truck. Everyone was still and silent until his truck rounded the bend. Jackson shifted and put his hands at her waist. Wyatt slapped Mack on the arm, and they retreated to his office.

"How do you feel?" Jackson asked.

She had to turn over and examine the jumble inside of her. "I feel like I can finally look forward and not worry about what's behind me. I feel . . . free."

It was the perfect word. Light and soaring like a bird let out of its cage. She tipped her head back and smiled.

"I suppose this isn't a good time to ask you to tie yourself down again, huh?"

Although the sky was cloudless and blue, she was sure lightning had struck. Her body was alive and electric. "Do you mean what I think you mean?"

"Hazel and Hyacinth are going to send their Bible study group over to take turns reciting scripture about sin if we keep on the way we've been doing." Were those nerves in his voice? He bit his bottom lip, the confidence that marked him as much as hair or eye color was gone, leaving her blinking at him in consternation or something closer to shock.

Would it be cruel to tease him a little? "Should I stop by Country Aire and see if my old trailer is available?" she asked with the innocence of a wolf in sheep's clothing.

"No!" He ran a hand through his hair. "That's not what I meant and you know it."

"Do I?" She linked her hands around his neck, popped to her toes, and kissed him.

"Willyoumarryme?" His lips moved against hers, the words slurring together.

"Yes." She pressed her lips against his cheek about where his dimple would be.

"I love you so damn much."

"I love you too." She kissed his jaw, the stubble rasping erotically against her lips.

"I don't have a ring yet."

"I can't wear a ring in the garage anyway." She took his earlobe between her teeth. His arms banded her close, his body hard in all the right places. Hers reacted swiftly and predictably. "Will Wyatt kill us if we go celebrate in the loft instead of watching him fire up the 'Cuda?"

"Something tells me he'll understand. Let's go." He grabbed her hand, and they quickstepped through the barn, heading toward the stairs to his loft.

She pulled him to a stop at the open doors in back. The woods stretched as far as she could see, the hint of new green interspersed with the dark green pines. Instead of making her feel boxed in, the expanse represented endless possibilities. The woods hadn't changed; she had. And the catalyst of that change had been Jackson. His faith. His patience. His love.

She laid her head on his shoulder, her eyes still on the horizon. "I don't want a fancy wedding like Sutton. Why don't we find a justice of the peace and get married tomorrow? Do they even have those anymore or are they—"

His kiss took her breath away and any logical thought with it.

She assumed that was a yes.